CW00828742

MURDER IN THE BOOKSHOP

A MISS MERRILL AND AUNT VIOLET MYSTERY

ANITA DAVISON

Boldwood

First published in Great Britain in 2023 by Boldwood Books Ltd.

Copyright © Anita Davison, 2023

Cover Design by Head Design

Cover Illustration: Shutterstock

The moral right of Anita Davison to be identified as the author of this work has been asserted in accordance with the Copyright, Designs and Patents Act 1988.

All rights reserved. No part of this book may be reproduced in any form or by any electronic or mechanical means, including information storage and retrieval systems, without written permission from the author, except for the use of brief quotations in a book review.

This book is a work of fiction and, except in the case of historical fact, any resemblance to actual persons, living or dead, is purely coincidental.

Every effort has been made to obtain the necessary permissions with reference to copyright material, both illustrative and quoted. We apologise for any omissions in this respect and will be pleased to make the appropriate acknowledgements in any future edition.

A CIP catalogue record for this book is available from the British Library.

Paperback ISBN 978-1-78513-313-8

Large Print ISBN 978-1-78513-309-1

Hardback ISBN 978-1-78513-308-4

Ebook ISBN 978-1-78513-306-0

Kindle ISBN 978-1-78513-307-7

Audio CD ISBN 978-1-78513-314-5

MP3 CD ISBN 978-1-78513-311-4

Digital audio download ISBN 978-1-78513-305-3

Boldwood Books Ltd
23 Bowerdean Street
London SW6 3TN
www.boldwoodbooks.com

For Katherine Pym, whose inspiration, encouragement, and wicked black humour I miss every day. RIP Kathy.

1

CHISWICK MALL, WEST LONDON, 9 SEPTEMBER 1915

Hannah woke to the sound of raised voices in a mildly combative tone. She glanced at her bedside clock and groaned in protest at the early hour. The journey from her parents' home in Surrey the previous evening had been exhausting, fraught with delays and cancellations due to troop trains on their way to the coast being given precedence. It was fully dark by the time she crept up the stairs, avoiding the loose floorboard so as not to wake her Aunt Violet.

Sliding from the warm cocoon of covers, her toes curling on the cold floorboards, she groped for her dressing gown, jammed an arm awkwardly into a sleeve and unhooked the window latch with the other. Her maid, Ivy, a rail-thin woman in her early twenties with frizzy mouse-coloured hair and unremarkable features stood at the wrought iron front gate, the post boy straddling his bicycle on the other side.

A cool, wet summer had swelled the Thames thirty feet away, and grey-green algae-filled water lapped the grass verge between the path and the low wall enclosing the front garden. A sudden cool breeze ruffled the surface of the water and lifted long strands of unbound hair across Hannah's face.

'How do you know? Unless you've got pigeons in your muvver's loft.' Ivy chuckled at her own joke, which seemed to anger the post boy.

'It's true, I tell yer! Me uncle arrived this half hour since to tell us.'

Hannah pulled the edges of her dressing gown tight around her neck and leaned her forearms on the windowsill.

'Ivy!' she called, levelling her voice to a low, but fierce whisper. 'You'll wake my Aunt Violet. Why on earth are you arguing with the post boy?'

'That ain't likely, miss. She's dead to the world most mornings.' Ivy gripped the gate with one hand and twisted at the waist to call back at Hannah. 'And this here scamp's tellin' porkies.'

'I ain't, miss.' The post boy, a lad of fourteen, shoved his soft cap further back on his head and looked up at Hannah. 'The Germans went and bombed London last night. That's what.'

'Last night?' Hannah's stomach dropped, banishing the remnants of her early morning indolence. 'Do you know where?'

'Aldersgate area, near Smithfield Market got done. And a ruddy great bomb took out a whole row of 'ouses in Bartholemew Close.'

'And 'ow can you know then?' Ivy propped her hands on her hips, her head tilted at Hannah in a 'can you believe him?' look.

'I told yer.' The youth's face twisted in anguish. 'Me uncle was on 'is way to Smithfield to stock up his shop and said the streets are covered in rubble and broken glass. The fire wardens wouldn't let him through so he 'ad to come home. Not a window in one piece for miles, 'e said. The firemen have been fighting the fires all night.'

Aldersgate was a little over a mile from her aunt's bookshop in

Covent Garden, and Charing Cross Station where hospital trains brought in the wounded from the battlefields of France to the military hospital in the Strand.

'How bad was it?' Hannah asked, dreading his answer. 'Were many people killed?'

'Dunno, do I?' He threw a disdainful look at Ivy before adding, 'Though Uncle Bert said Mr Fenge from the Admiral Carter pub was killed.' His gaze shifted to the line of houses that curved away along the riverbank, apparently eager to spread what he knew at the next house. 'I'd better be off, then.' Kicking the pedal into its vertical position, he pushed off with the other foot, his bicycle wobbling precariously on the dirt path as he headed towards Hammersmith.

Hannah squeezed her eyes shut, her thoughts on flesh and blood, people crushed or blown up as they went about their daily lives. One minute they were asleep in their beds and then...

'Don't you go listening to that lad, miss.' Ivy wiped her hands on her apron as she wandered back down the path. 'Always got a story, that one. Last week, it was all—' Her next words were lost as Hannah banged the window shut and hurried to the bathroom.

* * *

Once dressed in a light wool navy blue jacket and matching skirt over a crisp white blouse, Hannah descended the stairs just as Ivy emerged from the kitchen.

'You don't need to be up this early, miss, not when you've just got back from your 'oliday. And what about yer morning tea? I always brings one first thing.'

'I've been waited on for days at my parents', which was pleasant, but quite wearing in its own way.' Hannah caught her reflection in the hall mirror, paused and tweaked a stray hair into place.

'I'm going into town to make sure my aunt's bookshop hasn't been damaged by the bombing.'

'Don't know as I'd take the boy's word fer it. If there was anything 'o that sort goin' on, you'll find out from the newspapers tomorrer.'

'I can't wait that long, Ivy. I feel responsible for the bookshop and would hate anything to have happened to it.'

'Ah, well, you knows best,' Ivy tutted, her tone implying she thought nothing of the sort, and cocked her chin at the ceiling. 'Do yer plan on tellin' 'er ladyship?'

Hannah hesitated. She was probably panicking over nothing. If there was an air raid on Holborn, the chances a stray bomb had hit the shop were slim.

'No, I won't disturb her, Ivy. Aunt Violet was out late last night. Let her sleep.' Hannah suppressed a smile, recalling the front door slamming at three that morning, followed by a heavy thump and a smothered curse.

'Humph. S'all right fer some,' Ivy muttered under her breath as she sauntered back to the scullery.

Hannah held her tongue on a reprimand, reminded that with so many young men enlisting and with better wages to be had in munitions factories, domestic staff were scarce.

After a makeshift breakfast, Hannah made the short walk to Stamford Brook Station where she joined the shopgirls, matrons, housemaids and middle-aged men in dark suits on the platform. Young men in workmen's overalls eyed soldiers in khaki with a mixture of envy and unease. Low voices speculated the distant fires during the night were anything from a gas explosion to a fire. Others claimed to be better informed and confirmed the post boy's story.

Fears grew in nervous whispers about relatives not heard from, while others expressed confidence the battery guns on the

Embankment would have shot down any encroaching zeppelins. Only the noisy arrival of the District Line train silenced the urgent chatter as the crowd surged forward to secure seats.

Elbowing her way through the press of bodies, Hannah headed for the last carriage, where she claimed a rare corner seat; her triumph was short-lived when a corpulent man in a black suit with shiny elbows plumped down beside her. He caught her ankle painfully with his walking stick; his impatient grunt implying she was at fault for being in the way. The train lights flickered as it left the sprawl of the West London suburbs and plunged into a tunnel with a rush of warm air; the odours of stale tobacco, human sweat and hair oil combining to increase her claustrophobia.

The red bar and circle symbol of Charing Cross Embankment Station slid past the grimy carriage window as the train juddered to a halt. Hannah's attempt to rise was thwarted as a fold of her skirt was trapped beneath her companion's expansive behind. Oblivious, the man stared at his newspaper, until, with a final hard tug, she broke free. Muttering sarcastic thanks which he failed to acknowledge, she shouldered through a wall of tightly packed bodies, her repeated requests ignored as they stoically refused to move.

She stepped onto the platform with seconds to spare before the doors slammed shut and the engines roared to life. With a rush of soot-filled wind and a screech of metal wheels, the train sped off down the tracks into the blackness of the gaping tunnel.

Blinking in the sharp daylight after the gloomy train, Hannah stepped into a wall of sound from horse-drawn carts, hackneys, motor cars and buses; the air thick with exhaust fumes, flower stalls, manure and soot smuts from the factories and residential coal fires south of the river. Posters of a moustachioed and pointing Lord Kitchener stared down at her from every hoarding, but apart from a fire engine speeding past, she saw no sign of damage to nearby buildings.

Her nerves settled as it became clear the attack, although real, was far enough away not to have affected the immediate area.

'More on *Lusitania* sinking!' A newspaper seller's shout erupted beside her ear on the corner of Villiers Street. 'Ship believed to be carrying munitions.'

Her sympathy rose for the twelve hundred souls killed by a German torpedo the previous May; an act of savagery still being talked about in shops, churches and around dinner tables.

'The Americans won't let an outrage like that go with so many of their countrymen aboard,' Hannah's father had snorted into his whisky at a family dinner. 'They'll enter this war now. Mark my words.'

Hannah joined the steady flow of pedestrians who walked four deep on the Strand, with its increase in the numbers of soldiers and nurses in short crimson cloaks and white caps, either in pairs or pushing wheeled bath chairs carrying patients with heads or limbs swathed in bandages.

She tried not to stare at their grey, haggard faces while anger burned in her. The war was supposed to have been a fast, brutal skirmish, easily won, yet a year had passed, and the fighting was not only worse, but the Kaiser's army had gained the upper hand.

A line of canvas-sided motor ambulances queued beneath the arch of Charing Cross Hospital; a fluttering white banner stretched across the entire road bearing the words, *Quiet for the Wounded.* Recruitment posters graced every hoarding, exhorting wives and mothers to persuade their menfolk to enlist, while garish announcements of current and future theatre productions swept by in a blur of colour.

A few harassed road sweepers attempted to clear up after the horses, the sharp tang of manure witness to their losing battle as steaming piles built up faster than could be removed.

Shifting from foot to foot on the pavement, Hannah searched for a gap in the heavy traffic. Spotting her opportunity, she darted into the road. Narrowly avoiding a boy on a bicycle and skirting behind a hackney, she reached the far side without mishap. She hurried down the side of the Strand Theatre into Catherine Street, her stride increasing to a run, her skirt wrapped around her legs threatening to trip her. Forced to slow down, her heart pounded as she turned the corner, a sense of hope growing as the row of shops seemed unscathed.

Despite the normalcy of the surrounding streets, a wave of relief washed over her at the reassuring sight of the untouched bookshop. The old-fashioned, multi-paned Georgian frontage of the Covent Garden Bookshop with its randomly placed bull-nosed panes winked back at her in the morning light. Exhaling a slow, relieved breath, her steps lightened as she shouldered her way inside, setting off the energetic jangle of the bell above the door.

2

'Miss Merrill!' A fresh-faced youth of medium height with a mop of unruly dark hair appeared from between a row of floor-to-ceiling oak bookcases.

'We... um... weren't expecting you back today. Did you have a pleasant time in Surrey?' He slapped dust from trousers an inch too short and tugged down his waistcoat.

'Morning, Archie. And my holiday was... uneventful, so I decided to cut it short.' She hung her jacket and bag on a hook beside the internal door leading to the upstairs flat. 'Is Mr Carstairs here?'

The sturdy oak shelves filled half the floor space, crammed together with barely room for a person to move between. Play sheets, scripts, posters, and theatre programs old and new occupied a wooden display; a tribute to the previous owner's enduring passion for the stage.

'Er... he's not arrived yet, miss.' Archie's broad smile faded, and he shot a fearful glance past Hannah's shoulder to the still quiet street. 'He probably had an errand to run.'

The surface of the desk was barely visible beneath a layer of leaflets, invoices, and what appeared to be the remains of a cheese sandwich on a piece of crumpled greaseproof paper.

'When did Mr Carstairs last put in an appearance?'

'Um… I'm not sure.' Archie removed a small pile of books from the corner of the desk and stared about as if in search of somewhere to put them before tucking them awkwardly beneath one arm.

'Archie?' she dragged his name out in a warning.

'Monday, miss.' His demeanour altered from sheepish to enthused. 'But he stayed the entire day.'

Today is Thursday. Hannah sighed, swept the stale sandwich crusts into an overflowing wicker waste bin, then arranged the scattered letters into an untidy pile.

'Do you know about the bombing?' Archie asked, eager to discuss the more exciting news of the day.

'A few rumours circulated on the train this morning, but no one had any details other than it happened somewhere in Smithfield? Do you know anything more?' Her interest waned slightly knowing her shop was safe, but that bombs had been dropped anywhere was still disturbing.

'A ruddy great bomb took out an entire row of houses on Farringdon Road.' His youthful face showed a mixture of horror and awe. 'I ain't seen nothing like it. St Bart's church has an enormous hole in the front now and *The Dolphin* pub has gone and the landlord copped it. There was rubble and broken glass all over the streets with fire engines and ambulances going all night.'

Hannah's hand stilled on the pile of envelopes she was sifting through. 'St Bartholomew's? That's in Holborn. I thought you lived with your mother in Somerstown?'

The youngest of a large family, Archie could relate stories about his relatives for a year and never repeat a name.

'Aye, but I stayed at our Ellie's last night. It was late when the whistle sounded, so we got the nippers out of bed and down to the tube station still in their jim-jams.' Archie chattered as he collected scattered books and arranged them in piles. 'It was so crowded, some brave souls stretched out between the lines. You won't catch me doing that. I'd not sleep a wink in case a train came. Me sister's goin' down there again tonight in case it comes back.'

'It?' Hannah said. 'One airship did all that damage?' Her thoughts went to the poor people who had huddled in dank, gloomy tunnels all night, only to emerge to find their homes destroyed.

He nodded. 'They say another one took off up north, but I didn't see it.'

'Speaking of destroyed...' she eyed the stained parquet and half-empty bookshelves where volumes leaned at all angles, the spines facing the wrong way and gaps in between like missing teeth.

'I've tried to keep on top of things, but...' He hunched his shoulders as if braced for a reprimand.

'I'm not blaming you.' She ran a finger across a brass light fitting, grimacing when it came away black. 'What happened to the cleaner my aunt employed?'

'Ah.' Archie scratched at his left ear. 'She and Mr Carstairs had a falling out. I dunno what was said, but there was lots of shouting and door slamming. She ain't been back since.'

Growing more despondent by the minute, Hannah strode to three full-height bookcases arranged in a 'u' shape around a high-backed wing chair upholstered in rich burgundy velvet. A low mahogany table and a brace of matching but smaller chairs completed a haven for mothers to read with their children, and nursemaids to keep their charges occupied.

'Mr Carstairs likes to sit there in the afternoons with his newspaper and a cup of tea.' Archie clutched a book protectively to his chest. 'I don't think he likes children much, miss. He caught two boys rifling through the books the other day and threw them out.'

Hannah surveyed the desecration with dismay. The wingback chair was sprinkled with a layer of cigarette ash. A deep imprint of hundreds of backsides had dented the faded velvet squab. Newspapers littered the floor like felled birds with their wings splayed and crumpled; a half-empty packet of garibaldi biscuits and a full ashtray on the mahogany table badly marked with water rings. The semi-circular drawer beneath had been jammed roughly closed, leaving it lop-sided.

Hannah gave it a frustration-fuelled tug, which had no effect. She pulled harder. The drawer was freed with a screech, revealing old invoices, receipts and an assortment of odds and ends, string labels, brown paper and crumpled leaflets. Inside, she found what looked like a deck of cards, tied together with a length of string. She pulled them free, noting they seemed larger than a standard pack and made of thick pasteboard.

'It looks as if Mr Carstairs spent his time less than productively.'

'Er... no miss, I—' Archie reached to take them, causing a brief tussle between himself and Hannah for possession. The string unravelled, sending the cards onto the floor.

Hannah bent to pick them up, but halted. At her feet lay a dozen or more photographs of naked women in a variety of shapes and sizes; from slender girls not yet out of their teens to buxom older ladies in seductive poses, lounged on a chaise or draped over armchairs with fans or feather boas positioned to emphasise their womanly charms.

'I assume these don't belong to you, Archie?' She resisted an urge to laugh at his mortified expression.

'Oh no, miss. I never—' He swallowed, his already flushed

complexion turning a deep red. 'Mr Carstairs sells them. He told me not to tell anyone. I mean – you. But since it was you who found them, he can't blame me, can he?'

'Does he indeed? I don't suppose Aunt Violet, I mean Miss Edwards, knows about it?'

'She hasn't been in all week. In fact, we ain't seen 'er for a long while.'

Aunt Violet, a dedicated suffragette whose militant activities had been curbed for the duration of the war, now channelled her boundless energy into the British Red Cross. She took little interest in the bookshop, which always made Hannah wonder how she came to possess it, but no explanation had been forthcoming. Hannah, however, loved the cosy shop with its polished oak shelves crammed with love stories, fictional adventures, and daring feats of endurance.

'Are there any other inappropriate publications on the premises?' Her gaze probed the shelves, as if the offending items might jump out at her.

'I dunno what those are, miss.' Archie scratched his head, ruffling his already wayward hair. 'Only them postcards.'

'I'll deal with these.' Hannah gathered the offending items together with a glow of satisfaction and stowed them in her handbag, which she placed beneath the desk with a sense of quiet triumph. At last, she had a credible reason to persuade her aunt to sack Monty Carstairs, who had single-handedly allowed the bookshop income to decline and, with a misogynistic fervour which infuriated her, refused all Hannah's attempts to improve sales and regulate the inventory.

'Archie?' An idea Hannah had been toying with for some time prompted her to ask. 'How do you feel about working for a woman?'

'What sort of woman?' Archie looked as if she had suggested he swim the channel.

'My sort. I intend to run the shop myself. With your help, naturally.' It wasn't as if she had anything else to do apart from scouring *The Times* casualty lists, hoping not to see the names of anyone she knew.

'*You*, miss? Does Mr Carstairs know?'

'Not yet. But he will.' The shop doorbell set off into its harsh jangle, bringing Archie hurrying to the front of the shop as the rhythmic click of a cane on floorboards announced the arrival of Monty Carstairs.

3

'What ho, young Archie!' Monty's cut-glass voice drew Hannah to a gap in the shelves from where she observed the bookshop manager.

In his thirties and of average height, his fedora sat at a jaunty angle on his heavily pomaded hair. A patrician nose and deep, wide-set eyes defined him as handsome; his good looks spoiled by a perpetual sneer below a pencil moustache that disguised a weak upper lip.

'Colossal cheek of those Huns to bomb us last night, what?' Tossing a folded newspaper onto the desk without looking where it fell, he followed it with his cane, which rolled off and clattered to the floor. 'A poor show we can't make bullets and bombs fast enough. I'll wager that's why we made such a damned mess of Aubers Ridge, not to mention that Neuve Chappelle fiasco.' He pointed a finger at Archie which he transferred to the cane in silent instruction.

Retrieving the cane, Archie cleared his throat noisily and flicked a glance at Hannah as she emerged from behind the bookcase.

'What's wrong, boy?' Monty nudged him playfully in the ribs as he placed the cane squarely on the desk. 'Lost half a crown and found sixpence, eh?'

He followed Archie's look and froze as he spotted Hannah , her shoulder against the sturdy upright.

'Hannah!' He flashed Archie an undeserved glare of accusation, grabbed the cane and limped towards her. 'How are Hector and the ever-lovely Madeleine?'

Monty's use of her parents' given names rankled with Hannah. As the son of her father's chief clerk at his merchant bank, Monty had attended university with her late fiancé Gerald and Darius Clifford, the son of her father's business partner Joshua Clifford. This connection meant he was often included in house parties and social events, mainly because he would simply turn up to inveigle himself.

Hannah pushed away from the bookcase and slowly approached the desk. 'My parents are well, thank you, Monty. It was a pleasant stay,' she lied. Her mother spent the entire time trying to persuade her to live with them in Surrey. Only the intervention of her benign and tolerant father convinced Hannah to continue her stay.

'Well, don't just stand there, lad.' Monty waved the cane at Archie. 'Fetch Miss Merrill and myself a cup of tea. There's a good chap.'

'There's no milk, sir.' Archie shuffled his feet. 'And the cash box is empty.'

'That's easily solved.' Monty tossed a few coins from his pocket into the air, which Archie caught as expertly as an outfield cricketer before he headed for the door, sending the bell into a frantic jangle as he left.

Monty flung himself into the leather wingback chair; an impressive piece of furniture her Aunt Violet had inherited from the previous owners. The seat swivelled one hundred and eighty degrees and had a reclining back that Monty tilted as far as it would go, his ankles crossed on the desktop, arms bent at the elbows and his hands clasped behind his head.

Resisting an urge to slap his feet from the tooled leather inlay, Hannah fetched a stool from the end of an aisle and sat. 'How have book sales been going lately?'

'Business isn't what it was before the war began.' He adopted a resigned expression he probably reserved for such occasions. 'Folks have too much on their minds than books these days.' He pushed off the desk with one foot and swung the chair in a slow arc.

'If that's true, why are dance halls, restaurants and every theatre on Shaftesbury Avenue full every night?' Hannah itched to shake him. 'Everyone needs a distraction from the threat of invasion.' After a year of the war, the Germans had gained the upper hand, and panic spread. Hannah's elderly neighbours had barricaded themselves into their house and only took deliveries of food through their front window.

'Invasion? Poppycock!' Monty rocked back and forth in the chair, yawning. 'Our army will see off the Boche by Christmas, you'll see.'

'Then what about this?' She plucked a sheet of paper from the desktop and held it out. 'It's an order from the Chiswick Hospital. They've had an influx of wounded from the Front and need reading material for the long-term patients.'

'Er – I must have missed that.' Monty cleared his throat. 'I'll see to it presently.' He went to take the paper which she deftly moved out of his reach.

'Don't bother, I'll do it myself.'

'You seem out of sorts, Hannah.' He halted the chair mid-swing. 'Is something wrong?'

'If I am, it's because the bookshop is losing money, and—'

'Ah!' He halted her with a raised finger. 'Don't you mean your Aunt Violet's money?'

'That's beside the point. I care about this business as much as she does.' She waved an expansive arm. 'I've only been gone a week and look at how disorganised and filthy it is.'

'I suppose it could do with a bit of sprucing up.' His nose wrinkled as he surveyed the shop with disinterest. 'I'll have a word with Archie when he gets back.'

'Cleaning isn't Archie's job.' Her voice held an edge. 'He's employed to learn the bookselling trade and handle customers. The slump in sales means we can no longer pay two employees, much less three. Therefore, I—My aunt has no choice but to reduce the staff.'

'That would be a shame. Archie loves working here.' A frown appeared, but faded in seconds. 'He'll get something else, no doubt. What with all these chaps enlisting, there are jobs to spare.' He stretched both arms above his head and yawned. 'Forgive me, Hannah, but can we discuss all this later? I only stopped in to check on things and ensure Archie wasn't slacking off. I'm due at Simpsons for luncheon with a friend.'

'You've only just *got* here,' she snapped.

'I'm a busy chap, you know. But seeing as you're here, could I ask a favour?'

'What sort of favour?' A tremor of alarm went through her.

'It's my lodgings.' He adopted a pained expression. 'My rooms are three floors up, and the stairs play havoc with my hip.' He gripped his cane with one hand and rubbed his left thigh with the other, wincing in emphasis.

'I'm sorry to hear it,' Hannah said carefully, aware it was only a matter of time before he mentioned his injury, one which prevented his serving in the army.

During their final year at Balliol, Monty, and their childhood friend Darius Clifford brought Gerald home for the Easter holiday. The three young men took a boat out to Chiswick Eyot. Darius and Gerald played a prank on Monty by leaving him stranded on the island. Monty panicked and instead of waiting to be picked up he tried to get back on his own, when the fast-flowing tide swept him against a metal ladder, badly damaging his hip.

He had spent a month in hospital, missed his final examinations and left university without a degree. Since then, Monty walked with a limp, and shamelessly exploited his friends' residual guilt. When he heard Hannah's aunt owned a bookshop, he wheedled himself into the position of manager, citing his role as a close family friend.

'How about I move into the flat above the shop?' Monty said with an air of surprise, as if he had only just thought of it. 'I could keep an eye on things for you from up there.'

'That won't be possible, or necessary.' Anger surged within Hannah at his audacity, but an image of the postcards returned. 'I'm sorry, but I—that is we, have no choice but to end your employment.'

'You're sacking me?' He slammed the chair back into an upright position, braced his arms against the desk and pushed to his feet. 'You can't do that! Who'll run the bookshop? Your Aunt Violet hasn't spent more than an hour in the place since she took over.'

'I will. With Archie's help. I've learned a good deal in my last few months of working here.'

'Don't be ridiculous, Hannah. Women don't run businesses.' He pointed to a copy of Kingsley's *The Water Babies* from the desk and held it up. 'I don't know why you're still selling that rubbish! It was published over forty years ago.' He tossed the book back onto the desk. 'You barely came near the place for a month when your fiancé got himself blown up in France. You and your aunt owe me.'

'How could you talk about him like that? Gerald was your friend,' Hannah spat, stung by his contempt for her late fiancé.

'A friend who helped get me this!' He slapped his left thigh with his free hand. 'If he and Darius hadn't been so reckless, I might be a captain by now!'

Hannah smothered a disbelieving snort at the notion Monty's bad hip had denied him a glittering military career.

'I'm sorry, but this decision is final.'

'You'll regret this!' He held a finger menacingly close to her face. 'You and that unnatural aunt of yours won't last a week.'

'I don't know what you're talking about.' Hannah glared at him, defiant. 'And in case you had forgotten, my aunt is your employer, so for that slur alone you deserve to be discharged.'

Hannah had always been aware of what people said about her Aunt Violet, who once shared a house with Eva Ledbetter; a striking redhead with an infectious laugh who was also a member of the Women's Political and Social Union headed by Emmeline Pankhurst. Their association drew speculation and gossip by some, including Hannah's parents.

'You're determined on this?' Monty's eyes hardened, then chilled when she stood her ground.

'I'm afraid so.' *Stay firm, he brought this on himself.*

'Have it your own way.' He limped to the front of the shop, the crash of the door slamming behind him hard enough to wrench it off its hinges. The bell jangled in protest, then faded into silence.

Hannah released a slow breath and leaned a hand on the desktop in relief, only to straighten again as the door flew open to admit Archie, a stoneware jug in one hand and a brown bag in the other, the paper darkened by a smear of grease. With both hands encumbered, he delivered a swift backwards kick to the footplate.

'Miss Merrill?' The youth stared at her, frowning. 'What's wrong with Mr Carstairs? He almost knocked me down in the street, then stalked off without a word.'

'He's gone, Archie. For good.'

'Never!' Archie cradled the milk jug with both hands and stared at the still shivering shop door, then held up the paper bag from which came an enticing smell. 'That'll be just the two of us for tea, then? And bacon sandwiches from the café on the corner.'

Smiling, Hannah plucked the paper bag from Archie's unresisting fingers, reminded she had only toast and tea for breakfast, then remembered she had not asked Monty for his shop keys. But that could wait.

All she had to do now was tell her Aunt Violet.

4

Hannah left the underground later that afternoon and took the river path towards home; weary, but with a sense of satisfaction with her day's work. Not only was she now the manager of the Covent Garden Bookshop, albeit a self-appointed one, but with Archie's industrious enthusiasm, had begun its transformation into an emporium of classical and modern literature.

The hardwood shop floor and oak floor-to-ceiling shelves had been returned to a rich gleam with the application of soap, water and beeswax polish. The weak electric lights burned brighter, their soft yellow glow set behind sparkling clean glass; the combined smells of neglect, dust and stale food swept away in favour of leather, paper and lavender polish.

Their efforts were noticed by prospective customers, invited to browse at their leisure, seeming unperturbed at having to skip brooms or skirt round abandoned buckets.

On reaching home, she dropped her bag in the hall and entered the kitchen, her gaze going to a blue china bowl on the dresser that contained six creamy-shelled duck eggs with a note in her aunt's bold scrawl propped against it.

Darling Hannah

You had already left by the time I came down for breakfast this morning, but here is a small consolation for my not being there to welcome you home last night. I hope your sojourn in Surrey wasn't too arduous, but we both know my sister too well for that to be true.

A group of us went to the Carlton Club last evening, but it got a bit iffy when someone from the London Council of Morality, or whatever they call themselves, caused a scene, so we went off somewhere else and the night simply got away from us. Eva has tickets to a performance of Betty at Daly's Theatre tonight, so don't wait up.

Incidentally, Lily-Anne dropped by this afternoon saying she needed to talk to you urgently and was quite put out you weren't here. She refused to leave a message and was very flustered when she left. You might want to call on her when you can.

With love
Aunt Violet

Hannah re-folded the note, wondering what her friend wished to talk to her about. Experience told her Lily-Anne Soames's idea of urgent was fluid – anything from needing an opinion on a new dress to what flowers she should order for the house.

With the question of supper solved, she went to the telephone, lifted the earpiece and jiggled the lever and asked the operator to put her through to the Soames residence. The butler responded to her enquiry in formal tones that neither Dr nor Mrs Soames were at home.

Perplexed, Hannah asked him to inform Mrs Soames she had called and replaced the receiver.

Beautiful, wealthy Lily-Anne, who never missed a social occasion and loved being the centre of attention, creating dramas from the most trivial situations. In contrast, Hannah was the quiet, sensible one who calmed frayed nerves and restored order. Hannah marvelled their relationship worked, but somehow it did, for only Hannah knew how much Lily-Anne missed her parents, who spent most of the year abroad, leaving her with a companion in their townhouse. Hannah saw through the exquisite, sharp-tongued butterfly to the vulnerable girl beneath.

Lily-Anne met Cavan at a society party and, instantly smitten, they became engaged in weeks and married in what was seen by all in unseemly haste. He had been instantly drawn into the group of friends made up of Hannah, Mary and Robson Ewell, Monty, Darius and finally Gerald.

Had Lily-Anne changed her mind about needing to talk to her? Or had the situation, whatever it was, been resolved since then? She decided to call in on Lily-Anne on her way home from the bookshop the following evening and find out then.

* * *

The following morning, Hannah was buttoning her coat before the hall mirror when her maid, Ivy descended the stairs carrying a tray on which sat a single cup and saucer.

'Waste of me time, that were.' Her maid slammed the tray onto the hall table, spilling tea into the saucer. 'Her bed ain't been slept in.'

'Ah no, sorry Ivy.' Hannah winced. 'I meant to tell you. Aunt Violet won't be back until this evening.'

Reluctant to listen to Ivy's complaints about her aunt's irregular habits, Hannah waved a swift goodbye and hurriedly pulled the front door closed behind her, though not quick enough not to hear Ivy's aggrieved voice through the door.

'Good job I ain't begun cooking 'er breakfast then!'

After an uneventful journey into town, Hannah almost collided with a soldier on the Strand outside the station. His right arm was strapped to his chest in a sling, the white cloth stark against his khaki jacket. He tried to sidestep her, and when she mirrored his steps, to keep her balance she was forced off the kerb, almost into the path of a tradesman's horse and cart.

At the last second, she staggered, but rapidly regained her footing, her pulse racing at the near miss.

''Ere, you there, mind me 'orse!' the carter shouted, and sped by without slowing.

Ignoring the driver, Hannah smiled sympathetically at the soldier, who muttered something unintelligible she took to be an apology, but his eyes did not meet hers as he stumbled away down the street.

Her heart constricted as she watched him disappear into the crowd, unable to imagine what he had endured that turned him into the plodding, disengaged creature he was now. Would he recover from whatever trauma he had witnessed, or was he doomed to live in a horrific past?

'Excuse me, miss,' An aggrieved male voice beside her made her jump. 'You're blocking the doorway to my barber's shop.'

Mumbling an apology, she stepped aside to let him pass, resisting an impulse to tell him he was long overdue a visit as his hair was curling over his collar. On reaching the bookshop several doors away, it was no surprise to see it locked and empty with no lights showing as she had arrived early in the day. Fumbling in her bag for her keys, she let herself in, where morning light shone through the bow windows in the front, which made the rear gloomy in comparison.

Confident Archie would arrive soon, she tidied the desk and shelved a few books before entering the reading corner, only to find the wingback burgundy chair already occupied by a woman in a cream straw hat atop a cloud of pale hair scraped into a loose bun at the back of her head.

Hannah tried to recall if she had locked the door behind her, but assumed she had not and a customer had slipped in unnoticed.

'Excuse me, but we aren't open yet,' Hannah called.

The burgundy chair was set at an angle; the woman's face not fully visible, one hand on the chair arm that looked too pale to be real, which made her think a shop mannequin had been propped there.

Was this Monty's idea of a practical joke, or was it his twisted revenge for being sacked? She could not imagine Archie devising something so elaborate, especially if he was not present to see her reaction.

Not expecting a response, she approached slowly while taking in the mid-calf-length ecru jacket over a leaf green skirt, the high collar of a pale green blouse visible at the neckline; clothes too expensive to be wasted on a dummy.

A face beneath the wide-brimmed hat came into view, the visible eye closed, long eyelashes fanned on a face that was instantly familiar.

'Lily-Anne?' Hannah whispered, her vision tunnelled as her brain tried to process what she was looking at while the sounds of the street outside faded into a distant roaring in her ears, like being underwater.

She reached a tentative hand to a shoulder that felt stiff to her touch; the pressure, though slight, dislodged the arm from the chair. In what seemed to be slow motion, the arm fell from the chair and hung suspended over the floor, the fingers still and unnatural.

Hannah stepped back in shock that ran like heat through her veins as she caught sight of the embossed silver handle protruding from her best friend's chest. The handle of a paper knife her father had given to her as a gift when she began working at the bookshop.

She placed two fingers against the side of the exposed neck, but her heart thumped in her chest almost painfully, so a full minute passed before she was able to discern no heartbeat pulsed beneath her fingers. Lily-Anne's skin was cold, banishing her last grain of hope.

Panic and shock rushed through her in a warm, dizzying wave, just as the shop bell jangled obscenely in her ears. Archie paused on the threshold, directed a backward kick to the door while slapping dust from his too-short trousers.

'Sorry I'm late, Miss Merrill.' He angled his head to peer through the gap in the shelves. 'I stopped to get some milk for our tea.'

'Archie.' She backed away from the chair, turned and, resisting the urge to run, strode calmy to where he stood. 'I... I need you to do something for me,' she said, though her voice came out strangled and without volume.

'Are you all right, miss? You sound funny.'

'No, I'm not!' She fought down a rush of panic. 'Find a policeman and bring him back here straight away.'

'What for? Have we been burgled?'

'No.' Her throat dried. 'There... there's been a murder.'

'A what?' His toffee-coloured eyes widened as his mind grasped the concept. His gaze shifted over her shoulder to the reading corner. Before she could stop him, he strode past her, coming to an abrupt halt beside the wingback chair. 'Blimey! Where did she come from? Is that a knife stuck in 'er?'

'Would you please fetch that policeman now, Archie?' Hannah closed her eyes in an effort to keep her voice calm as hysteria built in her chest. She forced her breathing to slow as Archie fled without another word.

5

Hannah flicked up the latch on the shop door and pressed her forehead against the cool glass. Once her breathing slowed, she retreated behind a row of shelves that blocked her line of sight to the reading corner.

She only had a vague idea how long she sat there before a loud banging pulled her from her daze. Archie's face appeared through the door panel, his finger jabbing downwards in a silent request that she unlock the door.

Her fingers shook so badly, it took two attempts to release the latch.

'Sorry I took so long, Miss Merrill.' Archie rushed inside, followed by a policeman. 'This 'ere is Constable Jones. He don't do murders, so he sent 'is mate to fetch a detective.'

'My *superior officer* will be here directly.' Constable Jones emphasised the words in a polite but mildly condescending manner. 'Where is the body?'

'Over here, officer.' Archie led the way into the reading corner, the policeman's boots thudding on the boarded floor.

Hannah remained where she was, content to leave them to it, but hoping he might tell her it was all a horrible mistake.

'Yup. She's dead all right.' Constable Jones unbent from the chair, nodding sagely. 'Not much I can do until my superior gets here. Until then, no one is to go near the body.'

'Not much chance of that,' Archie muttered, his back to the policeman. 'Miss Merrill.' He eased to her side. 'I 'ave to tell you something. When I was closing up last night, Mr Carstairs came back.'

Hannah started. 'He was here? Whatever for?'

'I dunno. He didn't say. Just told me to go 'ome, and he'd lock up.'

'You left him here, alone?' She groaned, recalling he still had a set of keys. 'You shouldn't have done that, Archie.'

'He said you wouldn't mind, what with him being a friend of the family.'

'That's true. Was Mrs Soames with him?' At his confused frown, she added. 'The lady in the chair.'

'There weren't no lady here when I left.' He shrugged. 'Only Mr Carstairs.'

Outside, a man in a dark suit and matching fedora marched purposefully past the window and up the steps into the shop. He signalled to a second uniformed officer, who remained outside the door, hands behind his back and eyes front like a king's guard.

The first man briefly examined the contents of the wingback chair before approaching Hannah.

'Good morning, miss.' He removed his fedora and placed it on the desk between them. 'I'm Detective Inspector Farrell.' His short blond hair, bright penetrating blue eyes and clean shaven, youthful features struck Hannah that he was young to have achieved such a high rank, although his measured baritone instilled confidence.

Hannah's tongue clung to the roof of her mouth, so all she could do was nod in acknowledgement.

'What do we know, Jones?' He addressed the policeman, who repeated everything he had observed since his arrival.

'Is the proprietor present?' the inspector asked when Constable Jones had finished.

'That would be my aunt, Miss Violet Edwards, but she comes in only rarely.'

'And you are?'

'Merrill. Miss Hannah Merrill.' She nodded to Archie. 'This is my assistant.'

'Archer Root, sir.' He sprang to attention and thrust out his hand.

'Mr Root.' Inspector Farrell shook it briefly before withdrawing a notebook from a pocket, flicking it open one-handed. 'Were either of you acquainted with the deceased?' Retrieving a stub of pencil from another pocket, he licked the end and poised it over the page.

Hannah swallowed. 'I am... I was. Her name is Lily-Anne Soames. She was my best friend. We've known each other since school. She's also... was, my neighbour. At least, we live in the same road, which is quite a long one, so not close, as such, but...' she trailed off, aware the inspector was looking at her strangely. 'Sorry, I always talk too much when I'm nervous.'

Or upset, or angry or embarrassed.

'I understand this has been a shock.' His voice softened. 'The police surgeon has to confirm life extinct, but I could tell at first glance the lady has been dead some time.'

'She was killed during the night?' Hannah stared at him. 'I assumed she had been waiting for me and someone had broken in, and—'

'I doubt it, Miss Merrill. Now, is the apartment upstairs occupied?'

'Er, no, it's empty. Has been for months.' Her throat felt tight as she tried to process what he had said. 'There's um... an entrance at the side of the building, but an internal door over there also leads to the staircase.'

'Jones,' he nodded to his colleague. 'Search upstairs, would you?'

'Sir.' The constable nodded and strode away.

'Whoever killed her wouldn't still be here, surely?' Hannah swallowed, her gaze probing the ceiling.

'Unlikely, but it pays to make certain.'

'Is there a Mr Soames?'

'Dr Cavan Soames, yes.' She forced her voice into a more normal pitch. 'He'll be at his surgery, I expect.' Hannah recited an address on Wigmore Street, adding his and Lily-Anne's residence as an afterthought.

Constable Jones re-joined them and murmured at the inspector's shoulder loud enough for Hannah to hear. 'There's no sign of anyone in the upstairs, sir. Been empty for a while, I'd say.'

The inspector nodded, tore the page he had written on and handed it to the constable. 'Take the motor car and fetch Dr Soames. Tell him nothing, just get him here, Jones.'

'Yes, sir.' The constable scampered away like a Labrador eager to do his master's bidding.

'Aren't you going to warn him?' Hannah asked, perturbed.

'I prefer to give bad news face-to-face, Miss Merrill. First reactions can be enlightening. Now, when you found the body, did you touch it?'

'No! I... oh no, I did. I thought... hoped, she was asleep. I tried to find a pulse in her neck, but—' She wished he would stop referring to Lily-Anne as a body.

'Who closed up last evening, and when?' Inspector Farrell asked.

'I left at around half-past five,' Hannah replied. The direction of his questions jumped back and forth confusingly. Or was that deliberate?

'Mr Carstairs did,' Archie piped up before Hannah could answer. 'I left at six o'clock, or near enough.'

'And who is Mr Carstairs?'

'The bookshop manager.' Hannah moistened her lips. 'Former bookshop manager.'

'Miss Merrill told him to sling 'is—' Hannah nudged Archie with an elbow, cutting him off.

'He resigned his position?' Inspector Farrell looked up from his notebook. 'When exactly?'

'Yesterday. And he didn't resign exactly. I discharged him.' Hannah debated whether to mention the veiled threats Monty threw at her before storming out, but having dismissed them as a fit of temper with no substance, she remained silent. Making him a villain without proof smacked of spite. 'He left earlier in the day, but Archie said he came back last night after I had left.'

'Which means he still has access?' The inspector tapped the page with the end of his pencil and replaced the notebook into his pocket.

'I forgot to ask him to return his keys.' Something she planned to rectify as soon as possible.

'Did you arrange to meet Mrs Soames here yesterday?'

'No. Mrs Soames called in at my home yesterday but I've been in Surrey for a week visiting my parents. I telephoned last night, but her butler said they weren't there.'

'They? That's Dr *and* Mrs Soames?' At her nod he added, 'What time did you call?'

'Around six-thirty, I think. Maybe later. I'm not entirely sure.'

She had been late leaving the bookshop after all their hard work, making the exact time hazy.

'Is it possible Mrs Soames came here to see you, or Mr Carstairs?'

Hannah shook her head. 'We live within a hundred yards of each other.' Lily-Anne disliked Monty intensely because he abused their hospitality, but it was not something Hannah was comfortable repeating. Her mother's Victorian sense of propriety ran deep.

'And like I told Miss Merrill,' Archie interjected. 'I didn't see any lady last night. Alive or dead.'

'And the weapon? Have you seen it before?' the inspector asked.

'It's not a weapon!' Hannah insisted. 'Not until now, anyway. It's a paper knife my father gave me.' His accusatory tone put her on edge. 'I'm not sure what you're getting at, Inspector.'

'I'm merely establishing certain facts, which are,' he read aloud from his notebook, 'that Mrs Soames wished to discuss something with you, but you were not available. She came to the bookshop, possibly to speak to you or Mr Carstairs, but you claim not to have seen her although you left at around five-thirty? You were also the first to arrive this morning when you found Mrs Soames murdered, with your knife, inside your locked bookshop.'

'I resent your use of the word "claim", Inspector, but so far, you're correct.' Hannah folded her arms and mirrored his steady stare. 'Everything I've told you is the truth.'

'Except the part about confusing dismissal with resignation? Has there been any recent animosity between you and Mrs Soames?'

'Not that I recall.' *Not seriously, anyway.* She and Lily-Anne fell out like most friends, but not enough to result in murder. 'Do you actually think I killed my best friend?' Her voice rose slightly. 'Archie was still here when I left, so is he a suspect, too?'

'Oi! I never did anything!' Archie protested, just as the policeman at the shop door appeared at the inspector's shoulder.

'The police surgeon is here, sir.' He indicated to a portly man in a black suit and top hat using his Gladstone bag to clear a passage through the gathering crowd in the street, some of whom glared at him as they were shoved aside.

Hannah bit her lip at the sight of the postman and the baker's boy on his bicycle with its oversized basket, heads together with the lady who ran the florist's next door but one. Was the entire street gathered outside to gawk?

'Farrell.' The newcomer nodded curtly as he stomped dust from his feet on Hannah's clean floor. 'Where's the corpse?'

'Over there.' He cocked his chin vaguely behind him. 'Been there a while, I'd say.'

'I appreciate your input, Inspector, but I cannot have a plod doing my job for me. Right then. Let the dog see the rabbit.'

Hannah recoiled, but was powerless to prevent strangers from gaping at her friend like a specimen in a zoo. Archie crept as close as he was allowed without being shooed away, peering over shoulders as they worked, fascinated by the process as murmurings and the thump of booted feet circled the wingback chair in the reading corner. Hannah's high neckline suddenly felt too tight, making it difficult to breathe.

'Miss Merrill?' the inspector's insistent tone told her he had repeated himself. 'Are you all right?'

'Sorry? What did you say?'

'I asked whether Mrs Soames possessed keys to the bookshop?'

'Of course not. Why would she?'

His eyes closed briefly in exasperation. 'I don't ask these questions for my enjoyment, Miss Merrill, but to form a picture of what everyone connected with these premises was doing, when and why.'

'I'm sorry, but finding her like that... I imagined someone was playing a joke on me. Then when I realised—' She glanced past him through the bow window to the street, where a tall man alighted from a long black motor car. He paused at the bottom of the steps, frowning at the façade as if confused why he was there. Then he removed his hat, revealing dark hair with a distinctive white streak above his left temple.

'I take it this is the husband?' Inspector Farrell said, following the direction of her look.

'It is, yes.' Dread settled low in her gut as Constable Jones carved an opening through the crowd and Cavan Soames bounded up the steps into the bookshop.

6

'If you'll wait here, sir.' The officer at the door placed a restraining hand on the chest of a handsome man in an immaculate knee-length black overcoat.

'Wait? Wait for what? Why am I even here?' Cavan Soames's commanding tone would have cowed most people, but the young policeman held his ground and blocked his path.

'Let him pass, Jones,' Inspector Farrell interrupted, sending the constable back a pace.

Cavan threw the officer a disdainful look as he shoved past, then squared up to the inspector. 'Are you in charge here?'

'Detective Inspector Farrell, sir,' he responded without flinching, despite being several inches shorter. 'I appreciate your coming, Dr Soames.'

'I don't want your thanks. I want to know why some flatfoot turned up at my surgery with a vague tale about an incident he refused to explain. Then he brings me here, of all places.'

'My apologies for any confusion, but it was necessary.' The inspector stilled him with a look. 'However, I regret to inform you your wife has passed away.'

'Lily-Anne? What are you talking about?' Cavan's frantic gaze turned to Hannah.

'Cavan, I'm so sorry, I—' She reached to touch his sleeve, but withdrew her hand before making contact; it was a gesture that felt too intimate under the circumstances.

'My God, Hannah, what have you done?' His furious, accusing stare burned into her.

'What have *I* done?' Anger surged. 'How can you possibly think—' It was bad enough the inspector throwing accusations about, but he at least had an excuse. Cavan knew better.

'Dr Soames, Miss Merrill.' The inspector stepped between them. 'This is not the place or the time for emotional outbursts.'

'I apologise.' Cavan's complexion turned a dull red. 'I don't understand what's happening, and seeing Hannah here, I immediately thought—'

'What exactly *did* you think?' Hannah stepped closer and glared up at him, unintimidated by his superior height.

'This is absurd.' Cavan's hands flailed before returning to his sides. 'Lily-Anne was perfectly well when I last saw her.'

'Well, she isn't now,' Hannah muttered through gritted teeth.

'And when did you last see your wife, sir?' Inspector Farrell asked.

Cavan paused and licked his lips, seemingly unwilling to answer, but the inspector's hard glare dared him to refuse. 'Er – yesterday morning.'

The inspector's brows rose, causing Cavan's deep flush to reappear.

'Were you not alarmed when your wife failed to arrive home last night, sir?'

'Last night?' Confusion filled his eyes. 'What are you talking about? I thought she was found this morning?'

'She was, sir. However, Mrs Soames died last evening. She was discovered...' He consulted his watch. 'Approximately an hour ago. Am I to understand you were not aware your wife was absent from your home all night?'

'I... I slept in my dressing room. When she didn't appear at breakfast, I assumed she was still asleep. I assume she was here to see Hannah?' He looked away, suddenly sheepish after his previous outburst.

'I take it the last time you saw Mrs Soames was twenty-four hours ago?'

'Um... I suppose so, yes.' Cavan cleared his throat. 'Inspector, could you at least tell me how she died? Was it a heart attack or some sort of accident?'

'You wife was stabbed, sir.' He studied Cavan's face closely as he spoke.

'Stabbed!' Cavan inhaled sharply, his gaze going straight to Hannah. 'Here in the bookshop? How can that possibly have happened?' He looked about to say something more, but thought better of it.

'I'm trying to establish that, sir.' The inspector failed to mask his frustration.

'Where is she? Where's my wife?' Cavan made to move towards the activity in the room, only to be intercepted by Constable Jones, who halted him with an outstretched arm.

'First, I would ask you to relate your movements of yesterday,' the inspector asked.

'My movements... Er... I spent most of the day at my surgery. After luncheon I attended a patient and from there, I went to my club where I spent the evening.'

'And this patient's address?' Inspector Farrell held his pencil over the page in readiness.

'Is that really necessary?' Cavan turned a shoulder towards Hannah as if to create privacy, though the volume of his voice precluded it. 'My success as a physician relies on my ability to remain discreet.'

'This is a murder investigation, Dr Soames.' Inspector Farrell's world-weary sigh implied an experience of dealing with intransigent witnesses.

Reluctantly, Cavan rattled off a name and an address in Belsize Park, which Hannah immediately forgot, just as a deep masculine cough preceded the reappearance of the police surgeon. Now hatless, a sparse layer of grey hair combed across an almost bald head, he regarded them through small, round eyes like a friendly ferret. His shabby leather bag landed on the tiles with a thump, freeing the short-fingered, pudgy hand he offered to Cavan.

'Ridley. Police Surgeon. Allow me to offer my condolences, sir.' His tone held the respect of one medical man to another.

After a brief hesitation, Cavan took the surgeon's plump hand in his long-fingered, manicured one. 'Did...did my wife suffer?'

'I doubt it, sir. The fatal wound entered the front of the left side of the chest between the second and third ribs, most likely penetrating the right side of the heart, thus causing ventricular damage and bleeding into the lungs. Time of death is more difficult to discern, as rigor mortis is well established. Between eight and twelve hours ago, I would say.' Dr Ridley brushed off the flat surface of his hat with one hand and placed it on his head, giving it a sharp tap.

'Could you explain the lack of blood?' Inspector Farrell repeated Hannah's own observation. 'Unusual for a stab wound.'

'Corset!' the surgeon replied dispassionately. 'Laced tight enough to keep the wound under pressure. Same thing happened to Empress Elisabeth of Austria. She walked around for hours after a lethal stab wound. As in that case, a long, exceptionally thin blade was used, thus most of the bleeding was internal. I'll know more when I get her back to the mortuary.' He hefted his battered bag beneath his arm, raised his hat an inch with his free hand, and nodded at the inspector. 'Good day to you, Farrell.'

The shop door closed on him with the incongruous jingle of the doorbell.

'Who would want to kill Lily-Anne?' Cavan asked the question plaguing Hannah since her discovery. 'And why here of all places? *Your* bookshop, Hannah.'

'Technically, my Aunt Violet's bookshop.' Hannah sighed, growing increasingly annoyed at Cavan's frequent hard looks.

'Do you know where your aunt was last night, Miss Merrill?' the inspector asked.

'She was—' Where was Aunt Violet last night? Her note said she would be at the theatre and that morning Ivy said her bed had not been slept in.

'You were saying, Miss Merrill?'

'Nothing.' Hannah shook her head.

'You may see your wife now, sir.' Inspector Farrell gestured to the officer who guarded the burgundy chair.

Nodding, the officer stood aside, ignoring the dismissive grunt Cavan directed at him as he strode to the far end of the room. Immediately Cavan's demeanour changed, and he bent his head before slumping to his knees beside the chair, issuing a low groan, followed by a suppressed sob.

'He appears genuinely distraught,' Inspector Farrell said gently.

'Why wouldn't he be?' Hannah's voice trembled in empathy. 'He's just lost his wife.'

Perhaps it was true the police always suspected the spouse in a sudden death.

'Are you all right, Miss Merrill?' Inspector Farrell's brow furrowed as he asked, a hand on her forearm she was tempted to shrug off, but he seemed genuinely concerned.

'What are you like at making tea? I imagine we could all do with a cup.'

'I'm not a maid, Inspector,' she snapped, her former good opinion of him shrivelling.

'Well, no, but I thought—'

'I can, sir,' Constable Jones interjected. 'I do it all day at the station.' He flushed, indicating this might not be the most appropriate response.

'Good show.' Inspector Farrell appeared not to notice. 'I imagine you'll find all the accoutrements in the back room. See what you can rustle up.'

Cavan returned, looking to have aged five years in as many minutes. He had removed his jacket, his shirtsleeves slightly crumpled and his tie askew. His eyes were dull, his carefully coiffed hair in disarray from having his hand repeatedly pushed through it.

Hannah fidgeted, not knowing what to say. Offer condolences? Insist she had nothing to do with his wife's death? She settled on neither, turning her attention to a high-sided black wagon pulling up at the kerb. Two men in brown boiler suits emerged from the rear, a stretcher slung between them like a misshapen pantomime horse as they manoeuvred clumsily through the door and between the bookshelves.

'I'll also need Mr Carstairs's address.' The inspector produced the notebook again. 'Together with yours and your aunt's.'

'Monty – Mr Carstairs – lives in Bayswater. Albert Mansions. Number eight. My aunt and I live together.' She gave her address in Chiswick, which he transcribed carefully before consigning the notebook and pencil to his pocket.

A squeak of wood followed by a series of grunts and shuffles came from behind the bookshelves as the drivers completed their onerous task with the stretcher.

'Might I leave now, Inspector?' Hannah experienced an overpowering desire to be elsewhere.

'One last question.' He spoke with an air of having just thought of it, though Hannah suspected otherwise. 'What did Dr Soames mean when he asked what you had done?'

'I couldn't say.' Heat rushed into her face at the memory of Cavan's accusing tone. 'It surprised me too.'

'Hmmm. What sort of relationship do you have with Dr Soames?'

'What does that mean? He's my friend's husband. Or do I mean a widower now?'

'A simple enquiry.' His conciliatory smile failed to reduce the implication. 'What do your parents think of their unmarried daughter working?'

'That's three questions.' *Where did that come from?*

'Are you going to answer?'

'They disapprove, if you must know.' Hannah inhaled slowly before continuing. 'Unlike me, my older sister lived up to their ambitions by marrying into an aristocratic family. Her husband's elder sibling conveniently died, leaving him the estate.' Her cheeks warmed uncomfortably. 'Oh dear. Now I sound bitter, when I assure you, I'm not.'

'I'm convinced you aren't the bitter kind, Miss Merrill.' His brief but reassuring slip in his professionalism felt genuine, even compassionate. Or was he making fun of her?

The men in boiler suits had manoeuvred a long, wrapped shape on a stretcher through the shop door, and the slam of the ambulance door out on the street told her he had deliberately distracted her.

'Thank you,' she murmured, acknowledging his thoughtfulness.

'My pleasure.' He smiled and inclined his head. Perhaps he was human, after all?

The rattle of crockery announced the constable's return with a heavily loaded tray. 'Good timing, Jones.' Inspector Farrell acknowledged him with a nod, and an enquiring glance at Hannah.

'Er, no, I won't, thank you.' With a brief farewell to the inspector and a warmer one for Archie, Hannah pushed through the spectators on the pavement, her head down to avoid their curious stares, and ran all the way to the Strand where she hailed a waiting hackney.

'Where to, miss?' the driver called down from his seat.

Hannah hesitated. Aunt Violet was probably at one of her Red Cross meetings, and the thought of going home to an empty house held no appeal. She needed to talk to someone who had known Lily-Anne as well as she had. Monty was hardly a friend, and besides, she had sacked him and there was still a question about what he was doing at the bookshop last night. Gerald was dead, and her friend Mary Ewell was a dear, but hardly a confidant. Hannah imagined having to comfort her, not the other way around.

On an impulse she said, 'Ilchester Place, Holland Park please, driver.'

A hundred questions circled in her mind as the cab ate up the two-mile journey. Had Lily-Anne been so impatient to see Hannah, she came to the bookshop? Was she there when Monty returned soon afterwards? If so, how come Archie had not seen her?

And where had Aunt Violet been all night? At the theatre, like her note said, or somewhere else? Not that she could be considered a suspect, but Hannah would rather speak to her before the police did.

Nothing made sense, other than things not looking at all good for Monty.

7

'Mr Clifford is in the sitting room, Miss Merrill.' The butler admitted her with a smile of long familiarity. 'Shall I announce you?'

'No need, Travers. I know the way,' Hannah called over her shoulder as she crossed the wide black and white tiled floor of the triple-height entrance hall, illuminated by an impressive glass lantern two floors above. She entered the open door of a sapphire blue and primrose yellow sitting room that sported an impressive Adam fireplace at one end, where Darius Clifford lounged on a silk sofa reading a newspaper, his ankles crossed on a footstool.

Over six feet tall, broad shouldered and athletic, Darius wore his thick sable brown hair unfashionably long and, unlike his peers, eschewed the use of pomade. His imposing height and strong symmetrical features could unnerve on the first meeting, but his smile brightened the silvery flecks in his midnight blue eyes, engendering trust in the most hostile stranger. Hannah collected jokes and amusing anecdotes to tell him, purely to hear his laugh; a low, rolling growl that gave him the disposition of a friendly bear. She leaned a shoulder against the door frame, observing him silently, knowing she was about to ruin his mood with her news.

He seemed to sense he was not alone and twisted in his seat, his confused frown changing to delighted surprise. 'Hannah!' He crumpled his copy of *The Times* into an untidy heap, leapt to his feet, crossing the room in two strides to enfold her in an exuberant hug. 'What a lovely surprise.'

'I'm sorry to turn up with no warning.' Her voice cracked as she relished the clean linen and subtle citrus cologne he always wore. 'I needed to talk to someone, and I'm not sure where Aunt Violet is. It's... it's Lily-Anne, she—' Hannah's nerve failed her, and she clamped her lips together.

'Oh dear.' Settling her on the sofa, he took a seat opposite. 'What has the frivolous but lovely Mrs Soames been up to now?'

'Don't joke, Darius, please.' She blinked back incipient tears. 'She's dead.'

'Dead? What do you mean, dead?' His expression hardened into alarmed disbelief. 'Has there been an accident?'

'No... she was— murdered. Stabbed.' She had rehearsed what to say in the hackney on the way there, but saying it was still hard.

'What?' He blinked. 'Why would anyone kill Lily-Anne?'

'I've been asking myself the same thing since I found her.'

'*You* found her?'

'It was horrible. I'm surprised I didn't start screaming in the middle of the shop, but I just froze.' She launched into a garbled account of her encounter with Detective Inspector Farrell and Cavan's reaction to seeing his dead wife.

'What was Lily-Anne even doing there?' Darius asked when she had finished.

'The inspector asked me the same thing, but I had no answer.' She brought her clenched fists down onto her lap. 'Neither did

Cavan. The police surgeon said it happened sometime last night. She had been sitting there for hours, dead.'

'Where were you when it happened?'

'Darius!' Her chin came up. 'You sound like Inspector Farrell.'

'I'm sorry.' Darius left the sofa and came to sit beside her, his face close and one arm encircling her shoulders. 'I didn't mean to sound as if I was interrogating you.'

'No, I'm sorry for being so prickly.' She leaned closer, their foreheads almost touching, his closeness instantly calming her in a way Gerald had never achieved. *What made her think that at this moment?*

'You said Cavan was there.'

'Not at first. Inspector Farrell sent for him. He was terribly shocked, but then he attacked me.' At Darius's shocked expression, added, 'Not physically. He seemed to think it was my fault.' Darius protested, but she cut across him. 'He took it back straight away, but I felt he was deflecting his guilt onto me.'

'His guilt? Cavan couldn't have done this! He was devoted to Lily-Anne.'

Silently she agreed, but on some level, something struck her as wrong. 'He was... stunned, but also resigned. As if he expected something of the kind.'

'How does one expect the murder of one's wife?' His tone sharpened, but being Darius, he did not suggest she was being hysterical or misguided.

'No.' *Not unless they engineered it.* 'But isn't the husband always the first to be suspected?' He stiffened, and she felt immediately contrite. 'I'm sorry. I don't mean that, but he upset me.'

'My poor Hannah. It must have been awful for you.' He stroked her cheek with his free hand.

'It was.' Her eyes fluttered closed, and she leaned into his comforting touch.

The sharp click of the door preceded the entrance of a tall young woman on a cloud of a heavy, floral perfume.

Hannah jerked upright and Darius eased sideways, putting some space between them. 'Cecily!' His voice changed from surprised welcome to a question. 'Travers didn't inform me you were here.'

Darius's fiancée glided towards them in a beautifully cut calf-length burgundy coat trimmed with powder blue, over a matching blouse cut to emphasise a slender figure. She wore more make-up than was customary, her wide grey eyes outlined and full lips carmined a deep blood-red, though she wore it well. She stared at Hannah with mild contempt, as if she had encountered a kitchen maid in the drawing room. Hannah certainly felt like one in her now crumpled straight skirt and plain blouse.

'Because I told him not to.' Pouting, Cecily inclined her head to receive his kiss. 'How are you, Hannah?' she added as an afterthought, one raised eyebrow demanding an explanation. 'I thought you declined our invitation to join us this evening because you had other plans?'

'I did. I do.' Hannah scrambled to her feet, unwilling to admit a cup of cocoa and a Jane Austen novel were her only plans for the evening. 'I brought some bad news.'

'Oh dear.' Cecily halted, removing her hat. 'Does it concern anyone we know?'

'Yes,' Darius hissed the word. 'Lily-Anne Soames.'

'Gracious! What's she done now?' Cecily sighed and tossed the feathered confection onto the sofa and sat, one leg gracefully draped over the other at the knee. 'Don't say she's cancelled tonight? I suppose she regards Fred Emney and the Comedy Theatre below her?'

'Cecily!' Darius's warning tone cut through her chatter. 'Lily-Anne is dead.'

'Dead?' Cecily jerked upright; her eyes wide. 'How dreadful!' She made a grab for Darius's hand, which he accepted, if awkwardly. 'When did it happen? How?'

'Last night. Someone stabbed her.' Hannah hesitated, knowing what reaction her next words would bring, but could not avoid it. 'At the bookshop, with my knife.'

'Heavens! Will you need a lawyer?' Cecily's eyes rounded, a hint of glee in their depths. 'Darius knows several, don't you, darling?'

'Don't be ridiculous, Cecily.' Darius took a seat beside Cecily, his hands linked between his spread knees. 'You might be more sympathetic. It was Hannah who found her.'

'*You* were there?' Cecily's voice held a mixture of horror and disbelief.

Before Hannah could explain, Darius pushed to his feet, distracting her. 'What a dreadful host I am. I haven't even offered you a cup of tea.' He made a vague gesture towards Cecily. 'Would you ask Travers to send instructions to the kitchen?'

'That's what the bell is for, darling.' Cecily's girlish giggle failed to conceal her exasperation.

Darius stared at her without speaking until she took the hint.

'Oh, all right.' Reluctantly, she rose from the sofa. 'I'll telephone our other guests and tell them we'll only be a small party tonight.'

'Cecily!' Darius's sharp tone made Hannah jump. 'How can you possibly think we'll go ahead with our plans for this evening under such circumstances?'

'But I've made all the arrangements.' Halting mid-stride, Cecily turned pleading eyes on Darius. 'Your father is coming all the way from Hertfordshire for the night. I can't just—'

'My father will understand.' He gripped the back of his neck with one hand and inhaled slowly. 'He was extremely fond of Lily-Anne.'

Hannah silently acknowledged this was true. As Hector Merrill's business partner, Joshua Clifford attended all the same house parties and balls to which Lily-Anne and Hannah were invited.

'Of... of course.' Cecily visibly crumbled. 'Forgive me, I wasn't thinking.'

'I'll have a footman leave the tickets at the box office if anyone still wishes to go,' Darius added. 'No reason to spoil the evening for everyone.'

'No, darling. Only for us,' Cecily murmured, pulling the door closed behind her with a loud click.

A tic jumped at Darius's temple, confirming he had heard.

'I should go.' Hannah retrieved her bag from the floor and stood.

'Cecily didn't mean to be insensitive, only she's put a great deal of work into this evening.'

'I'm not leaving because of her,' Hannah lied. 'And don't be too hard on her, she didn't know Lily-Anne well.'

'It's no excuse. She's aware we grew up together; you, me, Monty and Lily-Anne. Even Gerald, although he was an afterthought.' He ushered her back onto the sofa, taking the seat opposite. 'Don't go yet.'

She sank down, her thoughts drifting. 'Talking of Monty, I sacked him yesterday.'

'Hah!' His bark of a laugh made her smile. 'Can't say I blame you. I'm surprised he lasted this long.'

'I know, you warned me he was work-shy, but it was Mother's idea. She insisted we needed a male assistant in the bookshop to make us respectable. In her opinion, two women owning and running a business were simply beyond the pale.'

Darius chuckled. 'Is she still trying to drag you to Surrey to hide away from the air raids?'

'She believes dutiful unmarried daughters should stay at home darning socks and running errands for their parents. Don't let me start on that subject.' She dismantled her smile. 'What would you think, if I told you Monty came back to the bookshop last night after I left?'

'What for? To ask for his job back?'

'I doubt it. He sent Archie home, saying he would lock up.'

'Was he there with Lily-Anne? Is that what you're thinking?'

'What other explanation is there? He might have been the last person to see her before she was killed. Either that, or—'

'Or *he* killed her. But why would Monty want to harm Lily-Anne?'

'It's more likely to be the other way around. She only tolerated him for Cavan's sake. He would always turn up uninvited just before meals were served. So rude, and yet Cavan seemed to enjoy his company.'

'Probably because Cavan was new to our small coterie and was too polite to throw him out.' Their mutual burst of laughter broke off as Cecily returned.

'The Crossleys weren't at home.' Cecily halted three paces into the room, darting a speculative glance between them. 'I left a message with their manservant. Poor Mary Ewell became hysterical, so Robson had to drag her away from the telephone.' Her hand went theatrically to her throat. 'Oh dear, and after all that, I forgot to order the tea.' Her air of martyrdom made Hannah think maybe she had listened at the door, but she dismissed it as paranoia.

'It doesn't matter.' Hannah's easy camaraderie with Darius now fractured, she rose for the second time. 'I'd better go. And I'm sorry you're missing Fred Emney this evening.'

'Compared to what's happened to poor Lily-Anne, it's unimportant.' Cecily had apparently sorted out her priorities.

'Must you, Hannah? It's barely six o'clock.' Darius intercepted her before she reached the door. 'Why not stay for supper?'

'Not your best idea, darling.' Cecily raised an artfully pencilled eyebrow. 'I've just cancelled our table at Elena's, and as Cook won't have anything in, we'll have to find somewhere to dine as it is.'

'Ah, yes, of course. I had forgotten.' His scowl was reminiscent of a small boy reprimanded by his nanny.

'No, really, I should go,' Hannah insisted. Her modest house with its overstuffed furniture and temperamental geyser was exactly where she wanted to be.

'We can't have you hunting for a cab in the street.' Darius strode to the door. 'I'll get Travers to order a motor car.'

'What a horrible thing to happen to someone we know.' Cecily's pose of anguished concern dissolved as soon as the door closed. She eased onto the sofa and plucked a sugared almond from a blue glass bowl at her elbow, nibbling at it. 'It's bound to get in the newspapers. Murder always does. No doubt the family will hush it up to prevent awkwardness.'

'The Benthams are still in the Far East, but they will need to be informed.' Hannah said, her voice tight. 'They've not seen Lily-Anne since the spring, and now they never will again.'

'If they insist on spending their life traipsing around the world, life will go on without them. Or in this case, death.' Cecily popped another sugared almond into her mouth just as the door opened to admit Darius. 'I was just saying about Lily-Anne's parents, darling.' She angled her neck to stare guilelessly up at him over her shoulder. 'There'll have to be a post-mortem, won't there?'

Darius shook his head at her, his eyes narrowed, and though Hannah appreciated his attempt at discretion, Cecily's careless words made her stomach knot at the thought of her best friend being treated by a stranger like a slab of meat on a cold mortuary table. 'I'll wait outside for the car.' Rising, she made for the door. 'Goodnight, Darius, Cecily.'

'Are you sure, Hannah?' Darius followed her into the hall.

'I'll be fine.' She pulled on her gloves, mainly to avoid looking at him. 'Please forget what I said earlier about Cavan. I was... overwrought.' Without waiting for a response, she swept past the footman at the same second Darius's Swift 15 motor car drew up at the bottom of the marble steps.

As the motor car pulled away, she risked a glance at the front window where a curtain moved, obscuring the figure behind it that could only be Cecily.

'I wish I could like her, if only for Darius's sake,' she murmured to herself.

'Did you say something, miss?' The chauffeur half-turned from his position behind the steering wheel, an eyebrow raised in enquiry.

'Er, no. Nothing.' She sagged with grief at not only the loss of her best friend, but Darius's recent announcement of his engagement to Cecily, which took her further away from him than ever.

8

Hannah closed her front door behind her and leaned against it. As she hung her coat on a hook by the door, she caught her reflection in the hall mirror and looked away, repulsed by the dullness of her own eyes.

Footsteps brought her attention to her aunt at the top of the stairs, looking down from the galleried landing. Taller than Hannah by three inches, her glorious tumble of red-brown hair, so like Hannah's own, was gathered in a low pompadour, full and high at the front with a soft, loose French bun gathered at the back above a long delicate neck.

She had kept the narrow waist and upright, slender figure of her youth that belied the fact she had recently reached her fortieth birthday; a fact she seemed strangely proud of and openly admitted to. A pair of finely arched brows over wide, luminous grey eyes puckered slightly in sympathy.

She did not descend the curved staircase, but swept down it, one slim hand sliding sinuously along the balustrade.

Reaching the bottom step, her hand lifted from the round newel to cup Hannah's chin, a soft comforting touch that was

Hannah's undoing. A sob issued from her chest and she leaned into her aunt's embrace. Her eyes fill with unbidden tears she blinked back quickly. 'I'm so glad you're here. Something awful has happened, and—'

'I heard,' Aunt Violet said gently, her low soothing tone indicating nothing more was needed. 'Darius telephoned a few moments ago.' No gushing sympathy or empty platitudes, simply practical comfort and pragmatic calm.

'That was kind of him.' Hannah summoned a smile, grateful and yet unsurprised. 'What exactly did he tell you?'

'That you sacked Monty yesterday, and this morning found Lily-Anne dead in the bookshop. I tried to ask questions, but Cecily was talking in the background, so I could barely hear him.'

Hannah stared at her aunt, her handkerchief clutched in her fingers. 'Um, yes, I did. Sack Monty that is. Are you angry?'

'Actually no. I'm quite proud of you. I didn't know you had it in you.'

'I held back because you seemed content to let him run things his way. You know he was making a terrible hash of it? If things continued as they were, he would have bankrupted you.' *He still might.*

Her aunt shrugged. 'It seemed easier somehow. Anyway, what decided you? Has he been filching the takings?'

'Something like that.' The postcards were the last thing she wanted to discuss right then.

'Oh, well, we'll talk about that later. Now come into the sitting room. You look as if you need to sit down.' She encircled Hannah's shoulders with an arm and guided her into the parlour where a fire crackled against the chill of a damp evening.

'The police surgeon said Lily-Anne died sometime last night,' Hannah said between sniffs. 'The police are demanding to know where everyone was. I know you said you would be at Daly's Theatre, but—'

'Don't say you're doubting me?' Her aunt's eyebrows lifted in wry amusement.

'Of course not. I don't believe for a moment that you weren't exactly where you said you were.'

'But you wanted to get my story straight before I speak to them? Understandable, if mildly insulting.' Her aunt guided her gently into the sitting-room where they took seats on opposite sofas. 'As I said in my note, Eva and I went to Daly's Theatre to watch *Betty* with the Hazelton's. We went back to their place for drinks afterwards, and didn't leave until the small hours, so I stayed in Mortlake. Now, I'll make some tea and you can tell me all about poor Lily-Anne.' She patted Hannah's cheek and rose, saying over her shoulder on her way to the door, 'Not because I'm a ghoulish busybody. Well, partly that, but because you need to talk to someone, and who better than your outrageous aunt?'

Too restless to sit, Hannah paced between the window and the fireplace until Aunt Violet returned with a loaded tray which she placed on a low table.

Having recounted the events of the previous day over two cups of strong tea and rendered a second handkerchief into a crumpled mess, Hannah felt, if not less shocked by Lily-Anne's death, but more resigned to her loss.

'What exactly did she say when she called here, Aunt Violet?' Hannah leaned her arms on the table that separated their chairs, a pot of cooling tea between them.

'I didn't memorise the conversation, but as far as I recall, she insisted on speaking to you. That it was important. I told her you weren't here and she became... flustered.'

'Not frightened?' Had Lily-Anne expected something awful to happen and needed her help?

'That's not the impression I got. More annoyed you weren't at her beck and call.'

'If only I had been. This might never have happened.'

'That's ridiculous talk, and untrue. You didn't kill her.'

'No, but whatever she wanted to tell me might have affected what she did next.'

'Hindsight is a wonderful thing. If I believed she was in some sort of danger, I would not have let her leave.'

'Oh no, I wasn't suggesting you would.' She dabbed away sudden tears. 'It was all so strange. I thought someone had put a dressmaker's dummy in the wingback chair for a joke. Then I saw the knife sticking out of her chest. My knife. The one Papa gave me. It was horrible.' She gulped a mouthful of tea, which was cold.

'A knife?' Aunt Violet leaned forward in her chair, her forearms on her knees. 'Darius didn't mention that part. I imagined it would be something more—'

'More what?' Hannah peered at her over the rim of her cup.

'Erm, nothing. I had no idea her death was so... brutal. Who could have hated her enough to stab her to death? She had a mean streak, but even so.'

'That's harsh, Aunt Violet.' Hannah lowered her cup. 'Whatever did she do to you?' She silently agreed that Lily-Anne could be abrasive, but it was a side of her most people overlooked.

'It doesn't matter now. I've forgotten all about it.' Her aunt waved her away.

'Obviously you haven't, or why mention it?' A thought struck her, and she inhaled a shocked breath. 'She made some crass remark about you and Eva, didn't she? Oh, Aunt Violet, I'm so sorry.'

'It's not important now.' Her aunt fiddled with the line of pearl buttons on her high neckline, her cheeks flushed. 'And Eva never got to hear about it. At least I hope not.' She changed the subject.

'Why was Lily-Anne at the bookshop in the first place? Had you an arrangement to meet her there?'

'Inspector Farrell asked me the same thing. But Lily-Anne never came to the bookshop. If we had lunch or shopped in town, we would meet somewhere else.'

'I'm interested to know what made you go running to Darius?'

'I didn't run!' Hannah snapped, avoiding her aunt's eye. 'He seemed the most obvious person, apart from you. 'Then Cecily arrived and glared at me as if I was a housemaid who had just dropped the best china.' She shook the image from her mind. 'She always makes me feel so clumsy and awkward. Like I can't compete. And the way she fawns over Darius is positively obscene.'

'Hmmm. A little of the green-eyed monster, perhaps?' Her aunt's mouth twitched at the corner.

'You think I'm jealous? What a ridiculous idea.'

'Methinks the lady doth—'

'And you can drop the clichés. You sound just like Papa.'

'I will, if you remove your "whatever-can-you-mean?" look. Darius Clifford has been in love with you for years and I've seen your attitude towards him change recently. Just a shame it happened after he got engaged, of course.'

Hannah stared into her teacup, her cheeks heating uncomfortably.

'I'll freshen this pot.' Aunt Violet withdrew, leaving Hannah to her thoughts.

Her growing affection for Darius confused her. They had always been close, but before he went away to university, he had asked her in the shy, self-effacing way he had, that once he had graduated and established himself in a career, they might be more than friends.

Hannah had thought of him as shy, awkward, Darius whom

she had known most of her life and had not placed too much expectation in his words. Then he had introduced her to Gerald, and everything changed.

Handsome, flamboyant Gerald made a beeline for Hannah, courting her with a dizzying intensity of well-planned outings, gifts, flowers and flattery. She had never commanded a young man's devotion and was naïve enough to believe compliments and romantic gestures indicated a man's true character.

Gerald applied for a commission in the London Regiment when war broke out and proposed to her on a platform at Victoria Station minutes before his train left for France. Hannah could not bring herself to refuse him, but as the weeks passed, her fears that she had committed herself to a life she had no heart for ended when Gerald was killed in Artois in the first weeks of the fighting.

Darius had embarked on what observers referred to as his lacklustre courtship of Cecily Prentice, so Hannah wrote him off as indecisive, even weak, but maturity told her he had acted in the only way an honourable man could have done. She had had plenty of time since, realising she had misjudged and underestimated him.

'Darius couldn't believe it, either.' Hannah took up her narrative when her aunt returned with the replenished teapot. 'Although he dismissed the idea Cavan had anything to do with it.'

'You think he killed his own wife?' Her aunt's hand on the teapot as she poured halted mid-way.

'I don't know. When Cavan told the inspector he had not known Lily-Anne had been out all night, I found it hard to believe him.'

'That does sound strange.' Her aunt regarded her over the rim of her cup. 'How did he explain it?'

'He said he slept in his dressing room so as not to disturb her.'

'I suspect there are many women who wished their husbands

would spend more nights in their dressing rooms.' Her scornful laugh ended abruptly as the growl of an approaching engine brought her to the window. 'Do you know anyone who owns a motorcycle?' Aunt Violet asked. 'There's one right outside.'

Garbed in an oxblood leather coat that skimmed his ankles, and gauntlet gloves, the rider kicked down the stand and dismounted the machine. Unclipping the chin strap of his round helmet, he tugged it off, revealing charmingly ruffled wheat-coloured hair streaked with yellow fire from the setting sun.

'Oh Lord,' Hannah groaned, joining her. 'It's Inspector Farrell. He said he needed to speak to you, but I had no idea he would come tonight!'

'He's the police, darling. They tend not to ask first.' She parted the curtain and strained forward for a better look. 'However, I don't think I've seen a policeman look quite *that* dashing.'

'Let me see.' Hannah shuffled into position at the window. His leather coat covered his high black boots, and wide lapels clung to his broad shoulders without a ripple.

He leaned the motorcycle against the stone wall, placed his helmet on the seat, and removed his gloves, slapping them together as his gaze swept the compact but elegant Georgian façade of the house. With the ease of a man confident in his welcome, he pushed open the gate and strode up the path.

9

'We can't just stand here staring,' Aunt Violet said. 'Oughtn't we to let him in?'

'You do it.' Hannah pouted. 'He's tricky. He asks innocuous questions, and it's only afterwards you realise they're a trap.'

'You forget, I've had experience dealing with the constabulary.' She strode into the hall, the sound of the letterbox rattling as she flung open the door.

'Good evening. Miss Edwards, isn't it?' the inspector said. 'I hope this is not an inconvenient time?'

'It is, and not inconvenient at all.' Aunt Violet crossed her arms and leaned against the doorjamb. 'I do like your motorcycle. A Triumph, isn't it?'

'Er, it is indeed.' He threw a bemused look over his shoulder which he transferred to Aunt Violet with admiration. 'She's a Trusty Model H Classic.'

'Horsepower?'

'Four, with a five hundred and fifty cc side-valve engine.'

Hannah split a look between them and tried to look interested, but they might as well have been speaking a foreign language.

'I wasn't aware the police force used them for transport,' Aunt Violet said, making no effort to invite him in off the doorstep.

'They're mainly used for carrying messages at the front line, but I purchased one for my use. With so few hackneys and taxis available these days, it's made my job easier.'

'Not to mention more fun.' Aunt Violet pushed away from the door frame and gestured him inside. 'May I take your coat?'

'Oh, yes, yes of course.' His cheeks flushed slightly, and he fumbled with two of the buttons of his greatcoat before relinquishing it into Aunt Violet's waiting hands. 'The Bedfordshire police are trying out an *Arrol Johnson* motor car. My commander has requested a loan to try it out.'

'Fascinating,' Aunt Violet raised a sardonic eyebrow. 'I'd love a trip out in one of those one day.'

'And I thought you preferred Black Marias,' Hannah muttered under her breath as she followed them into the siting room.

'Inspector,' Hannah asked before he had taken his seat. 'Has Monty Carstairs given a reason for being in the bookshop yesterday evening?'

'Hannah, dear, let our guest make himself comfortable.' Her aunt gestured him onto the sofa at right angles to the fireplace where he perched, dwarfing it, though he wasn't a tall man.

'This is more of an informal interview to cover all the bases.' He withdrew his notebook and pencil from his jacket pocket. 'However, you ask a pertinent question, Miss Merrill. I'd like to answer your question, but we've yet to locate Mr Carstairs. He left his lodgings early yesterday evening. However, there's not enough evidence to suggest he killed Mrs Soames.'

'Who else was there after closing time? Archie told you he saw him.'

'True, he did. But I cannot assume the veracity of his claim without confirmation.'

'Oh yes, I forgot. You don't make assumptions. But what sort of person thrusts a knife into a defenceless woman and then leaves her there all night?'

'Hannah!' Aunt Violet shooed her away. 'Make us some more tea while the inspector and I have our chat. Don't mind Hannah, Inspector, this whole affair has shaken her badly.'

Hannah did not hear his response as she was halfway to the kitchen before she remembered something. Swivelling on her heel, she marched into the sitting room and plonked down onto the sofa beside the inspector. 'I've remembered something. Monty was meeting someone at Simpsons for luncheon yesterday. Perhaps he kept that appointment?'

'Interesting. I'll be certain to check it out.'

'Tea, Hannah?' Aunt Violet pointedly raised her eyebrows.

Hannah stomped away, muttering to herself. 'As if we haven't just consumed about a gallon of the stuff.' Scraping the kettle noisily onto the stove, she loaded a tray, heedless of the risk to her delicate china, fretting as she waited for the water to boil. Voices reached her at intervals, the words indistinct, but punctuated by Aunt Violet's musical laugh and the growl of the inspector's baritone. When she returned with the tray, neither acknowledged her other than a silent nod from her aunt that even Ivy would not have tolerated.

'Thank you for your co-operation, Miss Edwards,' the inspector said as Hannah returned. 'I have a comprehensive account of your movements at the time of the murder as well as a list of esteemed names to check. Not that I anticipate any discrepancies.'

'I'm glad to help in any way I can.' Aunt Violet gave the tray a disdainful look. 'No biscuits, Hannah?'

'Hardly, Aunt Violet. There's a war on,' Hannah snapped,

glaring at her before turning to the inspector. 'How is your investigation going?'

'Since this morning?' He raised one eyebrow over his teacup, reminding her she was being unreasonable. 'Dr Soames did not spend the evening with his wife. In fact, he did not get home until late.'

'I know. I was there when you questioned him,' Hannah said, ignoring her aunt's fearsome eyebrow dance.

'As for Mrs Soames, none of the servants knew where she was going yesterday. Or claim not to.'

'You think someone is lying?' Hannah asked.

'Someone always lies, Miss Merrill. I need to work out who, and why.'

Hannah buried her nose in her cup and hoped he did not mean her.

'Did you ever contemplate the army, Inspector? Or have you always wanted to be a policeman?' Aunt Violet changed the subject, rather clumsily Hannah thought.

If she didn't know better, she would say Aunt Violet was flirting. And outrageously too.

'I'm from a military family, so I was in the London Regiment before the war began. I'm a reservist now, so I may serve again at some point.' He stirred sugar into his tea slowly. 'Do either of you ladies have menfolk at the Front?'

'Hannah was betrothed to a first lieutenant.' Aunt Violet jerked as Hannah's foot contacted her shin, but her smile remained in place.

'Ah, I see. But no longer?' His expression was sympathetic and mildly enquiring.

'Not any more,' Hannah said stiffly. 'Care of a stick grenade in Artois.'

'Hannah!' Aunt Violet gasped, but received a 'you started it' look for her trouble.

'My condolences.' He had the grace to blush. 'Unfortunately, such stories are becoming commonplace. I should have known better than to ask.'

'Think nothing of it.' Hannah experienced sympathy for his obvious discomfort, but was reluctant to revisit the subject of her late fiancé. 'When can I return to the bookshop?'

'I shall need access for another twenty-four hours, but after that, there's no reason not to open as usual. It might even help make the premises less of a focus of curiosity.'

'Huh, I doubt it,' Aunt Violet snorted. 'Covent Garden Bookshop will forever be tainted as being where a grisly murder was committed. Whether or not you catch the culprit.'

'Is Mr Root a reliable employee?' he asked, seemingly apropos of nothing.

'Archie?' Hannah frowned. 'I've no reason to think otherwise. He's always been loyal and hardworking.'

'Only no one else appears to have seen Mr Carstairs at the bookshop last evening.'

'If Archie says he was there, he was,' Aunt Violet interjected. 'There are three public houses on that street whose patrons rarely see anything other than the contents of their glasses.'

'Point taken.' The inspector flipped his ubiquitous notebook shut and stowed it in a jacket pocket. 'I think I have everything I need.'

'I'll show you out, Inspector.' Hannah could not help wondering why this man with his clipped tone and superior mien deserved her aunt's studied attention.

He placed his half-drunk tea on the table and rose, turning at the door. 'Oh, one more thing. Mr Root seemed concerned at the prospect of losing two days' pay because of the closure of the bookshop.'

'Archie doesn't have to worry about that,' Aunt Violet said with a wave of her hand. 'I wouldn't dream of docking his wages for something out of his control.'

'I hoped you would say that.' They exchanged an almost intimate smile. 'Thank you again for your hospitality, Miss Edwards, Miss Merrill.'

* * *

'What an interesting man,' Aunt Violet said as the phut-phut of the policeman's motorbike faded into the distance.

'Interesting in looks or what he had to say?' Hannah gathered up cups and loaded them onto the tray.

'Both. The fact Monty left his lodgings in a hurry suggests he's gone on the run. Not that I cannot see him as a killer. He's hardly a master criminal, nor is he accustomed to evading the police. It won't take them long to find him.'

Hannah wasn't convinced. With all the troops being moved all over the country and abroad, he might find it easy to travel undetected.

'Provided the inspector is actively looking for him. He might have already decided I did it.' Hannah slumped back onto the sofa, her hands on either side of her face, staring at the dying fire.

'Don't be so defeated.' Her aunt punched her lightly on the shoulder. 'It isn't always the person who raises the alarm is the guilty one.'

'You weren't there when he questioned me at the bookshop. He was... fierce. He even implied there was something inappropriate between me and Cavan.'

'I also learned a lot about motorbikes tonight. Inspector Farrell is quite impressive, for a policeman.'

'Pompous and taciturn would be the adjectives I'd use. Among others.'

'Don't be uncharitable, darling. He was only doing his job. You were quite sharp with him when he was being perfectly nice to you.'

'Really?' Her aunt's eyebrows rose at Hannah's comment. 'And did you *have* to bring Gerald into it?'

'I apologise. I was searching for subjects to converse about other than murder, and my tongue ran away with me. Anyway, he had a point in that we only have Archie's word Monty was at the bookshop at all when Lily-Anne was killed.'

'And he only has your word Lily-Anne came here the day before she was killed.'

'What *are* you insinuating?' Aunt Violet clutched at her neckline, but her mouth quirked upwards at a corner.

'Nothing at all, other than it's easy to misinterpret intentions. Besides, Archie's a terrible liar. He turns red and hyperventilates if I ask who ate the last of the biscuits. He certainly couldn't fool a seasoned policeman.'

'I wonder where Monty could have got to?' Hannah mused. 'It's not as if he has an army of friends he can cadge from apart from us.' She straightened and let her hands fall to her lap. He might not even know Lily-Anne is dead.'

'I'm more inclined to think Monty saw the killer and left town in fear of his own life.'

'I never thought of that,' Hannah gasped. 'He's lazy and arrogant, but I wouldn't wish him any harm. And, Aunt Violet, it didn't go unnoticed how very... coquettish you were with the inspector.'

'I was being disarming, that's all. It worked, didn't it? He didn't consider me a suspect for a moment.'

10

Waking the next morning, Hannah stretched her arms luxuriously above her head as she contemplated a few more minutes beneath the covers. Slowly, the fog of sleep in her head cleared, and the memory returned, bringing her bolt upright with a groan.

It wasn't a dream. Lily-Anne is dead.

Her pleasure in the coming day dissolved as she anticipated a round of ceaseless questions aimed at her when the news spread. Her involvement was bound to cause speculation, and Inspector Farrell had made it abundantly clear he would need to speak to her again. Would he call this time with a brace of uniformed officers in tow in sight of the neighbours, or summon her to the police station? Neither prospect appealed.

The police had commandeered the bookshop for another day to continue their investigation, so the day stretched in front of her with no purpose. Sighing, she shoved the bedclothes aside, just as the slam of the back door made her jump.

'I'll 'ave the kettle on in a mo, Miss Merrill.' Ivy's cheerful voice called up the stairs.

Hannah stumbled to the bathroom, resigned to her daily tussle with the water geyser, which behaved for once, allowing her to enjoy a hot, deep bath.

'Did you hear Dr Soames got brought 'ome by the police yesterday?' Ivy set a plate with the last of the duck eggs perched on a slice of toast in front of her. 'Their second 'ousemaid says he murdered 'is wife.'

And so it begins.

'It's bad enough Mrs Soames is dead without you gossiping, Ivy.' Hannah's tone brooked no argument.

'Didn't mean no 'arm, I'm sure.' Chastened, Ivy bundled a pile of laundry beneath her arm. 'I thought you'd know, seeing as she was a friend o' yorn.'

'She was. A good friend.' Hannah speared the bright orange egg yolk with a fork. 'And I don't want to talk about it.'

Ivy shrugged, but on her way out of the room, she turned back. 'Oh, I almost forgot.' She delved into a pocket of her apron, withdrawing a crisp white envelope she placed beside Hannah's plate. 'Letter for you.'

'Thank you, Ivy." Hannah recognised Iris's handwriting. 'It's from my sister.' Most likely another plea instigated by her mother to persuade her to live with them.

Ivy's face fell. 'I 'oped it might be from a young man, but I should 'ave known it were a lady's hand.' She flicked a loaded look at Hannah, who refused to be drawn. 'Never you mind, miss. Nice-looking young woman like you will find another beau before long. Not that the likes 'o me 'ave much chance with this blessed war.'

Hannah experienced a rush of sympathy for Ivy, whom nature had given few physical charms. 'The war cannot last forever, Ivy. And then all the men will come home.'

'*Who'll* be coming 'ome is what I'd like ter know?' Ivy muttered as she swept a loaded tray from the table and stomped into the scullery. 'It might be a bunch of them Huns.'

A creak on the loose floorboard in the hall announced Aunt Violet, rumpled from sleep with her hair flowing down her back and still wearing her dressing gown.

'You're very voluble this morning, Ivy, I could barely hear the other end of my telephone conversation just now.' She winced at the scrape of her chair as she dragged it across the flagstone floor. 'Just coffee for me, thank you.'

'Tea's all we've got.' Ivy sniffed, nodded at the teapot and gathered up the cutlery from Aunt Violet's place with more noise than was necessary, her mutterings about people who wasted her time clearly audible from the hall.

'Why haven't we got rid of her?' Aunt Violet moved her cup and saucer closer to the pot Hannah held up ready to pour.

'How would we replace her?' Hannah shrugged, although she found Ivy's pragmatic, no nonsense nature refreshing after the stultifying, "Yes m'am, no m'am" regime that prevailed in her parents' house.

Their household staff was sorely depleted since Hannah's lady's maid left to sew uniforms for the army, and their cook now worked as a bus conductor in Hammersmith.

'Ah, yes, I knew there was a reason.' Aunt Violet's eyelids slid closed over her cup. 'I'll give her the afternoon off so she won't bait me for all I know about Lily-Anne's murder.'

'There's nothing in the paper yet about the murder.' Hannah nodded to the copy of the *Fulham Chronicle* on the table between them. 'Who were you talking to on the telephone?'

'Eva. I'm meeting her for lunch. I don't want her finding out about the murder in the newspapers. By the way, does my darling sister know yet?'

'I haven't told her. And don't glare at me like that. Had I done, she would be on the next train demanding I return to Surrey because the city is full of scoundrels and deranged murderers.'

'She's not wrong. Besides, she's bound to find out. Farnham isn't exactly Brazil.'

'Brazil would be preferable. Farnham is so dull. And look at this.' She held up the letter. 'It's from Iris. She never writes, so I assume Mama has inveigled her into her scheme to entice me back home for good.'

Her aunt grinned at her. 'That's the nice thing about letters.' Aunt Violet pushed her cup away and rose. 'You can throw them in the fire and forget they ever existed.'

Aunt Violet left for her lunch with Eva, and Hannah filled her time with a slow wander through the shops in Chiswick High Road, but her concentration was too fragmented to make a decision on what to buy from shops with half empty shelves.

Returning home at teatime, Aunt Violet still had not returned so with Ivy gone for the day, she prepared a solitary tea on a tray she took into the sitting room. Belatedly, she recalled her sister's letter, and with a second cup of tea in one hand and the page in the other, she scanned the lines with growing dismay. The contents were exactly as she had expected: a diatribe on the dangers of a woman alone in London and an insistence that Hannah should abandon her ridiculous and misguided quest for independence and return home to Surrey. The style and phraseology were pure Madeleine Merrill; a mixture of guilt and concern guaranteed to make Hannah more determined to stay. Poor Iris; their mother must have practically stood over her as she could never imagine her sister actually thinking – let alone writing – this.

Tucking the letter into her pocket, Hannah went into the sitting room to look for her bag. Discovering it on the sofa, she went to pick it up, but knocked it onto the floor, spilling the contents. Sighing, she bent to gather an assortment of purse, hairbrush, and the postcards Monty had left behind. Each one had the name Hobart's Studio on the reverse side, together with an address in Soho.

They weren't the sort of thing she relished carrying around with her, but what should she do with them? Her first thought was to tell Inspector Farrell about them, but the thought of explaining Monty's nefarious activities stopped her. A few naughty postcards could hardly have anything to do with Lily-Anne being murdered, could they? But the thought of destroying them felt wrong when they did not belong to her. Suppose Monty came back to claim them?

Undecided, she bundled them roughly together into a pile, but in her haste, one dropped to the floor. She bent to retrieve the photograph of a woman in an Egyptian costume and noticed a loose corner where the photograph had separated from the backing. Inserting a thumbnail into the gap, she eased it apart, revealing a thin cavity which revealed a folded sheet of onionskin paper with three lines of looped handwriting on one side.

Imperative Suchscheinwerfer wurden Anfang Oktober für einen geplanten Angriff auf London deaktiviert. Die Ankunft von Ressourcen und Vermögenswerten steht unmittelbar bevor. Informieren Sie Ihren Ansprechpartner, wenn Vorkehrungen getroffen wurden.

The words "imperative" and "inform" stood out; a memory stirring from her schooldays that English had been brought to the country by Anglo-Saxon migrants hundreds of years before.

It was written in German.

Excitement mixed with alarm sent her running to the bureau from which she unearthed her old school German dictionary, a notebook and pencil. Pulling a chair up to the table under the window, she painstakingly transcribed the note.

Imperative searchlights be sabotaged early October for scheduled attack on London. Arrival of resources imminent. Inform contacts once arrangements in place.

Her pencil dropped to the desk with a click as she read her own writing with growing horror.

Monty was a spy.

She had barely spoken the words aloud when a loud bang on the front door made her jump and scatter the cards across the table.

Assuming her aunt had forgotten her keys, she scrambled to her feet, giving a cheery, 'Coming,' and flung open the front door only to be brought up short by the sight of Cavan Soames. Immaculate in a black tailcoat and white silk tie artfully folded between sharp collar points, he filled the door frame.

11

'Dr Soames?' Hannah took in his raven hair and dark eyes beneath his top hat that gave him an air of mystery; storybook villain or romantic hero, she couldn't decide. His eyes on meeting hers were dull and devoid of emotion, his usually broad shoulders hunched, diminishing him somehow.

'So formal, Hannah? You haven't called me that since we first met.' His wry smile did nothing for his dour expression. 'I thought we were better acquainted than that?'

'Yes, of course we were. We are.' She floundered, her hand gripping the edge of the door so hard her fingers cramped. Why was he here? To accuse her again? Demand answers she did not have?

'I won't come in.' He raised a sardonic eyebrow, reminding her she had not invited him. 'I only stopped by briefly to apologise for the way I treated you yesterday.'

'When you practically accused me of killing Lily-Anne?' The words came out before she could stop them. 'I'm so sorry, I didn't mean to—not when you are—'

'Grieving,' he finished for her. 'I imagine you are too? She was your best friend.' His doom-laden despair made her uncomfortable, combined with a lingering doubt around his involvement in his wife's death.

'I'm truly sorry about my behaviour yesterday. I thought—'

'Exactly what *did* you think?' Her anger returned. How could he believe she might have hurt Lily-Anne when he knew how close they were?

'I fear explaining my actions might make things worse. Therefore, I hope you'll forgive me and accept these.' He handed her a small blue velvet jeweller's box. 'You've always admired them, so Lily-Anne would have wanted you to have them.'

What did he mean? How could things be worse?

Absently, Hannah opened the box to find a pair of diamond earrings nestled on velvet, the stones of such size and brilliance, they sparkled in the fading light.

Silently, Hannah acknowledged he was wrong; Lily-Anne would have chewed off her own arm before giving these to anyone. Then tears welled at the thought her friend no longer had a use for jewellery.

'Lily-Anne didn't leave a will. I mean, why would she?' Cavan shrugged. 'She was only twenty-four.'

'Thank you, Cavan. I'll treasure them. Would... would you like to come in?' Keeping him on the doorstep seemed rude, although the postcards and Monty's note were in full view in the sitting room.

'Er, no I won't, thank you.' He cast a swift, nervous look over his shoulder. 'Inspector Farrell said Lily-Anne arrived unexpectedly at the bookshop. Is it true?'

'Yes, I still don't understand why she was there.'

'Someone must know.' His clipped tone displayed his frustration. 'She was going shopping in the afternoon and had been invited to have supper with friends, but did not say with whom.

I've spoken to as many of them as I could reach, but no one admits to inviting her.'

'I'm sorry, Cavan. If I knew anything, I would tell you.' She closed the velvet box with a firm click. 'If there's anything I can do, please ask.' Not that she could think of one thing he might need from her.

'I appreciate that.' He scuffed his shoe against the doorjamb. 'Well... um, I'll wish you a good evening.'

Sensing he wanted to say more, Hannah started to close the door, but paused. Instead of walking towards his house, he took the opposite direction to where his carriage waited on the road; a figure outlined in the rear window moved towards him as he climbed inside.

Hannah squinted to bring the pair into focus, but the low light of the coming dusk made it impossible to see if his companion was a man or a woman before the contraption moved off toward Hammersmith Bridge, just as her aunt's Sunbeam motor car pulled up beside the front gate.

'Was that our merry widower leaving just now?' Aunt Violet called from the driver's seat as she climbed out, slamming the door behind her.

'Don't call him that.' Hannah tried to sound stern, but her lips twitched. 'He looked dressed for an evening in town. And I could swear someone was with him in the carriage. Could you see who it was as you came past?'

'I looked, naturally, but the blinds were pulled down. However, I'd bet my Holloway brooch it was a woman.'

'What *is* the man up to?' Hannah shook her head. Had those questions he asked her been simply camouflage?

'Hmph. I'd say that was fairly obvious.' Aunt Violet nodded to the box Hannah still clutched to her chest. 'What's that you have there?'

'Cavan gave me a pair of Lily-Anne's earrings,' she replied, shrugging. 'A sentimental gesture to remember her by.'

'Huh!' Aunt Violet edged past her into the hall and hung up her coat. 'By sentimental, you mean "nothing of value"?'

'He made a point of telling me Lily-Anne had not made a will, so everything goes to him,' Hannah said, following her into the sitting room.

'Did he indeed?' Aunt Violet sneered slightly. 'And you got a consolation prize?'

'Not exactly.' To call a halt to her aunt's cynicism, she flicked open the velvet box.

'Oh, my goodness.' Aunt Violet's eyes widened. 'I take back every slight I've hurled at the man, which is not many. Although I find it crass that he's totting up his inheritance before she's even buried.' She relaxed on a sofa and kicked off her shoes. 'Put the kettle on, darling. I'm dying for a cup of tea.'

Hannah was reminded of the day Lily-Anne told her she and Cavan were to be married. 'He won't have a bean once his medical studies are paid for,' her friend had chattered excitedly. 'Not that I care. Papa is going to sign over the house to me and he's continuing my allowance.'

'Money is always a motive for murder.' Hannah murmured under her breath.

'What was that?'

'Nothing. Before I get the tea, Aunt Violet. I need to show you something.' She shuffled through the pile of postcards on the table, located the note, and handed it to her aunt.

Aunt Violet frowned as she unfolded the message, peering at the writing with little interest. 'I can't read this, darling. It's not in English.'

'No, it's German.' Hannah passed her another slip of paper. 'Now read my translation.'

Aunt Violet took the second note gingerly, her gaze skimming the lines before lifting to meet Hannah's, her full lips slightly parted.

'Where did you get this?'

'It was among these.' Hannah handed her the pile of postcards.

'Goodness!' Aunt Violet flicked through the pile, her expression changing from mildly curious to wide-eyed.

'Shocking, but strangely artistic.' She turned the card this way and that, inspecting it. 'Though I've seen better, to be honest.'

Hannah started, surprised: that was not quite the reaction she had expected. 'Monty was selling them in the shop. I doubt the proceeds found their way into the cash box, either.'

'The cheek of the man.' She nodded to the note Hannah held. 'Perhaps that's some sort of prank?'

'A prank on whom? No, Aunt Violet, Monty is involved in spying. I thought the postcards were rude but harmless, only I hadn't found the message by then.'

'You must give this to the police inspector. The longer you leave it, the worse it will look. He'll be at the inquest tomorrow, so do it then.'

'I will, only he might think I kept them from him on purpose.'

'You don't have a choice.' Her aunt shuffled the pack together again and handed them back. I suppose we'll have to find a replacement manager? Even if Monty does return, he'll have a lot of explaining to do.'

Hannah thought that was the least of his problems. 'About the bookshop... why don't I take over the day-to-day running? I'm sure I could improve things. Bring new life to the place.' She hesitated. Had she gone too far?

Aunt Violet remained enigmatic about how she had acquired a bookshop in the first place, so why she kept it was a mystery when she rarely set foot in the place. Whereas Hannah enjoyed trawling through publisher's catalogues in search of new titles, and the physical routine of arranging books on shelves complemented her love of order. Without Monty second-guessing everything she did, her imagination took flight.

'Are you sure, Hannah? It's quite a responsibility.'

'Perfectly, and I have Archie.' The thrill of a new opportunity ran through her. 'I've already made a start. I'll re-establish the reading corner; it was popular before Monty took over. Also, Monty consigned the Votes for Women and Britannia display to the back, so I plan to make them more prominent.'

'Well, if you're sure, but consider the fact not everyone approves of suffrage publications. You might lose more custom than you gain.'

'We'll see. I know it's frowned upon for a woman to manage a shop, even these days, but—'

'Goodness, Hannah, I'm not your mother! I knew you would find your feet once I got you out of darkest Surrey. I'd help more, but it would mean cutting my hours with the Red Cross and we're so busy right now.'

'Which is moderately better than harassing politicians.' Hannah chuckled.

'Don't be facetious.' Her aunt's smile negated any affront. 'Oh, did you know they've opened the National Gallery again? Eva wants to see the work of some obscure French artist who caught her eye, so we're going tomorrow. Why don't you come with us?'

'I have a bookshop to run now, remember? Are you sure they'll allow you in after the *Rokeby Venus* incident?' Hannah raised her eyebrows in ironic surprise.

The suffragette, Mary Richardson, damaged a Velázquez in protest at Mrs Pankhurst's arrest the year before. When five of Bellini's works were defaced that same month, the gallery closed.

'You cannot blame me for that, and I'd come with you to the

inquest, but I promised to accompany Eva to the dentist. The poor thing is nervous, and I can't let her face it alone.'

'I shall be fine on my own, and more than glad to get rid of the wretched postcards. I still find it hard to believe Monty's working for the Germans.' Hannah sighed.

'Not if they were paying him.' Her aunt handed the message back as if it might burn her. 'Now, where's my tea?'

'Of course, sorry.' Hannah fled to the kitchen.

12

Hannah arrived at the West London Coroner's Court, breathless from her last-minute dash from the tube station, conscious of critical looks turning her way as she took an empty aisle seat.

Dr Ridley, the police surgeon, was giving a bland, if chilling, account to the coroner of Mrs Soames's injury, the time it would have taken to render her deceased and what weapon was used.

His voice droned on, expounding medical details which went over Hannah's head, until his unexpected announcement that Mrs Soames had ingested an amount of cocaine in the hour before she died.

Hannah's jaw went slack as a ripple of surprised interest ran through the onlookers, dying down quickly when the coroner called Dr Soames to the front of the room.

Hannah paid scant attention to his initial testimony as she tried to process what she had heard. Lily-Anne took drugs? Or was it a single, never to be repeated event in unfortunate circumstances? Where did she get them or did someone give them to her? Monty? Certainly not Archie.

Under questioning, Cavan admitted to being aware his wife

occasionally used laudanum as pain relief, and cocaine for congestion, but refuted the suggestion she had progressed to stronger substances; claiming to have stringently discouraged her. The coroner thanked him for his candour and said he could go. Released like a greyhound from a trap, Cavan resumed his seat in the row behind Hannah, who stoically refused to turn her head, stunned at his revelation; Lily-Anne had lived a lifestyle she had known nothing about.

The Soames's servants gave similar versions of the same story, although none of them claimed to have been aware that Mrs Soames had gone to the bookshop, or why. Nor did they think it unusual when their mistress did not return home that evening.

The youngest maid claimed in a high-pitched, tremulous voice, that in her opinion that Mr Carstairs chap might have upset her as she was always angry after he called and often complained about him to her lady's maid, who passed it on in the servants' hall.

The coroner roundly chastised her, insisting he required only the facts.

Thus, when Hannah's turn arrived, she recounted the events exactly as she remembered and with no embellishments so as not to attract a similar rebuke.

Mrs Lily-Anne Soames's death was declared to be murder by a person or persons unknown, after which the proceedings ended.

In the marbled hallway, Cavan was instantly surrounded by well-wishers and friends offering condolences, while Hannah scanned the faces in search of Inspector Farrell. She spotted him at the far end of the hall, engrossed in conversation with a group of serious-faced gentlemen. He gave no sign he had seen her, so she backed into a discreet alcove to wait. The main doors opened and closed at intervals, allowing the clamour of the busy street to intrude on the church-like silence.

'Hannah?' a familiar voice made her jump.

'Darius!' Annoyingly, her pulse raced as she took in his impressive height and broad shoulders, relieved there was no sign of Cecily. 'I didn't see you in the courtroom.'

'I wasn't called as a witness. But I came to give you some moral support.'

'Thank you. I appreciate it.' A rush of sheer pleasure went through her, certain she was blushing.

'Sorry.' Darius looked from the inspector to Hannah. 'Were you waiting to speak to Inspector Farrell?'

'I had planned to, but he's otherwise occupied. I'm sure we'll catch up at some stage.' She clutched her bag tighter, conscious of the postcards inside.

'It wasn't an easy thing to hear, was it?' he said into a brief but heavy silence that settled between them.

'About Lily-Anne using drugs? No. It was not.'

'At first, Cavan insisted to me that it was a legitimate prescription for congestion, but—'

'Wait a moment. What do you mean, "at first"?'

'She... um, developed a predilection for it. Hannah, do I have to spell it out? She started taking it for fun.'

'You knew?' Her chest felt tight, and the room seemed to spin. How was she the last to know?

'In what circumstances would I broach a subject like that?' Darius sighed. 'We hoped it was simply a phase she would get bored with. Cavan tried to break her of the habit, but in the end all he could do was hide it as best he could.'

'Then he was very successful, because I had no clue.' His use of the word "we" did not escape her. How long had he known and why did he keep it from her?

'I'm not naïve, Darius. I'm aware that this sort of thing goes on, but not Lily-Anne? She had a wonderful home and a husband who loved her.' Hannah's voice lifted in frustration. 'What was she doing?'

'Keep your voice down.' Giving the hall a swift glance, he tucked a hand beneath her elbow and guided her away from the steady stream of new arrivals.

'No, I won't be quiet!' She rolled her arm out of his grip and slapped him away. 'Besides, it will probably be in the newspapers tomorrow.'

'Don't blame Cavan for this. It's not his fault.'

'Is that why you came? In case I denounced your friend from the witness box?' He winced, and spurred on by his discomfort, she blurted, 'I knew it. You're not here to support me at all. You're here to protect your friend!'

'No, of course not!' Hurt darkened Darius's eyes. 'Only the other night, you seemed convinced Cavan had something to do with her death.'

'That isn't true.' She faltered. 'Well, maybe it is. But he accused me first.'

'Exactly, which is why I didn't want you to embarrass yourself in public.'

'Embarrass myself?' His words slammed into her. 'I'm already embarrassed and indeed hurt too, because she was my friend and no one told me. I might have been able to help her?'

'Look, Hannah, I—'

'No! I don't wish to listen to your secrets or justifications.' She darted a glance to where Inspector Farrell had moved to speak to a court official, but all thoughts of speaking to him dissolved in her overwhelming desire to get away. She broke away from Darius and stomped towards the bevelled glass doors, beyond which the street beckoned.

'Hannah!' Darius sprinted past her to open the oak door, but she swept past him without stopping. The released door swung back into the face of a middle-aged woman who shoved it roughly open again with an annoyed "tut". He offered a garbled apology, but by this time Hannah had descended the steps. She was twenty yards down the road before he caught up with her and blocked her path.

Forced to a halt, she clenched her fists and stared at the ground. Anger dissolved into hurt, bringing her close to tears. 'Don't worry, Darius. Neither you nor Cavan have anything to fear from me, but it won't stop me finding out for myself what happened to her.'

'That's not your responsibility. It's a job for the police.' Darius reached a tentative hand towards her, but withdrew it when she glared at him.

'She was killed in *my* bookshop with *my* knife and *I* found her. I don't even have a credible alibi.' A couple slowed as they passed, raised brows over sharp, enquiring looks directed at the quarrelling pair. 'Inspector Farrell made all those points clear, only he cannot prove it,' Hannah said when they were out of earshot.

That she had kept quiet about the postcards might convince the police she and Monty were working together. She had contemplated telling Darius about them, but not now.

'Would you let me pass?' She tried to sidestep him, but he mirrored her movements back and forth in an odd, stilted dance.

'Hannah, please listen to me. My motor car is on the next street. Let me run you back to Chiswick and we'll talk?'

At any other time, she would have accepted, but she was close to losing her temper and didn't want to say anything she might regret.

'I'm not going home.' Putting her head down, she shouldered past him, her feet pounding the pavement toward Walham Green tube station.

'Hannah!'

His plea scraped her heart, but she refused to turn back, her footsteps an accompaniment to her fury that the one person she had expected to be on her side evidently did not trust her.

* * *

Hannah felt calmer by the time she reached the bookshop, even summoning a smile for Archie as he waved at her through the front window.

'How did the inquest go, miss?' He took her bag and carried it to the desk like a prize, returning to help her out of her coat.

'Sad and oddly tedious, but with one or two surprises.' Bemused by his attentiveness, she relinquished it, along with her hat and gloves. 'The verdict was unlawful death by person or persons unknown.'

'Odd way of saying she was done in.' Archie nudged something behind the shelves with the toe of his boot. 'I expect you could do with a cup of tea?'

'I would indeed, but you're my apprentice, not a tea boy.' She set off towards the back room, but he darted in front of her.

'Let me, miss.' Giving a cheerful salute, he backed away, disappearing into the storeroom, from which came the clatter of metal on metal, together with the whoosh of gas.

She started entering sales details from copy receipts into the ledger Archie had arranged neatly on the desk, but found it hard to concentrate. The lines of figures blurred before her eyes, her altercation with Darius replaying in her head, accompanied by a wave of shame. He had attended the inquest as a kindness to her, and she had shouted at him for not confiding in her about Lily-Anne's drug use. She should have known Darius's loyalty to their friend would have kept him silent, and despite her irritation, admired him for it.

'I've never been to an inquest, but it doesn't sound much fun.' Archie placed a cup and saucer onto the desk along with a plate of biscuits.

'It wasn't. And I'd rather forget about it.' She slammed the book shut and massaged her forehead with one hand. 'It's no good. I won't get anything productive done today.'

Archie cast a nervous look over one shoulder, prompting her to ask, 'Is something wrong? You seem on edge.'

'Me?' Adopting an astonished expression which looked contrived, he pushed a hand through his hair, making his messy dark curls more wayward.

Hannah debated whether to offer to pay for a haircut, aware he gave most of his wages to his widowed mother, but dismissed the thought as too presumptuous. Caring for one's employees was one thing; patronising them was another.

'Miss Merrill. About our rodent problem. I wanted to ask you if—'

'That reminds me,' Hannah interjected. 'Did you put those traps down like I asked?' She bit into the biscuit and chewed, relishing its raisin sweetness. 'Can't have mice nibbling our stock.'

'Er... actually, I thought we might try something else.'

'Not poison?' She shuddered and returned the biscuit to the saucer. 'Mice are a menace, but I'd hate the thought of any living creature dying a painful death.'

'Um... not exactly.' Archie disappeared behind the nearest bookshelf, reappearing seconds later with a covered wicker basket in his arms. It wobbled as she looked at it, then issued a chirruping noise.

'Is... is that what I think it is?' Hannah eased backwards away from him.

'I thought we might try him out, like,' he said, sheepish. 'In the shop.' Archie opened the flap and removed a coal black, chunky cat with bright blue eyes and a neat satiny nose.

'How do you try out a cat?' Hannah eyed the animal warily, as it perched contentedly in the crook of Archie's arm. It had a solid, compact body covered by a thick, glossy pelt and four perfectly rounded paws with claws mercifully drawn in. A snake-like tail slowly wrapped itself neatly around Archie's forearm.

'He's a solid little fella, isn't he?' Archie held the cat towards her. 'Go on, miss. Give him a cuddle. He's friendly.'

'No, I don't think— oh!' she gasped as the bundle of fur hurtled into her arms, a plump front paw clamped on each shoulder. Round blue eyes studied her intently for a moment before a slightly moist nose nuzzled against her neck, the sturdy body below it vibrating happily.

Her experience of felines was the slinky, long-haired variety with bones sticking out beneath a loose-fitting coat. This one had some weight to it and fitted comfortably in the crook of her arm.

'He belonged to a man who lives on my road,' Archie explained, his eagerness to please clear in his face. 'It's his son's cat, by rights, but he was killed at Ypres. The old man blamed the cat on account of it being black. He was going to drown it.'

Hannah stroked the animal's thick, soft fur, her fury at Darius dissipating rapidly. 'The poor creature. Why are people so cruel? Will you take it home?'

'No go, I'm afraid.' Archie's mournful expression begged for sympathy. 'Even if Mam didn't hate cats, we couldn't afford to feed one. Not with food in such short supply. He might help keep mice away from the bookshop.'

'Help?' Hannah snorted. 'If he's given the job, I expect him to achieve it on his own.' She ran a finger beneath the cat's pointed chin as the purring escalated. 'I suppose he is quite sweet. Has he got a name?'

'Why don't you choose one?'

Admiring Archie's tactics, but refusing to be manipulated, she handed the compliant cat back.

'You're responsible for keeping him fed and free from fleas. I don't want him sharpening his claws on the bookshelves, either.'

'Thanks, miss.' Archie grinned and held the animal up to his face, their noses touching. 'How about we call him Bartleby?'

'I didn't know you read Melville, Archie?' Hannah said, impressed.

'Not the story about the whale. That's too long, but there's a copy of *Bartleby the Scrivener* out back. I read it once during my lunch break. The name stuck with me and it suits our gentleman here.' Lowering the cat, he tucked it beneath one arm where the animal purred happily.

'Call him what you like, but if I see a mouse anywhere in this shop two weeks from now, Master Bartleby will have to go.'

13

A crack of thunder sounded overhead just as Hannah exited the station the next morning. Spotting a gap in the traffic, she set off at a run across the Strand, but had barely gone five paces when the squall turned into a torrent. Figures darted for cover in all directions, newspapers and shawls held aloft as feet splashed through rapidly forming puddles. She sprinted the last few yards and burst through the bookshop door, wiping dripping strands of hair from her face.

Detective Inspector Farrell sat at the desk with Archie, the two empty mugs between them showing they had been there for some time. Archie leapt to his feet and bore her wet coat away to the storeroom, returning with a towel.

Murmuring her thanks, she applied it to her face. 'Archie, would you mind the bookshop while I talk to the inspector?' Jutting her lower lip, she blew an upward breath, inwardly groaning at what she must look like with strands of wet hair clinging to her neck and forehead.

'Of course, miss.' Archie retreated, taking their empty mugs with him.

'This is a surprise.' Hannah dabbed at her neck with the towel while avoiding his eye. 'I assume you got my message?' She took the smaller chair and gestured for him to take the burgundy wing-back. She could not sit there since the day Lily-Anne died. Would she ever again?

'I didn't mean to ignore you at the inquest, Miss Merrill,' he began in a more conciliatory voice than she had heard so far. 'I would have spoken to you after the proceedings, but you seemed... somewhat distracted.'

'Oh.' Her cheeks flamed that he must have witnessed her altercation with Darius.

'Had I expected this weather, Miss Merrill, I would have offered to bring you into town.'

'On your trusty motorcycle?' she asked, suspecting he was making fun of her, a thought which hardened as a fat drop of water dripped off her forehead onto her lap.

'Why not? I fitted the sidecar this morning.' His eyes sparkled with mischief.

'Don't tell my Aunt Violet or she'll want to go for a run in it.'

'That doesn't sound too arduous.'

'She'd insist on driving.'

'Ah. That might be less enticing. Now, are you going to explain why you wanted to see me?' He tugged up his trousers and relaxed into the soft upholstery, looking quite at home there.

'It would be easier if I showed you.' She retrieved the doctored postcard from her bag and handed it to him.

'Um, very... er... artistic.' His lips quirked in a sardonic smile. 'However, I fail to see—'

'The subject is irrelevant. Pull the loose corner and you'll see what I mean.'

'How very creative.' He removed the sheet of onionskin paper and studied it. 'Where did you get this?' he asked after a moment, his tone stripped of his former light-heartedness.

'Apparently, Mr Carstairs sold them here in the shop. The message says—'

'I know what it says,' he interrupted without looking at her.

'You speak German?' she asked, surprised, but not knowing why. From her aunt's descriptions of her treatment at suffrage marches, Inspector Farrell did not share the brutish confidence of the average bobby on the beat.

'You were right to bring this to me,' he said, making no attempt to explain. 'Although this might be a hoax designed to keep our defences occupied while the Germans attack a different target.'

'But you won't ignore it?' Her confidence in him took a nosedive.

'Not at all. However, the War Office will have to establish its authenticity before taking action. This rather changes our priority on finding Mr Carstairs. I'll have to apply to have more men involved now I have this.'

'Monty could be a victim too, couldn't he?' Her stomach knotted as she recalled her conversation with her aunt. 'Suppose he saw whoever killed Lily-Anne, and they threatened him? He would have no choice but to go on the run with his own life in danger.'

'Sounds like you've been reading too many of your own mystery books.' His mouth twitched as he fought a smile. 'In my job, jumping to conclusions can be counterproductive.'

'And what exactly is your job?' Hannah bridled at his levity. 'To hunt theoretical spies or find my friend's murderer?'

'My duties cross barriers since the war began, so they could be the same. The War Office also has everyone on high alert to spies passing themselves off as foreign nationals of allied countries. Could you discern a Dutch accent from a German one?'

'I'd like to think I could, but I see what you mean.'

'You claim these postcards belonged to Mr Carstairs, and yet they are in your possession?'

'If I'm the spy, why would I relinquish them to you?' Was he being deliberately obtuse?

'Even so. I'll need to establish a connection between him and this message, genuine or not. The method is ingenious, since discretion is implied by the very nature of these photographs. Perhaps whoever it was intended for is eager to get hold of it.' He tapped the corner of the card rhythmically against his opposite thumb. 'Are there others?'

'About a dozen. Three others have compartments, but they're empty.' Hannah withdrew the bundle from her bag and handed it to him, only to find herself at the end of his accusing glare. 'Yes, I looked. Wouldn't you?'

He did not reply, simply shuffled the cards as if dealing them for a game of bridge, holding each one up to the light for scrutiny before dropping them into his jacket pocket.

'Do you still think I'm a secret agent for the Kaiser?' Hannah said, only half-joking.

'What I think isn't important, but you should consider my position. It was you who discovered the body of Mrs Soames, stabbed with a knife belonging to you, in premises which you own and run. Then there are these.' He tapped his pocket pointedly. 'I am, however, prepared to give you the benefit of the doubt if you agree to co-operate.'

'Co-operate?' Hannah stared. Was she about to be manipulated into helping the police?

'I'd like to install Constable Jones here in the bookshop. Should anyone enquire about the postcards, simply direct them to him. He'll know what to do. You are also forbidden from discussing this arrangement, or the investigation with anyone.'

'Do I have a choice?'

'That's settled then.' Ignoring her question, he rose, replaced his hat and tugged down the front brim, peering at her down his nose. 'Oh, and thank young Archie for the tea for me.' He snapped her a salute before stepping into the street.

She watched him stride towards the Strand, unable to believe what had just happened. She had hoped to pass the problem the postcards presented to him, and not be dragged into it.

Archie appeared from behind a bookcase, his sheepish expression showing he had eavesdropped. 'Is Mr Carstairs a spy? Like that Carl Lody bloke? The one they shot at the Tower?'

'Don't, Archie.' Hannah shuddered, the thought she might have sealed Monty's fate weighing heavily. 'I hope you also heard what the inspector said about not discussing this with anyone.'

'You can rely on me, miss. I can keep my mouth shut when I need to.'

* * *

'I'm sorry I haven't been around for the last couple of days,' Aunt Violet said as they adjourned to the sitting room after supper one evening, though she did not explain her absence. 'Was Darius at the inquest?'

'Yes, but not as a witness. He claimed to be there for my benefit, but I suspect he was more interested in covering for Cavan. I'm afraid we argued.'

'Ah, which explains your current dark mood. Are you going to talk about it?'

'Darius or the inquest?'

'Either, or both.'

'It was pretty unpleasant, actually.' Hannah shivered as she recalled the coroner's sombre, uncompromising words. 'He revealed "evidence of habitual laudanum and cocaine use." What's worse, is that I had no idea. Once it reaches the newspapers, everyone will know. I feel bad for her, even if she is dead.'

'How did you leave it with Darius?'

'Horribly.' Hannah threw herself onto a sofa, wincing at the sharp pain as her corset dug into her ribs. 'He knew about Lily-Anne, but chose not to tell me. It's why we fell out. Am I being a prude about the cocaine thing?'

'No, darling. I'm afraid to say it's becoming quite commonplace among the nightclub set. A certain earl's daughter throws cocaine parties in Mayfair. It can be dangerous if misused, but I'll bet we have a bottle of cough mixture somewhere that contains cocaine.'

'Not one I take to parties,' Hannah murmured under her breath. 'When I first told you about Lily-Anne, you seemed surprised at how she died. Did you know what she was doing?'

'I suspected something of the sort, but chose not to mention it so as not to worry you. Lily-Anne was always so animated on social occasions for it to be simply high spirits, and too sullen on others. I never quite understood your attachment to her.'

'I thought it was simply high spirits and a reaction to missing her parents. Drugs did not occur to me, which makes me not only an awful friend but unobservant. I doubt we would have been friends at all had not Mama insisted. She and Louisa Bentham were always close and before their first trip abroad, Louisa enrolled Lily-Anne at my school mid-term. Mama insisted I help her settle in and our friendship developed from there. Sometimes I forget she's gone, and it will hit me from nowhere when I least expect it.'

Since her death, Hannah avoided the Soames's house on her riverbank walks; the drawn blinds and wilted black ribbon on the door knocker evoked a range of emotions that varied from anger at Lily-Anne's rash choices, to guilt at having let her down.

'She wasn't always an enigma. We had things in common. I liked to read novels, and she loved poetry. Did you know that?'

Her aunt shook her head. 'What sort?'

'Christina Rossetti, Emily Dickinson. We'd read them together in her first floor sitting room or the garden and compare inspirational phrases, mostly romantic ones. She told me not to accept Gerald's proposal, but it was too late as he had already left for France.'

'She did? Why?'

Hannah shrugged. 'She didn't explain her reasons, other than I shouldn't accept the first proposal I received. If only I had listened.' Had she done so, perhaps Darius would not be engaged to Cecily now? Not that Lily-Anne followed her own advice, but in her case her marriage was a success. Or was it?

She had not dismissed Cavan as a suspect either. If he was having an affair, would he be ruthless enough to preserve his reputation by disposing of his wife? If so, had he purposely chosen a location which neatly deflected suspicion from himself? The way he turned on her that day at the bookshop still made her go cold.

'Inspector Farrell called into the bookshop today.' Hannah changed the subject. 'I gave him the message I found inside the postcard.'

'What did he say?'

'He's going to reserve judgement until it can be verified. He also said Monty hasn't been seen recently. He seems to have disappeared.'

'What do you mean, disappeared? He's not a genie!'

'That's not even mildly amusing, Aunt Violet. The police are now actively looking for him.'

'Which makes him a potential traitor, but not necessarily a murderer.'

'The police are going to watch the bookshop in case he comes back for those postcards. I shall be graced with Constable Jones's presence for the foreseeable future.'

'He's using the bookshop as a trap?' Her aunt's eyes rounded. 'Doesn't he need *my* permission for that?'

'He didn't exactly give me much of a choice, Aunt Violet. He seems far more interested in catching spies than murderers.'

'Maybe, but I might have a serious talk with him.' A smile flickered across her aunt's face. 'I'm not sure I approve of him putting my niece in danger from German spies.'

14

Hannah's black gown grew heavier with each step as she and Aunt Violet made the short walk to St Nicholas Church on a morning unusually warm for late September. Hannah's scalp beneath her hat was itchy, with pins required to keep her soft bun in place.

The pampas grass lining the riverbank swayed in a wind that carried a hint of decayed moss and the sour smell of silt exposed by the outgoing tide. Welcoming an excuse to delay her arrival, Hannah paused beside the sparkling water, shielding her eyes with one hand to watch a lone heron, a dark stripe over one eye, dive for a fish from the eyot mid-river. The slender bird tucked in its head and lifted from the ground in a slow flap of wings before tilting on the wind to glide over the trees, its long spindly legs trailing behind.

Her aunt tucked her arm through hers, the lightness of her touch reminding Hannah she was there, and they set off through the lych-gate into the churchyard where mourners gathered in small groups. Mahler's soulful *Adagietto* drifted from the open church door that gave an uninterrupted view of the cherry-wood coffin swathed in a black pall on a trestle in the central aisle, a spray of white roses piled on the lid. Hannah's heart thumped painfully in her chest while she became vaguely aware of her aunt murmuring something to her before she moved away to talk to an acquaintance.

She stood frozen at the end of the aisle between two urns on pillars overflowing with creamy white lilies, their heady perfume filling the air. Despite the sadness of the occasion, it was a beautiful sight. Hannah's sympathy rose for the industrious soul whose task it was to remove the orange stamens from the hundreds of flower heads.

'You look as if you're planning to bolt,' Darius said from behind her making her jump. 'If so, it's too late.' He placed a hand on her arm that felt so natural and comforting she had to stop herself from leaning into it.

'I'll admit, I'm tempted.' Her cheeks warmed at the thought of their last encounter, but she forced herself to relax, though smiling was out of the question.

'I want you to know I felt terrible after the inquest, Hannah. I didn't mean to upset you.' His dark blue eyes clouded as they searched her face. 'You're not still angry with me, I hope?'

'I'm the one who should apologise. I shouldn't have reacted the way I did. Nor did I thank you properly for being there.'

'No thanks needed.' His expression softened. 'I'll always be there when you need me.'

'Is… is Cecily here?' she asked, unsure how to respond, though her heart raced.

'She is.' He cocked his chin to where his fiancée stood in the church porch talking to someone Hannah did not recognise. Only Cecily's profile was visible, but she exuded a nervousness clear in the set of her shoulders, her fingers like claws on her bag.

'She seems tense. Is she all right?'

'Cecily's always all right,' he replied with a note of asperity. His gaze shifted past her, and he nodded. 'Here's Cavan, poor chap. Do excuse me a moment, Hannah. I must speak to him.'

The two men, one dark, the other fair, performed the male ritual of quiet murmurs, back-patting and sober nods over clasped hands.

'Funerals are so much worse when it's someone you know,' Cecily said, making Hannah jump. *Where had she come from?* 'Odd that Monty hasn't been seen since it happened. Perhaps he couldn't face the disgrace of being sacked?'

Cavan had delayed the internment to allow time for Lily-Anne's parents to return, but after almost three weeks, they had yet to be located.

'No one knows,' Hannah replied vaguely. 'It's all speculation at the moment.'

Hannah was about to ask how she knew about Monty, but refused to give Cecily the satisfaction of thinking she was embarrassed, and instead nodded or smiled to mourners she knew as they filed past her into the church.

'It's not as if you couldn't afford to employ him,' Cecily continued, her voice grating. 'After all, your father owns a merchant bank.'

'Half a merchant bank,' Hannah muttered under her breath, resisting the urge to bring the solid heel of her shoe down hard on Cecily's toe. Her father was in partnership with Joshua Clifford, and as Darius's wife, Cecily's connection would become permanent.

To Hannah's relief, she spotted Darius stroll towards them. His gaze went to his fiancée then shifted back to Hannah. The emotions on his face shifted faster than she could interpret them.

'Why don't you go inside, Cecily? I'll join you in a moment.'

Cecily's lips parted, then clamped together on whatever protest she was about to voice. 'Of course,' she murmured, giving Hannah a withering look as she entered the church.

'What did she say to you?' Darius asked, his voice sharp.

'Why do you think she said anything?' Hannah knew better than to criticise his fiancée, although something she said niggled at her. 'Did you tell her I sacked Monty?'

'If you think I discuss you with Cecily, you're wrong, Hannah. I would never—' He broke off to draw her aside just as Cavan passed them with a woman whose veil was so thick, her face was totally obscured.

'Have you seen that woman before?' Hannah nudged him, nodding to where Cavan was. On his progress down the aisle, he stopped to shake an occasional outstretched hand and say a few words. Each time, his companion hovered a pace behind, but engaged with no one.

'I can barely see her now.' Darius frowned. 'She could be anyone beneath that veil.' Dismissing the unknown woman, he offered her his arm, which she took out of habit. 'Are you sure you don't want to sit with us?'

'I should join my aunt.' Hannah nodded to where Aunt Violet occupied an aisle seat, from where she gave gracious smiles and nods to those in the surrounding pews. 'But thank you for the thought.' She looked pointedly at his hand, and as if he suddenly remembered they were not alone, he rapidly removed it.

Hannah fled to the far side of the church, feeling the imprint of his arm against hers all the way to her seat.

* * *

As the strains of the final hymn drifted away to a rustle of bombazine, cleared throats, and the sound of hymn books hitting pews, the mourners filed out of the church and gathered around the two-hundred-year-old Bentham family vault like a swarm of black bees.

Fighting tears, Hannah clamped her lips together as the pall-bearers carried Lily-Anne's coffin into the mausoleum to lie forever on a stone shelf with three generations of her ancestors. The wrought-iron gate slammed shut with an ominous clang and she turned away, just as a pretty fair-haired girl with a perpetual expression of surprise approached them at a dainty run, dragging a fair-haired man along with her.

'Hannah, dear. And Miss Edwards. Lovely day, isn't it?' Mary Ewell greeted them in her breathless, high-pitched voice.

'I suppose you could say it is. For a funeral.' Aunt Violet regarded her with one raised eyebrow before tactfully stepping away to engage Robson in conversation.

'Oh, sorry. That was a silly thing to say, wasn't it?' Mary twisted her hands together in front of her, shoulders hunched in a child-like pose Hannah recalled from school. 'It's simply awful, isn't it?' Mary said, one hand clutched dramatically at the neckline of a black dress that made her look washed out, her looks redeemed, however, by her large cornflower blue eyes. 'I haven't been able to sleep properly since it happened. Who would have thought Lily-Anne would die so young, let alone be murdered?'

'I know. Awful.' This was the last conversation Hannah wanted to have today. 'Now if you'll excuse me—'

'I saw you the other day in the Strand.' Mary said, never one to pick up on body language. 'I called out, but you didn't hear me,' she said in a tone which held annoyance. 'Whatever were you doing on the Tuppenny Tube? Now, don't deny it. I saw you.'

'Why would I deny it?' Hannah bridled. 'I was on my way to work.'

'What?' Her eyes widened into saucers. 'Why ever would you need to?'

'I enjoy it. I'm running my aunt's bookshop.'

'The one where Lily-Anne? Oh—' Her hesitation was brief but telling. 'Is it true what everyone is saying about Monty?'

Hannah wished she would stop chattering, or at least lower her voice. People were staring. 'What are they saying, Mary?' She put emphasis on the word "they".

'That he killed Lily-Anne. Can you believe that about someone we know? Not that you can really know anyone. Not properly. But if that's true, I hope they catch him.' Mary had apparently destroyed her faith in her friends and her sense of loyalty in one brief sentence.

'The police are still investigating. Unless you know something about her death?'

'Of course not. I'm as shocked as anyone. Only...' She licked her lips, her head bent conspiratorially. 'The last time I saw Lily-Anne, she told me Cavan was behaving strangely.'

'Strange how?' Hannah's nerves prickled.

'She was quite vague, only that he was being secretive. He often came home late at night with no explanation. That sort of thing. It had been going on for weeks, apparently.'

'Are you sure about this?' Hannah's tone sharpened. Mary's reputation for embellishing stories was legendary, though rarely malicious.

'There's no need to be snippy,' Mary pouted, hurt. 'I'm surprised she didn't mention it. What with you being her best friend...' Her coquettish smile betrayed her delight at having scored a point.

'Have you told the police?'

'Should I have?' Mary clutched at her neckline, exaggerating her simpering look. 'Now, I must go.' She spoke as if it was Hannah who was keeping her and not the other way around. 'Robbie and I want to give Cavan our condolences.'

'Of course.' *And glean some more gossip by the sound of it*. 'Mary, one moment.' Hannah halted her. 'The woman who arrived with Cavan. Do you know who she is?'

'Darling, haven't you been listening?' Tutting, she smiled at Hannah over her shoulder as she rejoined her husband.

Deprived of her companion, Aunt Violet wandered back to Hannah's side. 'Do we have a new mystery, as in Cavan's lady friend? Or was that simply Mary being Mary?'

'A bit of both, I think.' Hannah wasn't sure what to make of it as they meandered arm-in-arm through the lych-gate towards the Soames residence; an imposing four-storey red-brick structure, straddled the corner opposite the church. A wrought iron overthrow and central lantern extended above the gate. A sturdy black front door between two stone urns bore a gleaming brass knocker in the shape of a snake wrapped around a staff in the rod of Asclepius; a tribute to Lily-Anne's doctor husband.

The mourners were being obsequiously greeted by the Soames's butler at the open door; Hemmings, a slight, somewhat stooped man, looked more like an undertaker than the actual undertaker did.

The inspector's expression was unreadable, but his gaze rested on where Cavan Soames stood. The grieving widower's expression was of pained resignation while holding court to a group of admiring middle-aged ladies. The same woman Hannah noticed earlier clung to his side, her heavy veil concealing her face, though her slender figure and the economical way she moved betrayed her youth.

'I would love to know who she is.'

'Unless you plan on trapping that veil in a door, I doubt you will today. I'm the last person to disapprove of a man bringing his mistress to his wife's funeral, but he might have exercised more discretion.' Aunt Violet suppressed a smirk as they reached

Inspector Farrell, accompanied by a policeman in uniform. The pair stood apart from the other mourners, their hats held respectfully against their chests.

'I didn't expect to see you here today, Inspector?' Hannah said.

His sombre expression changed to a beaming smile of welcome. Hannah had to admit he was indeed an attractive man. Something her aunt appeared to appreciate if her flirtatious manner was anything to go by.

'One never knows what one can discover at a victim's funeral, Miss Merrill,' he replied. 'In my experience, the guilty often overplay their role.' His gaze shifted to where Cavan stood with his entourage, before adding, 'I'm afraid we have yet to locate Mr Carstairs.' His jaw clicked, showing how much this irked him.

'A lack of success all round, it seems,' Aunt Violet said, though the slight uplift of her mouth showed she was teasing. 'I'm disappointed you did not ask my permission to use my bookshop to catch your spies when my niece's safety is my responsibility.'

'I mean no offence.' He swallowed rapidly, making his Adam's apple bob above his tie. 'Miss Merrill was amenable to the idea, and as Constable Jones was immediately available, I—'

'Inspector, when you know me better, you'll know when I'm teasing.'

'I shall look forward to it, Miss Edwards.' A spark of interest entered his eyes. 'Now if you ladies will excuse me.' He inclined his head and replaced his hat. 'I have a few more questions for Dr Soames.' Gesturing his companion to follow, he strolled away.

'Such an interesting man.' Aunt Violet watched his retreat with an enigmatic smile.

'You've said that before.' Hannah rolled her eyes, tucked her hand through her aunt's elbow, and guided her in the opposite direction.

They spent the next twenty minutes circulating among the

mourners, exchanging polite greetings to discover the identity of the unknown woman with Cavan, but no one appeared to know who she was.

'Isn't that her?' Aunt Violet drew Hannah's attention to a figure in black getting into a hackney on Church Road.

'I think you're right. Blast it.' Hannah watched, frustrated, as the vehicle pulled away.

'Language!' her aunt warned. 'Now, do we join the wake for overly sweet sherry and dried up cucumber sandwiches, or go home to tea and gossip?'

'Do you really need to ask?' Hannah sighed.

'Tea it is, then.'

15

During the coming week, the weather deteriorated to frequent rainstorms, the persistent damp sending Bartleby into permanent residence on a plump cushion in the bookshop bay window. The mouse population had decreased markedly, and the animal proved gentleman enough not to leave evidence of his nightly hunting expeditions about for Hannah to find.

Constable Jones made himself comfortable in the reading corner each morning with a newspaper, issuing frequent requests for copious cups of tea – a duty with which Archie wavered between resentment and friendly co-operation.

Only one enquiry came about postcards all week, which created a buzz of excitement, but turned out to be an ordinary customer in search of a photograph of Tower Bridge.

Archie had smartened himself up since that first day, his shabby waistcoat replaced by a brown belted jacket and a collarless shirt that looked as if it had had a passing contact with a smoothing iron. He had also combed a parting into his shaggy hair, which sported a sheen of hair oil.

Around mid-morning, a tall, angular woman paused inside the

threshold of the bookshop as the jangle of the bell faded away. Dressed in a severely cut, expensive coat and a wide-brimmed hat as wide as her shoulders, she slowly appraised the shop with the keenness of an auctioneer.

'May I help you, madam?' Archie asked, a smile of welcome on his boyish face.

'The only way you can help me, young man, is to put on a uniform.' The woman looked him up and down like one might a chimney sweep in a ballroom, pulled a long white feather from a capacious handbag and tucked it firmly into the top button of his moleskin waistcoat.

Archie's mouth worked, but no sound came out as he looked from her face to the offending feather, a mixture of bewilderment and shock distorting his face.

'I would appreciate you not bullying my assistant.' Incensed, Hannah approached the woman, halting within a foot of her. 'I'll have to ask you to leave.'

'I don't think I like your manners.' The newcomer's ferret-like eyes narrowed over a bird-like nose in contemptuous scrutiny. 'It's unpatriotic to encourage cowards to shirk their duty. You should know better.' The woman's lip curled in distaste. 'I'll leave when you have assured me that this young man will enlist.' She waved to where Archie had removed the feather from his lapel and stared at it, confused.

'He's fifteen, and too young to enlist.' Hannah's fury intensified, and she snatched the offending feather from Archie's unresisting fingers, grabbed the woman's arm and frog-marched her to the door. Had the woman been less taken aback she might have resisted, but in seconds she was propelled through the door and onto the front steps. 'And you can take that with you.' Tucking the feather into the front of the woman's coat, she gave it a firm pat and slammed the door in her face, rattling the glass.

The woman's outraged, 'Well really!' could be heard clearly from the street.

Archie's height and build made him look older, but there could be many reasons he was not in uniform. Most young men raised in poorer homes were malnourished and had health problems which might make them ineligible.

'I'm not a coward, miss.' Archie's lower lip trembled. 'I tried to sign on down at the recruitment office, but they turned me away. I could go to another one and try again.'

'You aren't to do any such thing!' Recruiting officers rarely asked questions until an anxious parent turned up waving a birth certificate. 'I hope this whole horrible war is over before you are old enough to join the army.' A sentiment which sounded hollow even to her own ears just as the doorbell clattered again.

'I'm not too early, am I?' Aunt Violet glided forward with a look of enquiry. 'Hannah, your face is all red. Has someone ruffled your feathers?'

'Don't talk to me about feathers.' Hannah returned her hug. 'Are you too early for what?'

'You've forgotten, haven't you?' Aunt Violet's frown dissolved. 'Or was it me? I've asked so many people to give donations to the Endell Street Hospital library. I must have thought I had mentioned it. Incidentally, was that Gladys Mullinson I saw leaving? She walked straight past me without a word. Whatever did you say to her?'

'Nothing she did not deserve.' Hannah gave her aunt's black coat, with its trimmed black fox fur, and matching wide-brimmed hat a swift up and down look. 'Why the drab outfit? The funeral was last week.'

'Ooh, sharp.' Her aunt sliced her an oblique look. 'Haven't you seen the warnings everywhere telling us not to wear bright clothing or carry torches? After that message you found, I'm not taking any chances.'

'Airships use the River Thames to navigate by, not suffragettes in white dresses.' Hannah failed to suppress her smile. 'And it's daytime.'

'I know that, but dark colours have always suited me.' Pouting, she adjusted her hat in the wall mirror behind the desk. 'Good morning, Archie,' she said to his reflection over her shoulder. 'You've become quite handsome since I last saw you.'

'Yes, miss.' Archie's cheeks flushed bright red as he peered through the circle of his raised arms as he hauled Bartleby from the top of a bookshelf where he had sought refuge during Mrs Mullinson's verbal attack. 'I mean, good morning, miss. Thank you, miss.'

'If you wouldn't mind, Archie, Aunt Violet and I could do with some tea. I imagine you could do with some as well? You've had a difficult morning.'

Archie ducked his head away and retreated into the storeroom, the black cat slung over his forearm.

'Is he all right?' Aunt Violet mouthed, turning from the mirror.

'Not really,' Hannah replied. 'I'll explain in a moment. What's this about a hospital? I thought you were helping with the Belgian refugees at the Exhibition Hall today?'

'I've just come from there, actually. Delightful people and so grateful for everything we do for them, but when it comes to packing OXO cubes and Sunlight soap in boxes, my mind wanders. I've started collecting donations for the Endell Street Hospital.'

'I suppose it's better than smashing mummy cases at the British Museum.' Hannah raised an eyebrow.

'I'll not even attempt to respond to that.' Aunt Violet sniffed, taking the chair on the other side of the desk.

Hannah had visited the museum a few days after the suffragettes were arrested to see how much damage they had caused, but was turned away. The curator informed her in an uncompromising tone that women were admitted only if they possessed a ticket. There being no ticket offices on the premises, Hannah asked where to acquire one, only to be told she needed a recommendation from a gentleman willing to be responsible for her behaviour. Furious, but impotent against him, Hannah had stormed out and not gone back since.

'So, a hospital? I didn't know you were interested in nursing,' Hannah said.

'I'm far too squeamish to be a nurse, but you ought to come with me and see what goes on there. It's a military hospital run by two women doctors at the St Giles and St George's premises.'

'The old St Giles workhouse that was closed last year?' Hannah scoffed. 'Is that the best the great war machine of the nation could do?'

'Typical, isn't it?' Aunt Violet laughed. 'Had it been male doctors who put the idea forward, no doubt they would have made the Ritz Hotel available. But I expect they imagined women were bound to make a mess of it so gave them the first run-down premises they had to hand.'

'Who are these doctors?'

'Louisa Garrett Anderson and Flora Murray. Elizabeth Garrett Anderson is Louisa's mother, who was the first woman in England to qualify as a doctor. Elizabeth is an inspiration as she founded the London Women's Hospital over forty years ago.'

'Of course, that's where I've heard of her. I thought the name was familiar.'

'They need books to fill the library, so naturally I came to see if you are willing to part with any.' Her aunt removed her gloves and dropped them on the desk. 'The recovering soldiers are desperate for something to occupy them. Are you sure I didn't mention it?'

'You might have done, I cannot remember.' Hannah nodded to a wicker basket she had placed beside the storeroom door. 'I was going to dispose of those. Some have water stains on the covers and one or two have had the corners nibbled by mice. I can't sell them, but they're still readable.'

'The soldiers won't mind that. They've had far more to cope with than a little damp. Now.' Aunt Violet swept her trailing scarf over one shoulder. 'Are you going to tell me what Mrs Mullinson did to upset you?'

'Ah yes, that.' Hannah cleared her throat. 'Who is she? I don't recall you ever mentioning her.'

'She's a member of the Women's Emergency Corps. They do aid work, but you have to be a lord's daughter to qualify, partly because they have to buy their own uniforms at two pounds each. Gladys is the treasurer, which has gone to her head as she's always throwing her weight about. I'd love to see her put in her place.'

'Then you should have been here ten minutes ago.' Lowering her voice in case Archie heard, Hannah explained the incident with the white feather.

'Oh no, poor Archie. How awful for him. I hope he doesn't take himself off to the recruitment centre, just to prove that old busybody wrong.'

'I hope so too.' Hannah sifted through the envelopes on the desk. 'You don't mind me attending to the post while we talk? Only there's so much more to do now we are actually selling books and not just storing them.' Hannah pushed the letters aside to make room as Archie reappeared and placed a loaded tray on the desk. 'Thank you, Archie, that's just the ticket.'

'Bartleby needs feeding, miss, so I'll be out back if you need me.' He retreated, his blue-rimmed enamel mug clutched in both hands.

'No matter how many times I invite him to sit with me, he always takes his breaks in the storeroom.' Hannah handed her aunt a china cup and a matching saucer.

'He's been taught to know his place, darling. He probably doesn't feel comfortable with us. I suggest you leave him be.'

Hannah complied, knowing Archie's confidence had taken a dive because of the awful Mullinson woman.

'What was I saying?' Aunt Violet propped her elbows on the desk, the cup held between both hands. 'Have you heard any more from Inspector Farrell?'

'Nothing at all, although Constable Jones will be back in a few minutes. He stepped outside to scout the outlying streets for loiterers. Why do you ask?'

'You don't appear to be taking this spying matter seriously. They are real, you know?'

Hannah sighed. 'It was exciting at first, but maybe we got it all wrong. Suppose Monty had no idea what he was involved in and has no interest in the postcards? The whole thing might be a useless exercise. In the meantime, Lily-Anne's murderer is still out there.'

'You don't think Monty killed her?'

'I'm not convinced Monty did anything. No one has been near the bookshop in days, and Constable Jones is becoming bored.'

'You should trust Inspector Farrell's judgement. There's something deeply intuitive about the man.' Her aunt waved a hand in a circular motion beside her cheek. 'He weighs his thoughts before voicing an opinion, and he listens. Men rarely do.'

'I think he's rather pompous.' Hannah braced for a contradiction, which never came. 'I wonder if I did the wrong thing? I mean, Monty might not have been aware of that message I found.'

Aunt Violet lowered her cup. 'Perhaps you should leave Inspector Farrell to complete his investigation. There's a lot about this case we don't know, including that Lily-Anne indulged in cocaine,' Aunt Violet said as she packed books into the basket.

'I know.' Hannah bit her bottom lip. 'I haven't been able to stop thinking about it. She was always adventurous, even a little wild, but drugs? Could that have been what she wanted to tell me that day?'

'We discussed this, Hannah. Her death was *not* your fault.' Her aunt unbent from her task. 'Now, any more and I won't be able to lift it.' She glanced up at the clock and started. 'Oops. I'd better be off. Apart from my visit to Endell Street, I have a few things to do before my suffragette luncheon.' At Hannah's sideways look she added, 'Don't look so worried. We aren't planning to lay siege to parliament. We're simply a group of like-minded women putting the world to rights over a plate of vegetarian stew.'

'I daren't ask what vegetarian stew comprises.' Hannah grimaced.

'You may scoff, but you'll be glad of it when supplies of fresh meat dry up because it's being sent to the troops.' She adjusted her hat and pulled on her gloves. 'By the way, have you advertised the flat at all? It's a shame to leave it empty when it could add to the income from the bookshop.'

'I planned to, but Inspector Farrell asked me to hold off until all this was over.' Hannah hefted the basket of books into her arms and walked her aunt out to the door.

'Accommodation in this part of the West End is scarce. Ooh, I know.' Aunt Violet came to an abrupt halt, forcing a bowler-hatted gentleman to take evasive action. 'That young song writer, Ivor Novello, lives above the Strand Theatre just around the corner.'

'Who?'

'You know, he wrote *Keep the Home Fires Burning*. You hear it all the time these days. Maybe he'd like a quiet apartment above a bookshop in which to write his songs?'

'I'm sure he's quite happy where he is, Aunt Violet.'

'I suppose so. And now I think about it, he shares the flat with his mother. I doubt there'll be room for both of them above the bookshop.'

16

The afternoon continued quietly, with few customers apart from a gentleman in a black overcoat and Homburg hat pulled low over his brow. He rudely dismissed Hannah's offer of assistance, demanding he be served by a male assistant. Hannah attributed his brusque tone to the presence of a black armband above his left elbow, which prompted her sympathy and a rapid retreat. Promptly forgetting him, she gave a bored Constable Jones approval to wander Catherine Street, ostensibly in search of suspicious characters, but more, Hannah suspected, for an uninterrupted smoke. On his way out, he held the shop door open for an elderly lady who declared an enthusiasm for Anna Katherine Green's detective stories.

Hannah obliged with a thorough search and after an in-depth discussion, the lady left with a sizeable pile of books which more than made up for Hannah's last encounter.

As she carried the rejected choices and climbed the library ladder to replace them on the higher shelves, a deep masculine cough directly below made her twist around sharply. The books beneath her arm threatened to fall as she stared into Darius's eyes.

'I didn't see you there.' She swallowed, her heartbeat ranking up a notch 'Why didn't you say something?'

His summer-weight charcoal grey coat fitted his powerful build without a wrinkle over a matching waistcoat and dazzling white shirt; a custom-made fedora at a perfect angle sat on his brow.

'I enjoy watching you work.' He gripped the ladder with one hand to steady it; the other, he extended to help her down. His hold was firm, confident, and she didn't want it to end, but when it did, she surreptitiously checked her appearance in the front window and groaned inwardly. Her soft bun had worked loose, and she had a smut of dust under one eye.

'Am I keeping you from a lucrative sale?' He cocked his chin toward the black-clad man, who rummaged through a rack of theatre posters.

'I doubt it.' Hannah lowered her voice. 'He prefers being served by a gentleman, so I'm leaving him to Archie.'

'Is that usual?' Had the man not had his back turned, he might have felt the weight of Darius's disapproval.

'More often than I'm comfortable with, but I don't let it bother me. Anyway, what brings you to Covent Garden?'

'Cecily's shopping in Regent Street, so we arranged to meet here later.'

'How nice.' Hannah broke off their steady eye contact and busied herself arranging the books on a wheeled trolley. He stood close enough for his cologne to be both familiar and intoxicating.

'I'm not here purely for her benefit,' he added. 'I'm on an errand for my Great Aunt Christabel who is laid low with influenza.'

'Oh, I'm so sorry.' She softened, being fond of his octogenarian great aunt.

'She's recovering, but extremely bored, so I agreed to pick up some new reading material for her.' He glanced down to where the black cat's tail wrapped around his left trouser hem. 'And who's this sturdy chap?' The cat leapt onto the desk, his substantial weight landing with a thump, and planted both front paws on Darius's chest. Undeterred, he ran a firm hand along the feline's back, eliciting a loud, contented purr.

Archie emerged from the storeroom, slapping bits of hay from his hands. 'The unpacking's done, Miss Merrill. Only those law books to deliver to Temple.' His smile faded, and he swept the cat from the desk, depositing him on the floor, ignoring a hiss and a sharp mewl of protest. 'I'm sorry, sir. If he takes to you, he won't leave you alone.'

'You must be Archie?' Darius leaned a hip against the desk. 'I've heard you're quite an asset to the premises.'

'Archer Root, sir. Thank you, sir. I mean Mr - er... ' He stammered, red-faced. 'And that there's Bartleby.' He nodded to the cat wrapped around his ankle.

'We've met.' He thrust out his hand. 'Darius Clifford. A pleasure to meet you, Archer.'

'When you've served that gentleman, Archie, you can deliver those books to Temple,' Hannah said, eager to enjoy Darius's exclusive company while she had the chance.

'What gentleman?' Archie scanned the shop briefly, but there were only the three of them.

'Oh, well, he was here a moment ago. He must have left.' She had been so absorbed she had not noticed him leave. 'Just the delivery then.'

'Are you sure, miss?' Archie gave Darius a guarded look.

'I'll be fine.' With Darius inside and Constable Jones lurking in the street, what danger could she possibly be in?

'C'mon, cat.' Archie made a clicking noise with his tongue,

which brought the cat running, black tail held up in a question mark.

'That was nice of you,' Hannah said as Archie and the cat disappeared into the storeroom.

'What was?'

'You know perfectly well. The only other person to acknowledge Archie as more than a piece of furniture is Aunt Violet.'

'Not a problem. Now, what do you suggest?' Darius asked.

'Suggest?' Hannah barely listened, so glad to have him there.

'Book wise. For my Aunt Christabel.'

'Oh, yes, of course. What do you have in mind?' She headed towards a rack of shelving to the section marked "Fiction".

'What's this one about?' He removed a linen-bound book from a shelf and held it up. *Max,* by Katherine Thurston was emblazoned across the cover.

'A Russian princess who escapes an arranged marriage by disguising herself as a boy.' Hannah speculated if his sudden need for a book was a conscious choice or a diversion. 'She runs off to Paris and becomes an artist. Thurston is very well thought of. Or she was. She died tragically young.'

'Fictional drama and an author with an untimely end. Perfect!' He grinned. 'I'll take it.'

Archie reappeared in his jacket and cap, a parcel of books swinging from his wrist by a string. 'Cat's been fed, Miss Merrill. I won't be long.' The door slammed behind him, leaving a faint waft of fish in his wake.

'Regard this as a gift from me, for being so understanding when I made wild accusations about Cavan.' She wrapped the book in brown paper, wound a length of jute around it and tied off the knot.

'Were they wild?' His hand brushed hers as he took the book from her, the contact light and quick, but as effective as a caress.

'Darius, may I ask you something?' She cradled her fingers in her other hand, as if to preserve the impression his touch made.

'Anything.'

'Did Cavan have another woman? If he told anyone, it would be you.'

'What makes you think that?' He fingered the length of jute without looking up.

'I heard some gossip recently. It occurred to me that if Lily-Anne was troubled because Cavan was philandering, perhaps—'

'She might have taken to drugs?' He sighed. 'I doubt that's the reason. I tried to warn her opium could be dangerous, but she just laughed.' His tone held all the frustration he must have felt then. 'Called me reliable old Darius who did not know what fun was.'

'Why didn't you tell me?'

'How could I?' He hunched his shoulders. 'I couldn't burden you with Gerald preparing to go to France. Then he was killed, and...' his voice tailed off and his gaze shifted to the front window for the third time in as many minutes.

'Is something bothering you?' she asked, mildly irritated his attention had wandered, then remembered. 'Of course, you're waiting for Cecily.'

'It's not that. I spotted a chap hanging about outside when I arrived. You know the sort. Hands in pockets, kept staring at the ground, but kept giving this place furtive glances. He's wearing a flat cap pulled low over his face.' He straightened. 'Hang on, there he is again. Stay here, Hannah. I'm going to have a word.' He sprinted for the door, but she darted after him.

'Darius, it's all right.' She grabbed his arm, hauling him backwards. 'He's supposed to be there.'

'An admirer, perhaps?' A teasing glint entered his eyes.

'Don't be ridiculous.' She slapped his arm playfully, but her stomach lurched. 'The police have assigned him to watch the bookshop.'

'Oh? Have you suddenly had a spate of educated shoplifters?' His mischievous smile reminded her of when she did not have to worry their affection might be misinterpreted. How many times had she seen that same look, only now was it too late to mean something?

'It was Inspector Farrell's idea.' She toyed with telling him about Monty, but recoiled from the idea of slandering his friend – the youth who followed him around because Darius was kind to the son of his father's clerk.

'Does he think Lily-Anne's killer will be back?' Darius stared at her. 'Then why are you still working here? You could be in danger!'

'The police are merely being careful.' It was not quite what she wanted to say, but it was better than explaining about German spies and secret messages.

'As long as you stay safe. What with the dire news about the war and now you involved in a murder, I feel pretty much useless.'

'You're not thinking of enlisting?' Her heart thumped in her chest, braced for his answer.

'Hah! My father won't hear of it. He goes into a spluttering panic if the idea is so much as mentioned.'

'You cannot blame him for that. You're his only son.' Hannah sympathised with the kindly, widowed Joshua Clifford.

'I cannot stay safe at home forever, Hannah, even if I wanted to. The government is bound to introduce conscription before long. The British Expeditionary Force doesn't have enough troops to rely on voluntary enlistment.'

She nodded, but her brain screamed, *Don't leave, I cannot bear it.* 'Why *are* we fighting, anyway? War is such a terrible waste of young lives.'

'We've no choice. We're pledged to support France under the

terms of the Triple Entente. I fear Asquith won't remain prime minister for much longer having ignored all Lord Kitchener's warnings about us not being equipped for war.' He kept his eyes on the window as he talked, oblivious to her mounting distress. 'We're abjectly short of ammunition, as well as everything from soldiers to trained medical staff and supplies.'

'Are you saying we might lose this war?'

'Heavens, no! We're British, aren't we?' His eyes softened. 'I'm glad Inspector Farrell is taking steps to protect you. Can't have my best girl in danger.'

'I thought Cecily was your best girl?' Did he mean that, or was it simply a slip of the tongue borne of long friendship?

His gaze met hers, and he looked about to say something else, but halted when the doorbell announced Cecily's arrival.

Hannah snatched her hand from his arm and summoned a smile, as Cecily, arms full of packages, collided with the door frame and had to manoeuvre sideways.

'Help me with these would you, darling?' Cecily gushed, though a tinge of annoyance sharpened her tone. Had she seen Hannah's hand on his arm, or had he not moved fast enough to help her?

Darius moved to relieve her of most of her parcels; the rest she heaved onto the desk, scattering papers. 'Oh, hello, Hannah,' she added, immediately dismissing her.

'Cecily.' Hannah pushed down her resentment, followed by a wave of emotion she refused to label jealousy, but wondered for the hundredth time what Darius saw in this glossy, but vacuous woman?

'My feet are so sore. I must have been to every shop in Regent Street.' Cecily grasped Darius's forearm, kicked off a shoe and rubbed her heel with her other hand.

'Did you find what you wanted?' His question was more polite than a show of genuine interest.

'Not really. There's so little in the shops these days, I had to make some compromises.' Cecily peered sideways at Hannah from beneath the hat she wore tilted over one eye, while still rubbing her foot. 'Has Darius told you our news?'

'No. What news?' Hannah braced herself to hear something she suspected she would rather not.

'It's not definite yet—' Darius began.

'I've booked the last Friday in October.' Cecily chattered excitedly. 'St Mary's is red brick, not stone, but we cannot have everything. You'll come, of course?'

'I should be delighted, Cecily.'

'I thought we agreed to wait until St Margaret's was available,' Darius snapped. 'Which won't be until next year at the earliest.'

'Darling, we cannot keep putting it off.' Cecily pouted and replaced her shoe. 'The way this war is going, we'll all soon be Lutherans and have to make our vows in German.'

Hannah looked at Darius and saw her own shock reflected in his expression, though he said nothing.

Cecily's mouth twitched at the corner as she split a pointed look between them. 'Oh, I'm sorry. Have I interrupted whatever it was you two were discussing so intently just now?'

'Not at all,' Hannah blurted. *Damn, she had seen.*

'We were catching up while I waited for you,' Darius added.

'As long as it was nothing important.' Hannah detected accusation in Cecily's few words. 'I don't mean to be a killjoy, but I'm exhausted. Do you mind if we go?' She headed down the front steps to where Darius had parked his motor car, while calling over her shoulder: 'Hannah, dear. We simply must have luncheon together soon.'

'I'll look forward to it,' Hannah replied, though inside her head she heard the words *not if I can help it,* repeated.

Darius paused in the doorway on his way out and turned back, his arms loaded with parcels. 'You'll be careful? And if there's anything I can do, you know where I am.'

'Thank you,' Hannah mouthed, her grateful smile fading as Cecily's sharp voice intruded.

'Do come *on*, Darius.'

His eyes met Hannah's and held for long seconds with a look she could not fathom. Regret? Disappointment?

17

Hannah watched from the front window as Darius's motor car disappeared towards the Strand. Seeing he and Cecily together always acted on Hannah like nails on a blackboard. Cecily's fake niceness made it impossible to like her, partly because her easy friendliness with Darius was doomed to end when they married.

She glanced at the desk to where he had left his great aunt's book and wondered if she might use it as an excuse to deliver it later. 'Red brick, not stone, but one cannot have everything.' She mimicked Cecily's sing-song laugh, but at a creak from somewhere she fell silent, her head cocked to listen. She waited for the sound to come again, but only the clop of hooves and an occasional motor car engine from the street broke the silence.

Bartleby padded out from behind a bookshelf. 'Was that you, cat?' She bent and gathered the animal into her arms, smiling as Bartleby butted her hand with his head just as the noise came again; it was like a weight pressing on a floorboard.

'Not you then?' Still holding the cat, her shoes clipped across polished boards to the staircase door which, by some peculiarity of the ancient building, opened outwards. She reached for the doorknob with her free hand, just as the door was flung open, hitting her with such force it slammed her against the wall, sending up a puff of plaster dust.

The cat squealed in protest and flew from her arms. Instinctively, she raised her hands, palms outwards to push the door back, but the thick crossbars pinned her to the wall sending pain through both wrists. The old door pressed into her hips and chest so she could not breathe. She grew dizzy, the smell of old plaster and dust in her nostrils adding to her claustrophobia. Panic surged, and just as she thought she might pass out, the harsh sound of the shop doorbell answered her silent plea for help.

'Oi! What d'you think you're doing?' Archie's furious yell accompanied something light hitting the parquet floor.

The weight against her chest lifted, her knees gave way, and she crumpled to the floor, heaving air painfully into her lungs while vaguely aware of the smell of liberally applied lavender polish.

The shop door banged shut with a harsh clash of the bell, followed by Archie's voice that seemed to come from far away. 'Are you all right, Miss Merrill?'

Winded, Hannah pulled herself to her knees and summoned her voice. 'Never mind me! Get Constable Jones.'

'He's not here!' Archie frantically scanned the shop.

She inhaled a ragged breath, aware her chest burned. 'Yell, then. He'll come running.'

Archie darted back outside, sending the bell into another frantic jangle setting Hannah's teeth on edge. 'I've always hated that bell,' she muttered, dragging herself to her feet. Her hip burned where the corner of the door had hit her, and a pain in her temple told her she must have hit her head. Without thinking, she slumped into the wingback chair, instantly stiffening, but unable to bring herself to move again. Instead, she leaned her temple against one wing, her eyes closed as she waited for the dizziness to recede.

A low mewling close by drew her attention to the floor where Bartleby sat, his paws drawn together and unconcerned blue eyes staring up at her.

'And where were you when I needed some sharp claws?' she demanded, uselessly.

The cat meowed, brought a paw to his mouth, and flicked his tiny red tongue around it.

Moments later, Archie staggered back through the door. 'I found Constable Jones. He went after the man, so I came back to see if you were all right.' His eyes darkened with concern. 'What happened? Were we robbed?'

'I don't think so.' Angry with herself for having dropped her guard, she brushed dust from her skirt, leaned an elbow on the armrest with her forehead against her hand. 'I think someone wanted those wretched postcards. I should have given them back to Monty the day I sacked him.'

'No, Miss Merrill.' Archie gasped. 'You did the right thing telling the police. Can't have the Huns getting one over on us.' He crossed to the door, clicked the latch and turned the "Open" sign to "Closed" before he headed for the storeroom. 'Well, if the coppers are on their way, I'd better make some tea.'

Hannah smiled. Tea was Archie's panacea for everything. She had never drunk so much of it since coming to work at the bookshop.

'Shall I fetch a doctor?' he called out above the rush of water followed by a scrape of metal on metal.

'Don't bother, Archie,' Hannah said, too weary to move from the chair.

Bartleby leapt into her lap, his warm weight a comfort. Archie placed the tea at her elbow, but she had barely taken a sip when a pounding on the shop door sent her cup jumping in her hand. Bartleby squealed, sank his claws into her thighs, and hot tea sloshed into the saucer and onto her white blouse.

'Whoever it is, tell them we're closed!' Hannah prised the cat's feet out of her flesh with her free hand and stared at the brown spots marring the delicate lace of her blouse with dismay, hoping Ivy had some magic to get them out.

Constable Jones stumbled inside, his breath heaving after his recent run. 'Sorry, miss. I lost him in the station tunnels.' He snatched off a crumpled Fedora and batted it against a trouser leg, sending up a small cloud of dust. 'Are you hurt, Miss Merrill?'

'What do *you* think?' Archie snapped. 'He tried to crush her behind that door.'

'I'll need to use your telephone to report this to Inspector Farrell,' Constable Jones said, wincing beneath Archie's furious glare.

Hannah nodded, her eyes fluttered closed, and she leaned her head against the chair.

'That's a bit of luck.' Archie pounced on the brown paper bag on the floor and peered inside. 'My Chelsea buns survived, after all. I'd better make some more tea now the inspector is coming. Anyone want a bun?'

Hannah shook her head, nauseous at the very thought of food.

'Inspector Farrell is on his way,' Constable Jones said as he strode back, pointing to the bag in Archie's hand. 'I'll have one!' He shrugged in response to Archie's surprised stare and Hannah's bemused one. 'And two sugars, please.'

* * *

Constable Jones leaned a buttock on the corner of the desk, a mug of tea in one hand, his left foot idly swinging, unaware of Inspector Farrell's arrival until he loomed beside him.

'What happened, Jones?' The inspector demanded, his critical glance on the half-eaten bun in the officer's hand.

'I saw him run out of the shop and guessed he was dodgy.' Constable Jones jumped smartly to attention. 'I gave chase but lost him at Charing Cross station.'

Inspector Farrell snorted in annoyance and strode to the reading corner where Hannah still sat, followed by the sheepish constable.

'I cannot apologise enough, Miss Merrill, although I'm glad to see you aren't badly hurt.'

'I'm rather sore, but more shocked than anything.' Hannah attempted a reassuring smile, but failed when her ribs protested.

'You were instructed to follow unobtrusively, Jones, not scare him off. Now he'll go to ground.' The inspector flung his hat onto the desk in a rare display of temper.

'Sorry, sir.' The constable swallowed his mouthful of bun. 'But he didn't get the postcards. They're still in the drawer where you put them.'

'Maybe if he had, you might have been quicker on your feet and caught him.'

Constable Jones looked about to say something else, but the inspector held up his hand to silence him. 'Save it, Jones. Explain what you were doing when this man attacked Miss Merrill.'

'Er, I stepped out for a moment, sir, so I didn't actually see him.' He withdrew a notebook from one pocket, and hunted through several others, finally locating a pencil. 'I only caught a glimpse but wrote what I could remember.'

'Let's hope you've got a good memory, then!' Archie's eyes glinted angrily.

'Archie!' Hannah flexed her throbbing wrists, hoping the aspirin would take effect soon. The pain blurred her thinking. 'He was in the shop earlier, but I paid him little attention. His hat was pulled down over his face and he wore a black armband. A nice touch for a potential spy. I was... occupied elsewhere and thought he had left.'

Inspector Farrell huffed a frustrated if controlled breath. 'Did it not occur to you that a man skulking among the shelves might have come for the postcards?'

'This is a bookshop, Inspector. Everyone skulks,' Hannah said. 'But you're right. I should have been more careful. He must have slipped behind the door to the flat to wait until we locked up. It's early closing day.'

'Hmm, there's nothing more to be done here, so I suggest you go home, Miss Merrill. You're quite pale.' He made an impatient gesture. 'Don't just stand there, Jones, find a hackney for the lady.'

Hannah was about to remind him she was always pale, but could not summon the energy.

'They don't come down here much, sir,' Jones replied. 'I could try at the station?'

'Well, get to it then, lad.' His sharp tone sent the policeman running into the street.

'Is, um, Miss Edwards not here today, Miss Merrill?' Inspector Farrell asked when Archie had retreated to the storeroom with their empty cups.

'My aunt?' Hannah's hand stilled in the cat's fur. 'She only stops by occasionally.'

'She was a suffragette, I believe?' He drummed his fingers on the back of a wooden chair, the sound ordinary yet strangely ominous.

'She still is. Mrs Pankhurst has called a ceasefire, but my aunt still meets with her friends to—' she halted. Much like spies, the police regarded women's suffrage as a threat to the nation and kept known activists under close surveillance.

'I appreciate your discretion,' he said with a smile. 'However, I'm an avid supporter of the women's suffrage movement.' At her surprised look, he added, 'Not their more violent activities, of course, but the principles of the cause. My mother pays taxes on a family business, but resents the fact she has no say in how the government spends them.' His voice contained quiet pride. 'Your aunt reminds me of her.'

His revelation lifted him higher in Hannah's estimation; a man who revered his mother was worth cultivating. She was about to ask him more about this business, but the return of Constable Jones prevented her.

'Found one, sir!' He slapped the sleeves of his coat to remove road dust. 'I hope you'll not object to a motor taxi, Miss Merrill?'

'Not at all, and thank you, Constable.' She placed the cat on the floor and eased to her feet, guarding her sore ribs.

'I suggest you remain at home for a few days.' The inspector regarded her levelly. 'In fact, I insist.'

'There's no need. I'm not ill, only battered. I'll be fine tomorrow.'

'The situation has changed, Miss Merrill. We've gathered more information about this network, compliments of those postcards you found. It's being run in London by a man named Herr Weber. The Home Office are monitoring him in the hope he'll lead them to the rest of the network. It would be safer for you if you stayed away for a while, at least until the entire network is in custody.'

'Have you found Monty?' She jerked upright but instantly regretted it as a sharp pain shot across her middle.

'I regret to say no. However, in my experience, the German high command does not tolerate mistakes. They will definitely try again. I'd put another man in the shop, but resources are stretched.'

'What about Archie? Can you guarantee his safety?' she asked as he escorted her to the door.

'Don't worry, miss. He'll be fine with me.' Constable Jones administered a thump to Archie's back that sent him staggering forward a few paces.

After taking farewells from Archie and the constable, the inspector accompanied her into the street and handed her into the idling taxi.

'What about the air raid mentioned in the message?' Hannah whispered having checked the glass panel between her and the driver was firmly closed. 'Can you stop it?'

'What do you suggest, Miss Merrill? An announcement in the newspapers?'

'You don't have to be sarcastic,' she snapped, though it was close to what she was thinking.

'Look, missus.' The taxi driver slid back the partition, an arm braced across the back of his seat. 'I ain't got all day. Are we going or not?'

Hannah slid open the panel and asked him to wait another moment before closing it again. The driver huffed an impatient breath and faced forward, his fingers drumming the steering wheel.

'Miss Merrill,' Inspector Farrell said with barely restrained patience, 'This is no longer exclusively police business. The Home Office is involved. Anti-aircraft guns are in position at vital military locations, and preparations are under way to handle potential damage, but there's a limit to what can be done.'

'I should have torn the wretched thing up in the first place and said nothing!'

'I hope you don't mean that.' His voice took on a hard edge. 'It would suggest you are less than patriotic. Now, enjoy your rest.' He banged the flat of his hand on the roof as a signal for the taxi to leave.

'About time,' the driver grunted as he pulled sharply away from the kerb.

18

Sunlight dappled the bed where Hannah unbuttoned her nightgown to examine the impressive purple and blue bruise on her torso; a trophy of the previous day's encounter that was thankfully less painful than appearances suggested. Hearing footsteps on the stairs, she bundled the blankets over herself just as Aunt Violet barrelled into her room.

'That's kind of you.' Hannah struggled into an upright position and reached to take the cup her aunt held towards her.

'Don't thank me. Ivy was on her way up, so I ambushed her for it. You had better come down for breakfast soon, or she'll be insufferable for the rest of the day.'

'You could be a tad more sympathetic, Aunt Violet. I'm still sore.' At least the tea was excellent.

'I expressed all my outrage and frustration last night. I'm not going through it again. No, come to think of it, I'm not finished. What on earth were you doing alone in the bookshop? You might have been killed.'

'I know, it was stupid, though I cannot help feeling it was all my fault anyway,' she said, thinking aloud.

'Why was it your fault?' Aunt Violet gestured for her to scoot sideways on the bed to make space for her and sat.

'I was knocked down, that's all,' she said, unwilling to describe it as an attack. 'I was angry at being dismissed by the police. I didn't give the man in the overcoat another thought. Thinking back, he even looked sinister. His hair might even have been a wig—'

'Hannah, you're waffling.' Her aunt placed a hand on Hannah's forehead. 'Maybe you have a concussion?'

'I do not!' Grimacing, she shoved her aunt's hand away in a gesture worthy of a five-year-old. 'I left him browsing the shelves when Darius came in and then wig—'

'Darius was there?' Speculations brightened her eyes. 'How nice.'

'You can take that look off your face. He came to buy a book for his great aunt. Then Cecily arrived and made a point of telling me about their forthcoming wedding.'

'Wedding? Huh! She wants to get him down the aisle before he changes his mind.' She placed a comforting hand on Hannah's arm. 'I know you'll deny it, but that must be a blow.'

'It's my own fault. I should have encouraged him when I had the chance. Now he's lost to me forever.'

'Not lost, darling. Temporarily unavailable. She hasn't got him down the aisle yet. Anyway, when are these doomed nuptials planned for?'

'Next month, and you don't know they're doomed.' That Cecily would make a beautiful bride made it so much worse. 'Could we please change the subject?' she snapped, aware she was the one who had brought it up. 'I'm miserable enough now Inspector Farrell has banned me from the bookshop. He wouldn't have known anything about the spies without me. Even Archie is still there, while I'm missing all the excitement. The inspector might as well have patted me on the head and suggested I knit socks for soldiers. And he's still not convinced it wasn't me.'

'Ridiculous, why would he think you killed your best friend?'

'Because the police latch onto the first available person? And she was stabbed with my knife in our bookshop. Then there's the small fact I found the body, alone. He isn't even looking into the husband's story. But then Cavan Soames is a respected doctor and pillar of the community. His word is bound to be accepted over mine.'

'You should be grateful he's keeping you out of it.' Aunt Violet raised a sardonic eyebrow. 'Hunting spies sounds like a dangerous occupation.'

'I can look after myself.' In response to her aunt's slow up and down stare, she added, 'I was distracted. If the intruder turns up again, I'll be ready for him.'

Her aunt issued a discreet but telling snort, and patted the bed cover. 'Come on, get up and dress. Some breakfast will make you less grumpy.'

'I am not grumpy,' Hannah retorted grumpily. 'Only hungry.' She eased off the bed slowly and pulled on her dressing gown. 'I hardly ate anything yesterday. When I got home, all I could think of was sleeping. I didn't even thank the driver of the motor taxi.'

'You came all the way from Covent Garden in a motor taxi?' Aunt Violet pivoted at the door; her eyes wide.

'I did.' Hannah slid her feet into a pair of pink silk slippers. 'Inspector Farrell paid my fare.'

'I don't suppose he mentioned me at all?'

'Actually, he did. He said you reminded him of his mother.'

'Wretch!'

Hannah ducked, just missing the hairbrush that came flying across the room, reassured her aunt was smiling at the same time.

* * *

'I'm glad you came to live with me, Aunt Violet,' Hannah said over a rare boiled egg and toast with real butter. 'But if you prefer to go back to your own house, I'll understand. Eva probably misses you.'

'Are you throwing me out?' Her aunt glanced up quickly.

'Of course not.' Hannah dipped a finger of toast into the runny yolk. 'You came to live with me to placate my mother, but you must miss your own house...'

Hannah's house by the river with its view of Chiswick Eyot had become her sanctuary since Gerald's death. Of course, at first she had had to find the courage to confront her mother and insist living alone was not a scandal because she was unmarried, and also remind her that many young women worked outside the home since the war began, taking jobs which had traditionally been a male prerogative.

'You always were happy in your own company, which surprised us all when you accepted Gerald's proposal.'

'That was a mistake.' At her aunt's enquiring look, she hesitated. 'It was wrong of me to encourage his courtship, but with Mother pushing me towards Darius with the determination of Mrs Bennett, it was a bid for my independence. He waited until five minutes before his train left for the Front before suggesting we get engaged. How could I refuse with his entire platoon watching? That would have been heartless.'

'I didn't realise. I imagined some sort of romantic setting and an emotional proposal.'

'It *was* romantic, sort of. Victoria station early on a spring morning; the air misty from smoke from the engine and Gerald looking dashing in his uniform leaning out of the train window.'

'He rather put you on the spot, didn't he?'

Hannah nodded. 'I feel terrible he's dead, but I could never have made him happy.'

'Then take comfort from the fact he was unaware of how you really felt. Or was he?'

'How could I do that to him?' Hannah fiddled with the cuff of her blouse. 'When he applied for a commission, he said it would change his life. He thought my wanting to change mine by working in the bookshop was an unladylike fad.'

'If it's actual change you wanted, you could have joined me in the WSPU.' Her aunt batted her eyelashes in mock innocence.

'I endorse women's emancipation as much as anyone, Aunt Violet, but some of the things you got up to shock even me. Damaging property and committing arson are counterproductive to getting one's point across.'

'We had to do something dramatic to make Asquith listen, but he ignored us anyway.' Her aunt played with the gold locket around her neck, her cheeks pink with annoyance. 'Hannah, about what you said earlier. Do you seriously believe Cavan might have been responsible for Lily-Anne's death?' Her eyes glittered with mischief. 'A man who gave you a pair of diamond earrings?'

'Yes. No. I don't know. If I really believed he was responsible, I'd hand them back immediately.'

'That's rather drastic, don't you think?'

'Don't tease, Aunt Violet. There's something odd about the whole Monty–Lily-Anne situation. They were always hostile towards each other. Mostly because Monty used his limp to leech off Darius and Gerald. But murder?' She shook her head, as if dislodging the thought. 'If she was upset about Cavan and another woman, maybe she came to the bookshop to talk to me about it, but I left before she got there? Then someone, either Cavan, Monty or a spy, killed her.'

'It certainly creates some intriguing questions.'

'Cavan also denied knowing Lily-Anne had not come home all night. And he had access to the drugs she was taking. As a doctor, you'd think he'd take better care of his own wife? Then there was the woman I saw in his carriage the day after she died.'

'Think you saw? You aren't even sure this person was female.' Her aunt held up a finger.

'You said you would bet your Holloway brooch it was.' Hannah glared at her.

'I'm playing devil's advocate. Don't spoil my fun.'

Hannah huffed an annoyed breath. 'And the veiled woman at the funeral? Who is she and what's her involvement in all this?'

'Only Cavan can tell us that, and if guilty, he's hardly likely to volunteer anything.'

'Perhaps it's not him we need to speak to,' Hannah said through a mouthful of toast.

Aunt Violet's cup halted halfway to her mouth. 'Then who?'

'His servants. If anyone knows what was going on, they will. We just have to make sure Inspector Farrell doesn't find out we're questioning his witnesses.'

'Afraid of a policeman?' Aunt Violet gave her an oblique look. 'And you call yourself my niece?'

'Will you come with me?' Her pulse leapt a notch at the idea she was going to do something positive to solve her friend's murder.

'I have nothing else planned for today, so why not?' Rising, Aunt Violet scraped back her chair. 'Ivy is out shopping, so shall we do the washing up before we go?'

'Goodness no. We might be spinsters without a lady's maid, but we haven't sunk that low. I'll stack the dishes on the draining board for Ivy to do later.'

19

Hannah and Aunt Violet arrived at the imposing Soames residence on the corner of Church Street, and the clack of the gleaming brass knocker in her hand echoed into the depths of the house, followed by a shuffling before it was opened.

'Dr Soames is rarely at home this time of day, Miss Merrill,' Hemmings, the Soames's butler, informed them in a tone of bored regret, his stooped posture mirroring his despondent demeanour.

'Actually, it's you we're here to see,' Hannah said, nodding at Aunt Violet. 'You've met my aunt, Miss Violet Edwards?'

'I have indeed. Good afternoon, Miss Edwards.'

'Mr Hemmings.' Aunt Violet acknowledged his obsequious bow with a nod. 'We hoped you might help us clarify a few things about the day Mrs Soames died.'

'I cannot imagine how.' A flash of alarm entered his eyes, his brow furrowed. 'Such a terrible thing that happened to her. No one in the house knew anything until Dr Soames returned with the police.' He split a worried look between them. When neither of them moved off the step, he nodded, resigned to the intrusion, and stepped back to allow them inside.

He led the way along a wide hallway arranged in the aesthetic design of twenty years before; a mixture of Japanese art and Middle-Eastern style that vied for attention in overcrowded rooms decorated in red, gold, and white.

Memories ambushed Hannah from every corner in rooms which once rang with Lily-Anne's laughter, but now seemed to hold their breath. Silent, oppressive. As if sensing her discomfort, Aunt Violet gripped her forearm lightly and squeezed.

'This house has become an unhappy place lately, miss,' Hemmings said, as if reading her thoughts. 'The master rarely entertains and two of the maids have given notice. They have jobs at the aviation company at Acton.'

'But he has some visitors?' Aunt Violet's reference to the mysterious woman did not go unnoticed by Hannah.

'Only the young lady who came to offer condolences.'

'Young lady?' Hannah's pulse raced.

'She's called twice since the funeral.' Hemmings flinched as if regretting having mentioned it. 'Dr Soames answered the door on both occasions, so I never caught her name.'

He halted between two console tables where vases of flowers long past their best stood. 'Might we talk in my pantry? The ground floor rooms aren't fit to receive visitors. The carpets haven't been brushed for days, but the housekeeper has not the heart to scold the girls, and I cannot interfere in her domain.'

'Of course, we understand,' Hannah said, frustrated he had moved on from the mysterious lady caller and wondered how to re-introduce her.

He led them into a masculine-looking room at the rear of the kitchens devoid of ornaments or knick-knacks, apart from a utilitarian clock on a plain wooden mantle. A single shelf above a square window onto a rear yard held several books, while two wheelback chairs were arranged on either side of a scarred mahogany table with its leaves folded down.

An ancient wingback chair with sagging upholstery was angled towards the fireplace, a grease stain on the upright where she assumed the butler's head had lain during his off-duty hours; a sight which made her inexplicably sad.

'Please sit, Miss Edwards, Miss Merrill.' He dragged a third chair into a semi-circle beside the empty grate. 'Might I offer you some refreshment?' He hovered between them until they were both seated, finally settling on the upright chair from which he regarded them with mild enquiry. 'They'll be glad of something to do in the kitchens.'

'Please don't bother for us.' Hannah laid her bag at her feet, recalled his comment about the cleaning, changed her mind and placed it in her lap before asking, 'Do you recall the day Mrs Soames died?'

'It was the day the butcher's boy called for the week's orders.' He propped his elbow on the arm, cradling his chin in one hand as he cast his mind back. 'Apart from the fact he was late, it was a day like all others.'

'Did Mrs Soames's mood alter at all in the days before she died?' Aunt Violet interjected.

He fidgeted with a shirt cuff, looked about to say something, but changed his mind and fell silent again.

'Whatever you tell us will go no further,' Aunt Violet whispered.

'Well, Miss Merrill, you were a special friend of Mrs Soames, and after everything came out at the inquest, I imagine there is no longer a need for secrecy.'

'Exactly.' Hannah nodded, relieved he was being so co-operative. 'Is there is anything you can tell us which might help find out who killed her?'

'I don't know if it will help, miss. Mrs Soames was a high-spirited lady, even a little wild.' He cleared his throat as if the words were stuck there. 'Dr Soames worked all hours, and she was alone a lot. She became restless and took to going out in the evenings to an establishment which provided jazz music until the small hours. She was always very excitable when she returned. Euphoric, you might say.' His voice trailed off, then he seemed to make up his mind.

'Dr Soames gave her medication, ostensibly to calm her.' His eyes sharpened, transforming him from hesitant to intelligent. 'She became rather too fond of it. There was... an incident.'

'I understand. Go on,' Hannah said gently, while Aunt Violet released a slow breath.

'Mrs Soames came home late one night in an excited state. Dr Soames and I had quite a task getting her to bed.' He threw a nervous look at the closed door, then back at Hannah. 'I did my best to ensure the rest of the staff were ignorant, but there was bound to be gossip, especially after the inquest. Servants read newspapers. She was such a sociable, popular lady. It was a dreadful shock to hear she'd been stabbed.'

He broke off at a perfunctory knock at the door that preceded the entrance of a slim, neatly dressed woman whose age could have been anywhere between thirty and fifty. Her uniform black dress fitted where it touched, her brown hair, streaked lightly with grey, was severely drawn back from a long, narrow face.

'Second post has arrived, Mr 'emmings.' She waved a sheaf of envelopes in one hand. Her pebble brown eyes widened in surprise when they alighted on Hannah. 'I'm so sorry. I had no idea you had visitors.' Her outward show of regret convinced Hannah the post was an excuse.

'It's quite all right, Mrs Daly.' Hemmings gave a backward wave of his hand. 'Leave them on the table. I'll see to it later.'

Nodding, she circumvented the chairs on her way to the folded table where she arranged the envelopes in a neat line more slowly than necessary.

'Did anything unusual occur in the days before Mrs Soames's death, Mr Hemmings?' Hannah asked.

'Nothing that I can recall. Other than the terrace door key that went missing at Dr Soames's supper party. A constable from the local station was summoned and police concluded it was how the burglars got in.'

'Burglars?' Hannah exchanged a look with Aunt Violet, certain Lily-Anne had mentioned no burglary. 'When did this happen?'

'About a month before Mrs Soames died. Dr Soames claimed two hundred pounds was taken from his study.'

'But that turned out to be a mistake,' the housekeeper interjected, apparently determined to contribute to the conversation.

'Yes, yes, Mrs Daly, I was getting to it.' Hemmings gave her a warning stare.

'Why was it a mistake?' Hannah prompted, keen to get to the point.

'Is there always such a large amount in the house?' Aunt Violet asked simultaneously.

'Not as a rule.' Hemmings looked abashed. 'When the London Stock Exchange closed last year, Dr Soames's bank refused to let him take his money out in gold, claiming it was unpatriotic with a war on. He was concerned still, so he withdrew banknotes instead.'

Hannah recalled her father saying the sudden demand for gold had caused a run on the banks. Fortunately, it did not last long or cause long-term damage.

'They never found the key, though,' the housekeeper added. At Hannah's enquiring look, she continued, 'The one for the terrace door. Someone took it.'

'You were going to explain this mistake?' Hannah asked again.

'It was the oddest thing,' Mrs Daly blurted, determined not to be cheated of her part in the story. 'Mrs Soames returned from a house party the morning the police arrived to say they had arrested a man in The Dove public house for breaking into the study. Mrs Soames was quite adamant money hadn't been taken at all. That she had, in fact, spent it herself.'

'That *is* strange,' Hannah said, thoughtful.

'Do you know the name of the man the police arrested?' Aunt Violet asked, pre-empting Hannah's next question.

'A chap called Reg Guppy,' Hemmings replied. 'Dr Soames asked for his address so he might apologise personally. He wrote it down.' He pushed to his feet and shuffled to the bureau where he rummaged through the top drawer. 'I'm sure it was here—ah yes, here it is.' He handed a scrap of paper torn from a notebook to Aunt Violet. 'He was worried the man might take action against Dr Soames for false arrest.'

'And did this man take action?' Hannah asked, examining the paper over her aunt's shoulder.

'I don't believe so.' He lowered his voice. 'The policeman mumbled a bit about wasting police time, but we heard nothing more about it.'

'Is it true what they're saying?' Mrs Daly ventured eagerly. 'That Mr Carstairs killed Mrs Soames? We all thought he and the master were friends?'

'I really can't say,' Hannah replied. 'The police don't discuss their investigations with us.' She gathered her things before they made the connection between Hannah and where their mistress had been killed. 'Thank you, Mr Hemmings, Mrs Daly. We appreciate you talking to us.'

'I hope I haven't spoken out of turn.' Mr Hemmings escorted them back into the front hall. 'If the master learned I—'

'He won't hear a word.' Hannah glanced up at the galleried landing. 'Mr Hemmings, would it be an inconvenience if I took one last look at Mrs Soames's room?'

'Well, I'm not sure.' His eyes flicked to the landing and back again. 'But seeing as it's you, Miss Merrill, I don't see it could do any harm.'

Hannah mounted the stairs while, after a knowing look, her aunt began a discussion with the butler about the problems of retaining good domestic staff. Her voice faded as Hannah took the hallway to the back of the house towards her friend's bedroom.

She eased open the door and instantly the air was squeezed from her lungs. Her head filled with memories of the time she had spent in that room with Lily-Anne; the lingering smell of her perfume made Hannah clamp her lips together to prevent a sob.

The room was decorated in shades of cream and dusky rose with an accent of sage green. A canopy hung over the bed beneath a gilt coronet, and a chaise and chairs were embroidered with flowers of the same colours. Watercolour drawings of countryside scenes adorned every wall, and china ornaments crowded every surface.

Lily-Anne had loved this house; the home she had grown up in. When her father offered to purchase another as a wedding present, Lily-Anne had insisted he signed this one over instead, telling Cavan she never planned to leave it. Hannah suspected the property was grander than anything he could afford, as he conceded without an argument and moved in after the wedding.

Hannah replayed an entire childhood of summer afternoons and winter evenings of their schooldays in her head, when she and Lily-Anne had giggled together over cheap novels in the chaise below the window, or had lain stretched out at right angles to share secrets on the vast bed with its goose down coverlet.

The ebony dresser with its arched triptych mirror was where

Lily-Anne sat to have her hair dressed for her wedding, while Hannah perched on the end of the bed in her bridesmaid dress. The dressing table lay strangely empty and infinitely sad without her friend's silver-backed brushes and hand mirrors. That Lily-Anne's things were no longer needed brought tears to her eyes.

Hannah reached to touch the only object on the polished surface she recognised – an inlaid wooden box in which Lily-Anne kept the sentimental trinkets not consigned to a bank vault with the rest of her jewellery. A cameo brooch she had received on her fourteenth birthday; a silver pendant from which hung a lapis lazuli stone; an ivory pin in the shape of a hand holding a flower; a dog-eared dance card; and an embroidered handkerchief.

Almost without thinking, Hannah pushed the catch on the underside that revealed a hidden drawer in the base where Lily-Anne kept notes from Cavan from when they were courting. On top of a thin pile of opened letters, a card lay face down, the words 'Hobart's Photographic Studio' printed on. Turning it over, she was unsurprised to see a sepia photograph of a pale-skinned girl dressed in Egyptian costume and sharply cut dark wig.

Footsteps in the hall prompted her to slip the card into her bag, close the box and make it to the door just as a maid popped her head around the jamb.

'Oooh, sorry, miss. I was just—'

'It's all right. Don't let me keep you from your work.' Hannah put her head down against incipient tears and eased past her. 'I was saying goodbye to my friend.'

'Of course, miss. Such a sad, awful thing. I expect you'll miss her.'

'Indeed, I will. I do.' Blinking back more tears, Hannah bid her a curt farewell before she hurried downstairs to where Aunt Violet waited with the patient Hemmings.

20

'A robbery that wasn't a robbery,' Aunt Violet said as they strolled beside the water's edge, where the quacking of ducks vied with mechanical bangs and shouts of workmen from the two large boatyards at Strand-on-the-Green upriver. Once, they produced pleasure craft, steamboats and sculls for the University Boat Race, but now only built defence vessels for the Royal Navy.

'Not to mention Cavan's mysterious lady visitor.' Hannah linked her arm through her aunt's elbow, slowing her brisk pace to ease the ache in her ribs. 'I'll wager it was the woman at the funeral. I wonder who she is? And no, I don't intend to ask Cavan.'

'So what now?' Aunt Violet shielded her eyes with a hand to watch as wherries, ferries and pleasure craft glided by on the water in both directions, loaded with salt, coal, or the decks crammed with passengers enjoying the unusually warm weather.

'That's easy.' Hannah plucked the piece of paper her aunt still clutched in her hand. 'We ask this Guppy chap his version of events.'

* * *

Number 73 Rivercourt Road was one of a row of late-Victorian villas, with well-maintained, though tiny, front gardens behind waist-high walls and wrought-iron gates. The short woman who answered their knock eyed them suspiciously. She wore her wavy mouse-brown hair scraped back from a high forehead; her youthful mien spoiled by a gruff voice with which she responded to Hannah's halting enquiry about whether her husband was at home.

'What do the likes of you want with 'im?' She leaned her shoulder against the door frame, her scrawny arms crossed beneath a small bosom encased in a cotton dress so faded it was impossible to discern what colour it had once been.

'We understand he came to the notice of the local constabulary fairly recently,' Aunt Violet said.

Two women carrying wicker baskets slowed at the front gate and whispered together, watching them.

'You'd better come in.' The woman jerked her chin at the hallway behind her and stepped back. 'I don't need any more gossip around here than there is already.'

She led them into a gloomy hallway decorated entirely in brown paint; an aroma of carbolic soap overlaid by wax furniture polish all mixed with a lingering smell of boiled cabbage instantly made Hannah feel claustrophobic.

'Reg is in the garden, but I'll have you know he had nothing to do with no robbery.' The sound of a door closing at the rear of the house brought a smile to the woman's face. 'That'll be him now.'

A lanky man in an ill-fitting suit hung his coat on one of a row of hooks in the rear hall, followed by his soft cap, revealing a fluff of sandy hair highlighted by the daylight from the glass panel in the door behind him. His complexion was deeply tanned with tiny white lines at the corner of his eyes, showing he spent a lot of time outdoors.

'Reg!' His wife's high-pitched shriek made Hannah jump. 'These ladies want to talk to yer. But you don't have to say anything if you—'

'All right, Mavis, don't take on.' He cut her off, his voice low and conciliatory. 'I'll talk to them.'

Mavis huffed an annoyed breath, but obediently slunk away along the narrow hall, muttering to herself.

Mr Guppy examined the visitors with mild curiosity while unwinding a grey scarf from around his throat. 'Don't mind Mavis. She's a mite upset about what happened.' He led them into the tiny front parlour that contained two armchairs set at angles by the fireplace with a handmade rug in between. An unhealthy-looking aspidistra in a blue and white pot stood in the square bay window facing the street, the light filtering through the plant's broad, tapering leaves.

Mr Guppy gestured them to sit. 'Take a load off.'

'Thank you for agreeing to talk to us,' Hannah said as she and Aunt Violet took the two chairs while Mr Guppy perched on a narrow, upholstered fender in front of the empty fireplace, knees spread and one forearm resting on a thigh. 'You aren't compelled to explain anything to us. We aren't the police.'

'Lady police officers,' he chuckled. 'Now, wouldn't that be something?' He brushed dust from his trousers. 'So, what's this about, then?'

'We're friends of the late Mrs Soames,' Hannah said.

'The lady from the big house in Chiswick Mall?' He shook his head sadly. 'Terrible thing what happened to her. I don't know what you want from me, but I know nothing about her murder.'

'We're not here to accuse you, Mr Guppy, but we were told you were arrested on suspicion of robbing Dr Soames's house,' Hannah said.

'And a big surprise it was an' all. I was having a drink down at the Dove, minding me own business, when I asked Edwin – he's the landlord – if he could change a note for me so I could pay me rent, when some off-duty copper having a quiet pint arrested me under this new "No treating law". I tried to explain, but he took me down to the station. When the custody sergeant saw the banknote I'd offered Edwin, everything went to 'ell and back.' He flushed. 'Er... begging your pardon, ladies.'

'He saw the money?' Hannah frowned. 'Why was that relevant?'

'The custody sergeant said some banknotes stolen from the doctor's house had his initials written on 'em, just like the fiver I had. Odd thing to do, I thought, but there you are.'

'Have you ever been to Dr Soames's house?' Aunt Violet asked.

'No. Never met the chap either. But they didn't believe me. Kept asking what I did with the rest of the money. I had no idea what they were talking about, so they banged me up in Pentonville for a week.'

'I don't mean to imply anything, Mr Guppy, but where *did* you get the five-pound note?' Hannah asked.

'Ah, well that's the thing.' He scratched his ear. 'I'm a boot polish salesman by day, but sometimes I moonlight for my brother-in-law. He owns a shop in Leadenhall, but most of his sales staff have enlisted, so he's in a pickle.'

'What does he sell?' Aunt Violet asked.

'Negligées, undergarments and the like.' He flushed beneath his tan, unable to meet their eyes. 'Good quality, no rubbish. I hawk 'em at the stage doors of theatres on Shaftesbury Avenue. Actresses are always up for buying a good quality piece of silk. I do well there.'

'Do you recall who gave you the banknote?' Hannah wasn't sure where this was going, but he had her attention.

'One of them chaps who 'angs around the stage door, waiting

for the girls to come out. He bought an oyster dressing robe and a matching nightgown. My best line, in fact. It was four pounds twelve shillings for both items, and he gave me the fiver. I told him I didn't have no change, and he said to keep it. Nice little earner, that was.' He pulled on his chin with a thumb and forefinger. 'Paid for it later, though, didn't I?'

'I'm sure it was an awful experience. But you were released,' Aunt Violet said.

'I was, and got an apology, too. The sergeant said all the charges had been dropped.'

'Did they explain why?' Hannah asked.

'Nope. Still got a warning about buying rounds of drinks, though. As if I could afford it.' He snorted a laugh. 'Even gave me the fiver back, which was good of them.'

'Can you remember what this man looked like?' Hannah tried not to sound too eager, but doubted she succeeded.

'Um, taller than me, and broader.' He stroked his chin thoughtfully. 'Expensive clothes with a nice diamond pin in his tie. His 'at hid most of his face and there ain't many street lights round the back of those theatres, what with the blackout.' He frowned, then straightened as if in recollection. 'Except, when the stage door opened for the girls, he took off his hat and he had dark hair with a white streak right here.' He tapped the side of his head with a finger.

'You've been most helpful, Mr Guppy.' Hannah rose and held out her hand. He took it and she could feel the callouses on his palms through her thin glove.

'Don't see it m'self. But if it helps find out who killed that lady, I'm 'appy to 'elp. My boss at the Cherry Blossom Factory took some convincing I weren't no burglar, but I'm back at work now.'

'We're relieved for your sake you were exonerated, Mr Guppy,' Aunt Violet said as they were showed out.

* * *

'I'm still confused about this so-called burglary,' Aunt Violet observed on their leisurely stroll towards home. 'But the story about the banknote was too complicated to make up. And he described Cavan perfectly.'

A scattering of small boats reared and bobbed against the ropes that held them to wooden jetties, their owners having finished work for the day.

'What happened to the money he reported stolen?' Hannah mused.

'Maybe it never existed?' Aunt Violet held down her hat with one hand as a gust of wind threatened to whisk it away.

'Hemmings said Lily-Anne claimed to have spent it, but she never used cash. She had accounts at both Harvey Nichols and Harrods. And if Cavan bought a negligée, he certainly did not give it to Lily-Anne. She had all her clothes made for her.'

'Obviously, he bought it for this other woman. And unless we intend to ask every actress in the theatre district if she received silk underwear from her lover, we'll never find out who.'

'Not so loud!' Hannah aimed a shy smile at an astonished passer-by. 'It might prove Cavan is a womaniser, though not necessarily a murderer.'

'Isn't that what I keep saying?' Her aunt tutted. 'If he had gone anywhere near your bookshop that afternoon, we would know by now.'

'I suppose so,' Hannah conceded. 'Wait, how do you know the inspector has checked Cavan's alibi? When I mentioned it, he dismissed me.'

'Did I say that? I meant it makes sense he would have. Don't be so pedantic, Hannah.'

Aunt Violet tilted her head in acknowledgement of a sharp

whistle from a young man from the deck of a passenger cruiser chugging downriver.

'You really shouldn't encourage men like him, Aunt Violet.' Hannah shook her head.

'I'm not encouraging him,' she replied, offended. 'I'm simply acknowledging his good taste.'

Hannah sighed, tucked her arm through her aunt's and pulled her away. 'Perhaps Lily-Anne was right. They say a wife always knows. And I thought Cavan was upright and respectable.'

'Lloyd George enjoys an intimate relationship with his secretary, and no one says *he's* not respectable.' Giving a disdainful sniff of contempt for society's double standards, her aunt flung open the front gate. 'Why don't we go out this evening?' Aunt Violet said as they relieved themselves of their coats and bags in the hall.

'Just the two of us, and without a male escort?' After her initial surprise, the idea definitely appealed to Hannah.

'London is full of unescorted women these days, so why not?'

'What are you up to, Aunt Violet?' Hannah joined her in the sitting room where her aunt eased off her shoes. 'I assume this plan has a purpose?'

'Not really, although if Lily-Anne spent so much time in the night spots of London, we might discover what she found so fascinating there. If not, we could simply enjoy a pleasant evening dancing to jazz music. What do you say?'

'I'm all for it, although I'm not up to anything too energetic. The last time you suggested an outing I sprained an ankle at Prince's Skating Club.'

21

Hannah wrapped her evening coat tightly around her and exited the Sunbeam outside a nondescript building that resembled the discreet entrance to a private bank. Aunt Violet pressed a brass bell set into the wall. Almost instantly, the door swung inwards, spilling a rectangle of warm yellow light onto the grey pavement to reveal a doorman in a calf-length navy blue coat with gilt buttons whose impassive face split into a wide smile as he bowed them into the building.

'Miss Edwards! We haven't had the pleasure of your company for some time.' A slight pause followed as he searched his memory. 'And Miss Merrill, how delightful to see you.'

'The same to you, George.' Aunt Violet handed him her coat. 'We aren't dining this evening, but would like a table not too close to the band.'

'Of course, Miss Edwards.' The doorman handed them off to a waiter who led them through a set of double doors that opened onto a world of light, music, chatter and bright laughter. A small stairway led down into a vast hall that rose to a twenty-foot ceiling from which crystal chandeliers reflected light from thousands of sparkling prisms onto half-panelled walls. Gilt-framed mirrors were set at intervals along the walls, a dining area on one side and the dance floor on the other, separated by a row of white plastered pillars and potted palms on plinths. Marble statuary of half-dressed ladies in provocative poses were arranged at intervals, their assets concealed by artfully placed white flowers.

A platform at the far end contained a six-piece band who played saxophones, trumpets and a banjo. An African gentleman at a baby grand piano teased a melodious tune from the keys. High female laughter mingled with male guffaws and low-pitched chatter, accompanied by the clink of glass and clatter of crockery.

Young men in formal black tailcoats, white bow ties with wingtip collars, and white vests sat with women who wore empire line gowns decorated with pearls, sequins and bows, and velvet or jewelled browbands or combs in their coiffed hair.

Their waiter led them to a table for four beside a round pillar wound with artificial vines, and as she took her seat, Hannah's gown of aquamarine silk shot through with gold thread that shimmered in the light received several admiring looks. The dress was her favourite, with hand-embroidered gold lilies around the hem, and a long peplum between the bodice and knee in the latest fashion.

Sliding into the gilt and black chair, she settled down to enjoy a rare evening of extravagant glamour where the war and all its misery seemed very far away, despite the number of men in uniforms.

Taking the chair opposite, Aunt Violet plucked the pasteboard drinks list from a metal prong in front of her.

'Good grief, have you seen how much they charge for a bottle of champagne? It's outrageous.' She looked up and smiled at the hovering waiter. 'We'll have two gin-and-its, please.'

The savoury odours of cooking food and cigarette smoke filled

Hannah's senses, along with something else she could not identify.

'What's that odd smell?' Hannah wrinkled her nose.

'I'm wearing Guerlain's Mi-Mau, so it cannot be me.'

'Different to perfume, but a spicy, musky scent with a herbal undertone.'

'I couldn't possibly say.' Aunt Violet fiddled with her necklace. 'Ah, here are our drinks.' The waiter placed two cocktail glasses before them filled with a clear liquid with slices of orange floating on the surface.

Hannah sipped the slightly bitter drink as the heady combination of exotic perfume, light laughter and clink of glasses proved cathartic, and before long, Hannah's foot tapped to the rhythm of the band. She sensed something panicked about the way couples threw themselves into the dancing with wild abandon, as if determined to enjoy themselves while the world crashed around them.

'Hannah, is that you?' A shrill, female voice carried above the noise as Mary Ewell descended on them with short, balletic steps caused by the figure-hugging oyster pink sheath she was wearing. 'How lovely to see you! And you, Miss Edwards. Robson, look who's here!' She called to a group of young men who talked in loud braying voices, the overhead light bouncing off their pomaded hair.

A blond head detached from the others and turned in their direction, a finger raised in a gesture that said he needed another minute.

'Have you only just arrived?' Mary surveyed the two cocktail glasses with a myopic squint. 'A shame you missed the floor show. It was stunning. You don't mind if we join you, do you?' she added, negating her own question by the fact she was already seated. 'Ah, here he is.'

Robson Ewell bounded towards them, pulled up a second chair, then repeated everything his wife had just said. 'Hannah!

Haven't seen you for an age. It must have been about the time Gerald copped it.'

Hannah froze and Robson's face fell as he realised his faux pas. 'Gosh, I didn't mean. Well, you know I thought Gerald was a top chap. I—'

'It's quite all right, Robson.' Hannah smiled up at him. 'I understand what you meant.'

'Might I impose upon you to get me a drink, Robson?' Aunt Violet interrupted him, although her half-full one was still in her hand. 'You know what I like.'

'Uh, yes. Yes, of course.' He scrambled to his feet and scuttled away, red-faced.

'He doesn't mean to be unkind.' Mary pressed Hannah's wrist on the table, apologising as always for her sweet, but slightly dim husband. Robson left university with a third-class degree and went straight into his father's business. He occupied an oversized office with an empty desk, with an underemployed secretary; his days comprising extended lunches and weekends at country house parties where he disparaged the working man for not knowing his place. Despite all this, Hannah could not help being fond of him.

A loud drum roll cut through the murmur of conversation as the tempo ramped up into the strains of *The Memphis Blues.* The piercing tones of a saxophone brought toes tapping, while chairs scraped back and couples took to the floor.

Robson returned with a cocktail glass he placed in front of Aunt Violet, but before he could resume his seat, Mary announced, 'Robson, I'm parched. Order us some champagne, would you?'

'Right ho.' He only got three paces away before he was accosted by a trio of loud-voiced young men who greeted him with the gusto of schoolboys.

Aunt Violet chose that moment to scrape her chair back,

rising. 'You'll be fine with Mary and Robson. I'll be back soon.'

'Where are you going?' Hannah's tapping foot halted in mid-flight.

'I can see a few faces who might be amenable to a little light gossip.'

'She won't desert you.' Mary giggled at Aunt Violet's retreat. 'Anyway, it allows us to have a private chat.'

Hannah groaned inwardly. Mary's proclivity for asking inappropriate questions was legendary.

'Murray's isn't the same since poor, dear Lily-Anne got herself murdered, don't you think?' Mary's simpering voice fulfilled all of Hannah's expectations.

And there it was.

'She enjoyed coming here. I've only been a few times.'

'That was Gerald's doing. He always said—' Mary's hand flew to her mouth. 'I'm so sorry. I didn't mean to say that.'

'No, go on, Mary.' Hannah straightened. 'What did Gerald always say?'

'Nothing really, only that this sort of thing wasn't you. He said the music gave you headaches.'

'Did he indeed?' Hannah bridled. 'Was that often?'

'Oh, a couple of days a week, usually.' Mary adopted an expression of shocked embarrassment, but before Hannah could reassure her, Robson returned with a white-coated waiter who bore an oversized silver bucket.

Hannah never expected Gerald to spend his evenings away from her in front of the fire with his slippers, but why hadn't he invited her?

'Ooh, a magnum, darling. How extravagant!' Mary squealed in her little girl voice. 'And we'll need some extra glasses for the new arrivals.'

Hannah craned her neck behind her in the direction Mary was

looking and stiffened.

Darius, handsome in black tie and crisp white-collar points, his hair darkened from a discreet application of pomade, approached with Cecily on his arm; her ivory gown reminiscent of a wedding dress, fastened so high at the neck she looked as if she might choke if she moved her head.

The heat of embarrassment flooded Hannah's cheeks at the thought that she was sat draped sideways, one arm over the back of her chair with her foot tapping, her shoe half off. She straightened abruptly in her seat and one flailing elbow sent her bag onto the floor.

'Allow me.' Darius retrieved the beaded bag, their fingers touching briefly as he handed it back, making her face flame more.

What was wrong with her? She had known Darius all her life. Why was she behaving like a love-struck schoolgirl?

'Hannah, how nice.' Cecily broke the spell. 'We haven't seen you here in ages.' She made it sound like an accusation, one she diluted by air-kissing Hannah's cheek, her breath heavy with an odour of spirits. 'I so admire your courage to show the world you have nothing to hide.'

'Cecily.' Darius snapped, his voice tight. 'You're embarrassing yourself.'

'Darling, I'm only joking.' She slapped his arm playfully. 'No one really believes Hannah has anything to do with the murder. Even if it happened in her bookshop and with her knife.'

A brief, but loaded silence followed, during which no one seemed to know where to look. To Hannah's relief, Robson instigated the ceremony of opening the green and gold bottle, culminating in a discreet "pop" and a triumphant shout.

Tempted to point out a fizzy drink hardly warranted all the fuss, Hannah smiled brightly in all the right places. Once the full crystal coupes had been distributed, the waiter pocketed his tip and retreated.

Oblivious to Hannah's discomfort and Darius's furious frown, Cecily beamed at Robson who handed her a glass of champagne. 'How lovely, thank you, Robson.'

'Hey, old thing.' Robson eased his chair closer to Hannah's. 'I hear you also got clobbered by an intruder at your bookshop.' He rubbed his hands together as if readying himself for some juicy gossip.

'Robson! Who told you that?' Mary demanded.

'Miss Edwards did. A moment ago.' Robson gestured vaguely to where Aunt Violet was chatting to a tall, red-headed man, her head thrown back in uninhibited laughter.

Mary grabbed her husband's arm and dragged him onto the dance floor. 'Do excuse us, I simply love this tune.' Although appreciative of Mary's tact, Hannah cringed inwardly. But there was nothing for it but to endure the questions.

'What's this?' Darius's glass halted mid-way to his lips, a frown directed at Hannah. 'When did this happen?'

'How exciting! Do tell.' Cecily's champagne glass hit the table hard, spilling a few drops onto the white tablecloth.

'I was knocked over, nothing more. I'm fine.' She would certainly have a word with her aunt later.

'It doesn't sound like nothing.' Darius's raised voice attracted attention from nearby tables.

'Don't bully her, darling.'

Cecily waved her almost empty glass in the air at an approaching waiter. 'If she doesn't want to talk about it, leave her alone.'

'She's making light of it. And take it easy with that.' Darius firmly removed a newly refilled glass from Cecily's hand. 'This stuff is potent, and you aren't used to it.'

'I intend to become very used to it.' Cecily laughed hollowly. 'In fact, when we are married, I shall drink nothing else. Now, what about that dance you promised me?' She hauled on his arm, a grip he stoically resisted.

'Later, perhaps.' He waved her away, still looking at Hannah.

'Then I'll find someone else to dance with.' Cecily directed a pout at Darius over her shoulder as she pranced away.

Darius ignored her, the fingers of one hand drumming the tabletop.

'Tell me exactly what happened, Hannah?'

'There's nothing to tell. It's likely the man who shoved me was after the postcards, but he didn't get them.'

'So much for police protection.' Darius eased his shoulders, though his eyes remained wary.

'I appreciate your concern, but I'm all right, really.' She reached to place a hand on his arm, but thought better of it. 'I'm staying away from the bookshop until the inspector has finished his investigation.'

'That's something, I suppose. And concern doesn't begin to describe it.' He kept his voice low, but the music, loud chatter and the clink of glass made it too noisy for eavesdroppers. 'You could have been badly hurt.'

The dance ended and couples drifted back to their tables, including Aunt Violet, who greeted Darius with a warm smile and explained her absence was to catch up with some old friends. While Robson set about procuring more chairs, the band struck up a spine-tingling tango and Cecily abandoned her temporary partner and pounced on Darius. 'You must dance with me now. I've been practising especially.'

He rose slowly, almost reluctantly, his eyes still on Hannah as he entered the rhythm of the music with surprising skill and a firm walk to the on- and off-beat rhythm; the tilt of his head was just the right angle, his arm curved around Cecily in a firm, possessive hold. Hannah imagined what it might be like to be in his arms, the focus of the intense look he had given her a few moments before. A tiny flare of hope ignited in her chest but was extinguished immediately. All couples have their disagreements, and Cecily's over-consumption of champagne would likely be a source of embarrassment between them later.

'Why did you tell Robson about the man in the bookshop, Aunt Violet?' Hannah hissed.

'Oh sorry, it just slipped out.'

'Well, did you find out anything?' Hannah pushed aside the remains of her gin and topped up her champagne, feeling no guilt. Robson could afford it. From the corner of her eye, she spotted Darius sweep past with a stony-faced Cecily. Were they still arguing? Or had Hannah misinterpreted their mood because she wanted to?

'Actually, yes.' Aunt Violet clicked open a compact she held up to her face, peering at her reflection. 'I've just had an informative chat with three of the most empty-headed girls in London who told me they buy their stuff from a woman whose prices are more reasonable than the staff here.'

'The waiters here sell drugs?'

'Hush. Not so loud. But yes.' She patted her nose with an ostrich feather puff before lowering it again. 'I didn't get a name – that's reserved for those in the know – but that could simply be...' her voice faded into the clamour of the room as Hannah's attention strayed to the door where a familiar face sent a jolt through her.

'Hannah? Did you hear what I said?'

'Aunt Violet,' Hannah said in a fierce whisper. 'Cavan Soames has just walked in.'

22

Aunt Violet turned ninety degrees in her chair, her elbow toppling a champagne glass from a passing waiter's tray that emptied onto a nearby lady's dress.

'How clumsy of me. I'm so sorry,' Aunt Violet gushed.

The woman huffed, made some exaggerated swipes at her skirt and stomped away, muttering to herself.

Cavan stepped back hurriedly to allow the disgruntled lady to pass, a bemused frown on his face that told them he had missed the small drama.

'Miss Edwards, and Hannah.' He inclined his head at an empty chair, then dragged it from the table and sat. 'What a surprise to see you here together.'

'I would say the same of you,' Hannah said, her smile guarded. She was about to ask what he was doing there when his wife had been brutally murdered less than a month before, when the toe of her aunt's shoe contacted her shin under the table, silencing her.

'It's lovely to see you, Cavan, and looking so well.' Aunt Violet scraped back her chair and stood, her gaze fixed on the far side of the room. 'I'm sure that's Raymond Asquith over there. You'll have to excuse me, Cavan dear, but I simply must ask if his father has reconsidered putting our petition to the Commons. Hannah, you stay and entertain Cavan. I'll be back in a moment.'

'Aunt Violet, I—' Hannah's protest fell on deaf ears as her aunt strode away.

'Was it something I said?' Cavan dragged out a chair and sat.

'No. You know she never keeps still.' Hannah fingered her half-full glass of champagne as she took in his immaculate evening suit and white tie, the white streak at his temple that gave him a sartorial look. 'She's right. You look well.'

'Is that a euphemism for "what is a grieving widower doing in a notorious nightclub"?' His mouth twitched at the corner in a cynical smile.

'Sorry. I didn't mean to be unsubtle.' She chewed her bottom lip, annoyed with herself at being so transparent.

'It's a fair question. Truth is, I cannot bear that empty house. Lily-Anne loved this place. The lights, the music and dancing. Being here somehow brings me closer to her again for a while.'

A wave of shame flooded through her at the sincerity in his voice. She had not thought of it that way. Why wouldn't he seek the places they were happy?

Or was he simply an accomplished actor?

'No need to look embarrassed.' He looked up to acknowledge the waiter who placed his whisky in front of him before leaving. 'You're only thinking what everyone else is.' She fumbled for a response, but he was speaking again. 'I'm also heartily sick of that chap, Farrell.' He withdrew a gold case from his pocket and fumbled it open, plucked a cigarette and tapped the end on the table, an eyebrow raised in her direction in a 'do-you-mind' look.

She nodded, despite hating the smell.

'He keeps asking the same questions, as if he's trying to trap me into giving different answers.' He produced a flame from a matching lighter and lit the cigarette, inhaling deeply as if drawing strength from it before slicing her a sideways look. 'I saw your face at the inquest. You really didn't know, did you?'

'About Lily-Anne's... medication?'

'You could call it that.' He tapped the cigarette smartly in the astray on the table but did not look at her. 'My wife had taken to... experimenting with her friends. As you and she spent so much time together, I assumed you were one of them, thus my reaction at the bookshop when—' He broke off, as if saying the words was still painful, took a drag of his cigarette and blew a controlled stream of tobacco smoke into the air.

'At the inquest you claimed you prescribed it for congestion ' Her words came out sharper than she intended, though he did not appear to notice,

'I did, at first. Then about a month before she... died, I called in to Savory and Moore to collect some supplies and the pharmacist asked after my attractive assistant.' His lips quirked into a sardonic smile, the cigarette hanging precariously from one corner. 'My assistant is forty-five and has a squint. I almost asked for the poison book to check how much she had bought but couldn't bring myself to.' He swept his glass into his free hand and took a mouthful before setting it down again. 'I went a little crazy when she was killed. I hope you'll forgive my behaviour on that day?'

He stubbed out his cigarette, although it was only a third burned down. 'You look lovely this evening, by the way.' He covered her free hand on the table and squeezed. 'Gerald was wrong, you know. This place suits you.'

She summoned a weak smile. *How many more times would she hear those words this evening?* 'I have been here before, you know?'

'Er yes, of course. But—'

'Gerald was a more frequent visitor?' He looked about to

speak, but she shook her head. 'Don't worry. I've learned more about him since he died than I did when he was alive.'

'Don't judge him too harshly. Gerald was a good person, but... a little lost. Fear invades every aspect of our lives with this war. No one knows what is going to happen, and with these blasted airships dropping bombs on civilians, can you blame people for trying to find some pleasure in life before the inevitable happens?'

'Inevitable?' A lance of fear went through her. 'Do you believe there will be an invasion?'

'No. I think we'll beat the Huns, but it will take time. And morphine plays a part in that.'

'I... I don't understand.' Though deep down she did, but needed him to lay it out for her.

'This is a dirty war, Hannah. One we must win by any means possible. Opiates and cocaine help to mitigate the paralysing terror of battle. Hand-to-hand fighting and bombardments that last for days are crippling for those men in the trenches. I doubt many could face those guns, much less run at them, without it.'

'I didn't think of it that way. It must be terrible.'

He nodded. 'The anticipation of attack is cruel enough, but exploding shells and machine gun bullets do terrible damage to human flesh. Morphine sulphate is the most effective painkiller we have.'

But Lily-Anne wasn't fighting a war. Why did she need to escape her life?

'Cavan? Do you think Lily-Anne's habit contributed to her murder?'

He glanced at her sharply. 'I don't know. I hope not, but it's possible. If she mixed with the wrong sort.'

'Is that really why you're here? To discover who she was mixing with?'

'Is it that obvious?' His smile enhanced his startling good looks, but was also sad.

'What am I thinking, sitting here in my cups when you should be dancing? Shall we?' He nodded to the crowded dance floor where loose-limbed young men twirled their partners dangerously on the polished floor to a lively rendition of '*Alexander's Ragtime Band*'. By some miracle, no one crashed into one other, although there were a few near misses.

'Would you mind if we don't? I'm not quite in the mood this evening.' Her bruises now barely troubled her, but she had no intention of explaining the incident at the bookshop.

'Not at all. I only asked to be chivalrous. I haven't danced at all since—' He left the thought unspoken.

'Cavan?' Impulse drove Hannah to ask. 'Do you think Monty killed Lily-Anne?'

'I honestly don't know.' He propped an elbow on the table and massaged his forehead. 'Had he not skipped out, I would have said it was out of the question.' He sliced a sideways look at her, filled with a mixture of hope and unease. 'Something happened at the house once, which I attributed to him, but Lily-Anne convinced me I was wrong. However, the longer he stays away, the more explaining he has to do.'

Was he referring to the robbery? The weight of her knowledge made her uncomfortable. 'What will you do now? When this is all over?'

He inhaled a slow, deep breath, as if considering his response. 'You should probably know I've applied for a commission in the Royal Army Medical Corps.'

'You're going to the Front?' Despite the warmth of the room, a sudden chill went through her.

'Eventually, I expect. I'll need training in battlefield injuries for the first weeks, but depending upon how long the war continues, I'll probably be needed overseas.'

Lily-Anne had once scornfully told her his work consisted entirely of handing out tonics and pills to neurotic wealthy women. Hannah's shocked reaction prompted Lily-Anne to rescind the remark, but it had stuck with her. Was she completely wrong about him? Was a man willing to face the arena of a bloody war the type to stab his own wife?

'This has been nice, Hannah.' He slapped his knees, pushed to his feet, and plucked her hand from the table. Dropping a kiss on her knuckles, his gaze flicked to meet her eyes. 'Nice to see you wearing them.'

'Ah, yes.' She brought her other hand to her ear where a diamond earring sat. 'Thank you again. I truly treasure them.'

Straightening, his gaze fell on Hannah's handbag on the table where the corner of the postcard she had taken from Lily-Anne's room was visible. But before she could react, he leaned forward and withdrew it.

'Where did you get this?' His brow furrowed as he stared at the girl in the Egyptian costume.

Hannah thought quickly. 'It fell out of Lily-Anne's bag the last time she visited my house. I was going to return it but—well, you know. I don't suppose you know why she would have such a thing?'

'I can only assume one of her friends gave it to her as a prank.' His cheeks paled, his gaze fixed on the photograph, although his mind seemed to be somewhere else.

'It's rather lurid. I'm surprised Lily-Anne kept it.'

'So am I,' he whispered. He looked as if he was about to put the card in his pocket, but at the last second handed it back. 'Well, um... I'm sure we'll see each other soon. Goodnight, Hannah.'

'Goodnight, Cavan.' She grasped his forearm as he turned

away. 'I'm truly sorry about what happened to Lily-Anne. I really miss her.'

He nodded, his lips pressed tightly together, and his eyes suspiciously wet as he turned and shouldered his way between the tables. Hannah barely lost sight of him in the crowd, when a young man she knew by acquaintance bounded to her table and asked her to dance.

'It's Howard, isn't it?' She smiled up at him, hoping her memory had not failed her.

'Well remembered.' He stuck out a hand as the band struck up a waltz. Relieved it was not a foxtrot, she allowed him to pull her to her feet. His unusual height meant her chin did not quite reach his shoulder, giving her a feeling of peering over a wall. However, his firm grip around her waist and the musky smell of his cologne reminded her of how long it was since she had been held by a man, let alone danced with one.

'I heard about Gerald,' he said, his face softening in sympathy as he swept her into the swirl of dancers with a competence which impressed her. 'Thought I'd better get it out of the way at the start.'

'Thank you, Howard. It's happening to too many people we know these days.'

'Gosh, yes. Chaps like him put the rest of us to shame. I've been thinking about applying for a commission myself, mainly to please the pater. No one believed the fighting would go on this long. Now look at us, a year in, and it's worse.' He dropped his voice to a little above a whisper. 'Pity about Roland McKay. You know he copped it at Cuinchy last month?'

'Poor Roland, although I didn't know him well. He got married recently, didn't he? To Daisy Banks?' Hannah concentrated on not stepping on his feet as he resumed the dance.

He nodded. 'It was quite a blow, and so sad for Daisy.' His Adam's apple bobbed as he fought for control.

'I must write and send her my condolences.' Her throat prickled as she recalled the lines of khaki-clad young men who boarded trains at Charing Cross on one platform, while the wounded arrived, dirty, ragged and silent on another. As these thoughts intruded, she caught Darius's intent look as he swept past with Cecily on his arm on their way back to the table. His head turned towards Hannah as he held her gaze until Cecily pulled him away.

'Superb fellow, Darius.' Howard cocked his chin at the retreating couple. 'I always thought you and he would, well... you know.' His slight shrug conveyed more than his words. 'Bit of a surprise all round when you and Gerald got engaged.'

'Life never quite turns out how we expect it.' Hannah's chest tightened, and she looked away quickly, surprised at how pragmatic she sounded. 'Darius is engaged now, you know.'

'Hmm, yes, I heard. Her name's Prentice, isn't it? No idea who her people are.' He looked about to say more, but just then, the music ground to a halt before moving seamlessly into a blues number. 'Shall we go again?'

'Thank you, but I can see my aunt beckoning me. I should join her.' She ran a hand over her nape to ease the knot in her neck. He was indeed very tall.

'Ah, that's a shame.' He walked her back to the table. 'And by the way, you're an excellent dancer, no matter what Gerald says.' He raised a hand in farewell before disappearing into the crowd.

'Was that one of the Randalls I saw you dancing with?' Aunt Violet asked as Hannah slid into her chair.

'It was. Despite my fiancé informing everyone what an incompetent dancer I am.'

'What are you talking about?'

'Nothing. I recognise that smug look, Aunt Violet. What have you been up to?'

'I've been doing a little eavesdropping, and it seems there's been some trouble between Darius and Cecily.'

'Really?' Hannah's nerves prickled as she surreptitiously searched the room, but they were nowhere in sight. 'What kind of trouble?'

'Darius went to make a telephone call and Cecily complained of neglect, so he insisted they leave. She wasn't at all happy about it.'

'That's a shame. I wanted to say goodnight.'

'Of course you did, dear. You and Cecily are such good friends.' Aunt Violet slid into her chair and eased close. 'Now, what did you and the merry widower talk about?'

'Don't call him that. And there's nothing merry about him.'

'Charmed you, did he?' Aunt Violet rubbed her right ankle with one hand. 'I haven't danced like that for an age. I forgot how hard it is on the old ankles.'

'No, he did not charm me. And there's nothing wrong with your ankles. We had an interesting conversation.' Although it was more something he didn't say, which intrigued her. And the look on his face when he saw the postcard.

'How enigmatic. Do you still see him as a wife-killer?'

The lights dimmed, and the band began packing up their instruments while a lone saxophonist played a slow number. Tables emptied and waiters collected dirty glasses, plates and discarded bottles. A yawning Robson draped an arm around his wife as they returned to the table. Mary was subdued and had trouble keeping her eyes open. 'Actually, no.' Hannah lowered her voice to a whisper, but the pair did not appear to be listening. 'He cannot see Monty as a murderer, and when you think about it, if Cavan killed his wife, wouldn't he be eager to put the blame on someone else? Monty seems the prime candidate, seeing as no one knows where he is.'

'Good point. Did he say who he thinks killed her?'

'No. But he believes Monty carried out the robbery. At least I think that's what he meant.'

'They could be one and the same.' Aunt Violet consulted her wristwatch. 'Goodness, it's almost two.' She scraped back her chair and rose, her elbow catching an urn of peacock feathers that teetered dangerously before settling back in place. Hannah thanked Robson for the champagne and wished them both a goodnight as they weaved between tables, pausing occasionally to exchange air kisses with several acquaintances on their way to collect their coats.

Hannah hugged her fur-lined coat around her as they emerged into the street, shivering as a gust of sharp wind swept litter along the gutters, the dark night strangely oppressive after the bright light, noise and colour of the club.

Aunt Violet retrieved the starting handle from the Sunbeam's footwell, bunched her long skirt in one hand and inserted it into the notch beneath the radiator. 'Damn and blast it! I can't see what I'm doing.'

'Let me.' Nudging her aside, Hannah placed one hand squarely on the bonnet, and gave the handle a firm turn. Instantly, the engine coughed into life before settling into a low, rhythmic chunter, a stream of smoke emerging from the exhaust. 'Get in, Aunt Violet. I'll drive.' Hannah withdrew the handle and tossed it into the footwell before she settled into the driving seat.

'Are you insinuating I'm intoxicated?' Aunt Violet caught her heel on the kerb, and staggered, but quickly righted herself.

'I wouldn't dare.' Hannah shoved open the passenger door as undaunted, her aunt swept the flap of her wide coat to one side and half collapsed into the leather seat, declaring, 'I knew it was a good idea teaching you to drive.'

'I dread to think what my mother would say if she knew.' Hannah revved the engine and pulled away with a screech of tyres.

'She won't hear it from me,' Aunt Violet said as Hannah negotiated a sharp turn into a virtually deserted Regent Street.

Hannah pressed down on the accelerator and urged the Sunbeam towards Kensington High Street, swinging wide to overtake a Rolls-Royce Silver Ghost full of noisy late-night revellers hanging out of the windows. When she pulled in sharply ahead, their indignant driver squeezed the car horn, making her smile.

23

After a late breakfast, served by Ivy, who failed to hide her irritation at the fact her routine was disrupted once again, Hannah showed Aunt Violet the postcard she had found in Lily-Anne's room.

'Where did you get this, and why haven't I seen it before?'

'From Lily-Anne's room the day we talked to Hemmings. And don't scowl at me like that. I kept quiet because everything is complicated enough already. However, now I feel it might be significant after all.'

'What changed your perspective?'

'I've thought about that a good deal. Suppose Lily-Anne found it among Cavan's belongings and jumped to the most obvious conclusion?'

'I know what I'd think. That this woman with no clothes on was his paramour?'

'No one uses words like "paramour" any more, Aunt Violet.' Hannah sighed 'But I intend to find out if my theory is true.'

'How? You don't know anything about her.'

'Not yet.' She turned the card over and pointed to the writing on the bottom.

'Hmm. I don't think you should keep evidence from the police.'

'Says the champion of the WSPU, who once set fire to post boxes.' Hannah smiled when her aunt poked out her tongue. 'Anyway, it's not evidence. This card is intact, so it wasn't used to pass messages.'

'How did Cavan get it then? Do you suppose Monty gave it to him?'

'Sold it to him, more like.' Hannah snorted. 'And I kept it to myself because, if you knew, then Inspector Farrell would, too. You've become pally with him recently.'

'I agree we have certain mutual interests.' Her aunt glanced down at her plate, but failed to hide the slow flush that crept into her cheeks.

'I showed the card to Cavan last night at the nightclub.'

'Really? I wish I'd been present at that conversation.'

'I lied about where I got it, but that it was Lily-Anne's. He looked stunned at first, but then shrugged it off as a prank played on her, though I'm convinced he's seen it before. Suppose this was what she planned to tell me the day she died, and he killed her to prevent it?'

'Rather drastic, don't you think?' Aunt Violet slathered a piece of toast with raspberry jam. 'Most men buy their wives jewellery to obliterate their indiscretions. It's how most of my married friends have built up such impressive collections.' She bit into her toast and chewed. 'I still think you should inform Inspector Farrell.'

'I can imagine his response if I hand him another piece of evidence I just happen to have stumbled across and didn't tell him about.'

'Hmm, I can see why it wouldn't sound too good.' Her aunt placed her hands on the table and pushed to her feet. 'You'll have to decide what the best approach is. I've been invited to a house party, so won't be back until Monday.' She slid the postcard back across the table. 'Unless you want me to cancel?'

'No, of course not. You enjoy yourself. Is it anyone I know?'

'Unlikely, they're Red Cross bods I haven't seen in a while. Now, I had better pack a bag. I was going to ask Ivy, but she'll probably bite my head off.'

Hannah retrieved the postcard and studied it again, but the reverse was clean apart from the name of the studio where it was taken. Where did Lily-Anne get it? Cavan's suggestion of a prank did not hold true, and she was certain he knew more about it than he claimed. But then if the woman was his mistress, he was hardly likely to admit it to her.

On Sunday morning, a low grey sky sagged over the river; the surface whipped into grey waves where lapwings and moorhens huddled on the bank, reluctant to venture into the open. Hannah pottered around the house, enjoying the silence of her own company. By late afternoon the sky had cleared, leaving patches of blue which faded into a grey and pink dusk. The light faded quickly, and preferring the soft, intimate light of an oil lamp to the flickering electric ones, she arranged her solitary tea of duck egg sandwiches, garibaldi biscuits, and a rare fruit cake from Fortnum's. She was settling into her favourite chair with a copy of Anna Katharine Green's *The Golden Slipper* just as a heavy knock at the front door interrupted her thoughts.

Sighing, she unfurled from the chair and entered the hallway, only for the knock to come again, louder. 'All right, I'm coming, don't be so imp—' Her jaw went slack with shock at the sight of Monty stood on her doorstep. He leaned one shoulder against the door frame, his body hunched as if trying to make himself invisible. His gaze scanned the road with fear, as wordlessly, she took in his rumpled suit, his pallor and purple bruises beneath his eyes. His black hair, usually worn slicked back and applied with pomade hung over his forehead showing he had not been near a barber in weeks.

'Well, don't leave me out here, Hannah.' Snatching off his hat, he shoved past her, aiming a backward kick at the door, which slammed shut, almost taking her thumbnail with it.

His cane bounced off the door frame as he made his way clumsily into the sitting room. 'Shut those curtains, would you? I do not want anyone seeing me. I'm guessing you're alone, as I didn't see your aunt's motor car.' He tossed his hat on the floor and slumped into her chair. 'I could do without Violet Edwards tackling me to the ground and sitting on me until the police get here.'

'What makes you think *I* won't do that?' Hannah snapped, instantly regretting her tone when he could well be a murderer.

'You, Hannah?' He snorted. 'You're a girl.'

'Aunt Violet is also a girl.'

'More a commando in disguise,' he muttered under his breath, then louder, 'I thought I was being followed when I left the station, but my nerves are shot, so probably imagined it.'

'Where have you been, Monty?' Anger surged at his casual audacity. 'Every policeman in London has been searching for you.'

'Don't you think I know that?' He dry-washed his face with shaking fingers. 'I stayed at a boarding house on the east coast. God-awful place it was, too. Even in summer, the wind comes off the sea like a knife. Have you got anything to drink?'

'Sherry or brandy?' Ignoring his casual reference to knives, Hannah headed for the sideboard.

'What do you think?' He massaged his forehead with his free hand. 'I need something stronger than Amontillado.'

'Why are you here?' Hannah focused on pouring a large measure of Aunt Violet's best Napoleon into a crystal glass. Handing it to him, she perched on the arm of a sofa opposite.

'Because I need your help.' He took a gulp of the spirit and shuddered. 'I want you to tell the police I didn't kill Lily-Anne. I burgled their house, but I never touched her.'

So Cavan was right, at least about the robbery.

'Why would Lily-Anne protect you?' She refilled his glass three-quarters full without asking. He looked as if he needed it. 'I would have thought Lily-Anne would have jumped at the chance to get you into trouble. You two weren't exactly close.'

'She persuaded Cavan to tell the police it was a mistake.' He paused long enough to swallow a large quantity of brandy. 'Provided I did what she wanted.'

'She blackmailed you?' Hannah perched on the arm of the sofa. 'What did she want you to do?'

'It's not important, but it's why I could never have killed her. I would be in prison right now if not for her.' Clutching the glass to his chest, he went to the front window where he stared into the darkening street through a gap in the curtains. 'Believe me. I've done some bad things in my past, but I've killed no one.' He rubbed the back of his neck with his free hand. 'Look, Hannah, I apologise for what happened at the bookshop the other day.'

'That was you?' She frowned. Surely not. The man who pushed her to the ground did not limp.

'With the police swarming all over the bookshop? Not ruddy likely! I refused to go back there, so the chap I worked for sent someone to retrieve something I had left behind.'

'The postcards?'

'You found them?' His expression cleared and hope entered his eyes. 'Where are they?'

'The police have them.'

He growled a low, colourful curse.

'This man you work for. Is his name Weber?' His chin jerked up, and she nodded. 'The police know about him. They have the message he was looking for.' If he saw how hopeless his situation was, perhaps she could convince him to hand himself in.

'It's all your fault!' He dropped the curtain back into place and returned to his chair. 'Had you not fired me, I would have handed it over and none of this would be necessary.'

'How did you get involved with German spies?' Her nervousness dissolved as his expression looked more desperate than threatening.

'I didn't know. Not at first.' He gulped down another mouthful of brandy before answering. 'He approached me with a scheme to sell the postcards. He'd tell his regular clients where to come and I'd hand them over. It seemed like a good wheeze and he offered good money.' He held his now empty glass out for a refill. 'My God, he'll kill me for losing the message. He said it contained details of his next job.'

Hannah fetched the decanter from the bureau, snatched the glass from his hand, and poured him another hefty measure. She slapped the glass into his outstretched hand, splashing his trousers before slamming the decanter back on the bureau. Maybe he would drink himself into a stupor, making persuasion redundant?

'Quite a temper you've got there, Hannah.' Grimacing, he swiped at the spots before tossing a good measure of the brandy down his throat.

'Technically, I'm harbouring a fugitive, so I'm in no mood for comments on my personality. Now, tell me everything.' She moved to take the seat beside him, thought better of it, and remained standing. 'Did Lily-Anne find out what you were doing, so came to the bookshop that day to confront you?'

'She came to confront me, but not about Weber.' He paced the floor nervously. 'No, she had her own agenda. And I didn't kill her!'

'Then who did?' Lily-Anne's dislike of Monty's parasitic nature suggested having something to hold over him would have suited her.

'I don't know!' He slammed the glass on the side table hard enough to break it, though by some miracle it remained intact. 'Lily-Anne knew nothing about the postcards. I didn't know what was going to happen or I never would have—'

'Would have what? You're not making any sense.' Hannah's patience was growing thin, but she knew he was no threat. Just a man in a situation he could no longer control.

'The night—well, you know. I came back to get the postcards and told Archie I would lock up. He had barely left when the shop doorbell went.' He rested his forearms on his knees and leaned forward, the glass held in both hands. 'I assumed Archie had come back for something, but it was Lily-Anne.'

'Did she explain why she was there?'

'Sort of. She issued her demands, and, well there was someone else there.'

'Someone else?' Hannah frowned. 'You're not trying to say Archie killed her?'

'No! Look. I... I left for a while and when I went back later, she was dead in that chair.'

'I don't understand. Why did you then leave her? Was she hurt or dying? Did you think to try and save her?' She could not imagine Monty doing much on a practical level, but his conscience might have bothered him to some extent. The thought he had left Lily-Anne breathing her last and had fled without summoning help fuelled her anger.

'What could I have done? She had a knife sticking out of her chest. She was clearly dead.' He pushed a shaking hand through his hair. 'I got out as quick as I could and went home, packed a bag and took the first train up north.'

'Monty, you must tell all this to the police. Especially the part about another person being present. And why can't you tell me who it was?'

'Because I can't!' He swung around to face her, pure fear in his eyes. 'And I will *not* hang for a murder I didn't commit.' He placed his empty glass on the table, grabbed his hat and cane and shoved past her towards the door.

Hannah followed him into the hall, tempted to tell him he was more likely to be shot on Tower Green as a traitor before that happened. 'What do I tell Inspector Farrell?'

'If you won't help me, then at least say nothing.' He yanked open the front door, beyond which the sound of night birds and the rush of the river broke the tense silence. 'I'll sort everything out once I've—' He exhaled a slow breath and stared off over the river. 'I shouldn't have come. I'm sorry about everything, but I had no choice.'

Her mind raced as she tried to think of something to make him stay, but he was already halfway down the front path, leaving her front door still swinging on its hinges.

24

Grabbing a shawl from a hook in the hall, Hannah ran after Monty, pulling it around her shoulders against the mist-laden drizzle that swept off the river. She was about to call out his name, but the word died on her tongue. Suppose Weber had followed him and loitered close by?

She reached the front gate, noting he was two houses down just as hoofbeats and a rumble of wheels behind her made her turn her head. A horse-drawn van bore down on her from nowhere but showed no sign of slowing. It was almost upon her, the dilated nostrils of the horse and the whites of rolling eyes loomed inches above her.

Panic filled her, and instinctively she threw herself sideways, landing hard on the grass verge beside her own gatepost, her palms scraping the stone. A sharp tang of horse sweat filled her nostrils and a rush of wind blew strands of hair across her face as the tall side of a tradesman's van thundered frighteningly past beside her head. Then there was the sound of a whip cracking followed by a horse's whinny of protest and a thump before the van continued toward Hammersmith Bridge.

She could no longer see Monty, just a straight dirt path with houses on one side, the river on the other. She blinked rapidly, willing her eyes to refocus. Then she saw it – a mound in the middle of the road about thirty feet from where she stood.

'No, no, no,' she pleaded aloud as she hitched her skirt to her knees and pounded towards it.

Monty lay face down on the verge, the ground softened by the day's rain. His head turned to one side, one visible eye wide open, sightless, arms flung outwards, one leg bent at an impossible angle. His mud-splattered fedora lay on the verge, his walking cane resting beneath a garden wall on the other.

The sound of running footsteps brought her head around to a figure hurtling towards her from the same direction the van had come. The early evening light had faded to a grey and pink dusk, the sky darkened by scudding clouds, so the approaching figure resembled a shadowy bat-like creature, his coat-tails flapping.

She tensed, fearing it might be Weber, and made a grab for the cane, then relaxed as the man's face came into focus. Constable Jones halted beside her, bent at the waist and both hands braced above his knees, chest heaving. 'Is he dead?'

'I would say so.' Hannah averted her eyes. One look was more than enough. 'You were following him?'

'All weekend, hoping he was meeting up with Weber. At Charing Cross Station he bought a ticket for Stamford Brook, so I knew he must be on his way here. I alerted Inspector Farrell at Scotland Yard, who said I was to stick with him and he would drive over in the motor car. I lost Carstairs at Stamford Brook Station, but I knew you lived in this road, though not which house. Then I saw him come running into the street and hung back to see where he would go.' He groaned. 'I should have stopped him right then but didn't see the van, and—' He scanned the deserted road nervously. 'Inspector Farrell will have my job for this!'

The sound of a motor engine in the next street warned her Inspector Farrell was about to arrive.

'We cannot leave him like this. Could you fetch a blanket? There's one beneath the hall stand.' She cocked her chin at her open front door lit with a golden glow from within.

'There is a blackout on, Miss Merrill! The light could be seen from the sky by—'

'Oh, for heaven's sake!' Hannah snapped, her fragile nerves stretched to breaking point. 'Make yourself scarce so I can explain to your boss why you let his suspect get killed!'

'Ah... um, yes. Good idea.' Jones turned and fled.

The mechanical, rhythmic sound of a motor car grew closer, but without lights a square black shadow loomed out of the gloom into what resembled a crouched animal easing forward over the ruts in the road. The driver brought the vehicle to a halt at the grass verge and Inspector Farrell alighted, slamming the door shut behind him.

'Well, isn't this a fine mess?' He pushed his hat further back on his head and jammed both hands into the pockets of his trousers beneath his overcoat. 'I would have got here sooner had I not got lost in the dark of this blackout. Nearly ended up in the river at the corner. What happened?'

'A horse-drawn van ran him over.' Hannah fought down nausea, unable to look at the prone form of a man who had been shouting at her such a short time ago. 'It almost hit me too, but I got out of the way in time. And in case you're asking, I'm fine.' She did not bother to tell him about her scraped elbow or the mud on her skirt.

Constable Jones reappeared at a run, Hannah's best lambswool tartan blanket over one arm. Regretting he had not chosen the faded green one she had meant to throw out weeks ago, she forbore to mention it for fear of sounding unsympathetic.

'How did this happen, Jones?' Inspector Farrell demanded. 'You were supposed to stay with him.'

'I'm sorry, sir. I—' the policeman stammered.

'It wasn't his fault, Inspector,' Hannah interjected, sensing a lecture was about to begin. 'The driver didn't even slow down. We were both fortunate to have avoided it.'

'I see.' He conceded, albeit reluctantly. Inspector Farrell stared off across the river, his bottom lip held between thumb and forefinger. Then, dismissing whatever was going through his mind, he returned to where Hannah waited, guiding her out of earshot of both Constable Jones and a few curious onlookers. 'What exactly did you see?'

'Not much apart from being at close quarters with a horse.' Hannah rubbed her upper arms and shivered again as a spray-filled wind hit her face. 'I heard the cart coming up behind me but didn't actually see it happen. I had tried to keep Monty talking, but he ran out. And before you ask, he didn't say where he was going.'

'We'll never know now, will we?' Inspector Farrell huffed a breath and stared around. The only sound was the rush of the Thames a few feet away. 'It's fairly obvious someone other than us knew he was coming here.'

'He said one thing.' Hannah looked up into his face. 'On the night Mrs Soames was killed, there was a third person present. I got the impression Monty left Lily-Anne in the bookshop with this person.'

'Could it have been our spymaster, Weber?'

'He didn't mention a name. In fact, he refused to when I asked. But who else was Monty likely to obey? He was clearly frightened of him.'

Lights came on in nearby windows, and doors opened, disgorging figures onto garden paths. A voice asked if help was required, while another grumbled about excessive noise, 'And on a Sunday night too!'

'Was going fast enough to rattle the china on my shelves,' another neighbour observed to no one in particular.

'Well?' Hannah demanded. 'Are you going to look into it?'

'Naturally, but you'll forgive me if I don't go into details.' He gestured to Constable Jones. 'Move those people on, would you, Jones?'

Constable Jones obeyed, and with his firm encouragement the crowd dispersed. Doors closed again, but the more curious simply moved further back where they congregated on the other side of the street.

Monty's body was effectively hidden, but an image of his staring eye and mangled leg remained in her mind; ironically, his good leg. The wind picked up, and she rubbed her upper arms through her shawl. 'Inspector, might I go inside now?'

'Yes, yes, of course. Thoughtless of me. Would you mind if we use your house as a centre of operations? I'll need to use your telephone to call the coroner to remove the body. Then you can tell me whatever he told you, Miss Merrill.' Telephones were rare in the suburbs, and yet he seemed confident she owned one.

'Of course. It's in the hall.'

The knot of people Jones had corralled onto the far side of the road whispered among themselves but showed no sign of leaving. She was still a figure of speculation regarding Lily-Anne's death, and this latest drama would do little for her reputation. Maybe she would turn out as notorious as Aunt Violet.

Returning to her sitting room, Hannah retrieved her book from the floor and placed it beside her empty tea tray. Constable Jones had left the sitting-room door open; the fire burned down to silver ash.

'I'm afraid it isn't much warmer in here.'

Without a word, the inspector rolled up his shirtsleeves, hefted the coal scuttle into his muscled arms and replenished the fire in the grate. Selecting a poker from the fire irons, he applied it to the mound of shiny black that shifted with a whoosh and red flames shot upward.

He caught her watching him and grinned up at her over one shoulder, reminding her a handsome man hid behind a perpetually serious expression. 'Comes of a bachelor life,' he said, replacing the poker in the rack, then tugging up his trousers at the knees and taking the chair opposite hers.

'It wasn't an accident, was it?' Hannah's voice was barely a whisper.

'I doubt it.' He held his hands loosely between his knees, his eyes distant.

'Monty was afraid of Weber. He didn't intend to be involved in spying, but couldn't get out of it,' she said, experiencing a belated surge of sympathy for Monty. How did you know he was coming here?'

'We had lookouts at the major railway stations for Weber when Jones spotted Carstairs at Charing Cross and alerted me. I guessed he was headed here, so told him to stick with Carstairs while I drove the motor car. I was on Church Road when the van came past me and I guessed something had happened. Unfortunately, we appear to have lost track of Weber himself, and now we've lost Carstairs altogether.'

'The driver of the van wore a cap pulled down over his face and a long overcoat,' Hannah said. 'Might it have been Weber?'

'Possibly. He might show his face again before the next air raid. Then we'll nab him.'

'In the meantime, you're simply going to wait for the Germans to carry out their attack on London?'

'Doing nothing is the worst part of this job, Hannah,' he said, using her given name for the first time. 'Constable Jones? How about you do what you're best at and make us some tea?'

'Sir.' Jones sidled from the room, his expression reminiscent of a scolded puppy.

'Don't be sharp with him. It's not as if he lost Monty on his own. I had a small part in it.'

'I suppose not. Though it might make him buck his ideas up a bit.' He tugged his jacket flap from beneath his thigh and eased back in the chair. 'He's enjoying life in your bookshop far too much. He's even started quoting poetry.' His lips twitched at the corner, showing he was more furious with himself than with anyone else.

Hannah eased forward, her hands held out to the fire, which now pumped out an impressive amount of heat. With the curtains drawn, the lamps lit, and the distant clink of china from along the hall, Monty's death was effectively subsumed beneath a semblance of normality.

The sounds of vehicles arriving reached her from outside, followed by footsteps approaching the house. Two policemen entered the room, filling it, followed by a third figure, the sight of whom made Hannah gasp.

'Aunt Violet! Why are you here? I wasn't expecting you until tomorrow.'

'I was summoned.' Aunt Violet removed her coat and draped it across the back of the sofa before coming to sit beside her. 'I'm afraid I exceeded the speed limit on my way over by quite a lot.' Her tone lacked remorse as she tucked a strand of Hannah's hair behind her ear. 'It must have been awful for you.'

'You called her?' Hannah stared at the inspector. 'Why?'

'I thought it prudent to have someone with you.'

'That was thoughtful.' Her throat prickled at his unexpected consideration. 'I can't help thinking if I'd not been so harsh towards Monty, he might still be alive.'

'Nonsense. It couldn't be helped.' Aunt Violet looked up as Constable Jones reappeared with a heavily loaded tray. 'Ah, excellent, just what we all need. And I see you found some cake, Constable?'

'Found it on the kitchen table, ma'am.' He flushed beneath her aunt's flirtatious look.

'It wasn't lost.' Hannah murmured. She had hoped to make it last another day or two.

'I gather it was murder and not some unfortunate accident, or the van in question would still be present? Not to mention its driver.' Aunt Violet poured the hot, fragrant tea which she then handed out to those present.

'It appears so.' Inspector Farrell accepted a generous slice of fruitcake before resuming his seat. 'We have a description of the vehicle, but it might not get us far.' Taking a generous bite, he chewed slowly. 'Hmm, this is extremely good.'

'I'm glad to hear it,' Hannah replied grudgingly, eyeing the crumbs on his plate.

'What I don't understand, is why kill Monty?' her aunt said. 'Although, I suppose once he could identify the German, he became a liability, and therefore dispensable.'

'My conclusion exactly. Perhaps you should come and work for us?' He held up his empty teacup, an intense, admiring smile directed at her, which brought an attractive flush to Aunt Violet's cheeks.

'What an intriguing prospect, Inspector.' She sprang forward to refill his cup before settling back in her seat, her voice low and sensuous.

Hannah stared at her aunt, perplexed at the silent, almost intimate exchange. What was she up to, and with the inspector of all people?

A discreet knock at the door preceded the appearance of the police surgeon Hannah had met before, though his name escaped her.

Reluctantly, the inspector placed his empty plate on the table, slapped crumbs from his trousers and entered the hall where the two men held a muffled conversation.

'Darling, you look exhausted!' Aunt Violet slung a comforting arm around Hannah's shoulders. 'Why don't you have an early night? I'll clear up here and see the inspector out.'

'Thank you, Aunt Violet. I will.' Weariness flooded through her as she rose unsteadily and bussed her aunt's cheek. Bidding goodnight to Constable Jones, she nodded a silent greeting to the trio in the hall and climbed the stairs.

Hannah closed her bedroom door and leaned against it, fumbling with the buttons on her dress, groaning at the sight of a long, jagged tear at the hem. The accumulated tension of the evening made her tearful and in a flash of temper, she gave up trying to undo the buttons, yanked the garment over her head and let it drop to the floor. She scrambled into bed and pulled the coverlet up to her chin when a thought struck her. How did Inspector Farrell know where to summon Aunt Violet from? And when?

25

'D'you hear 'bout that poor man being run down last night?' Ivy bustled into the kitchen where Hannah sat with the morning newspapers. 'Did you see what 'appened?'

'Not really, Ivy.' Hannah focussed on the newspaper in front of her, hoping Ivy would lose interest.

The rattle of the letterbox announced the post boy, giving Hannah an opportune moment to leave. 'I'll get the post on my way out,' she called, heading to the front door.

Charing Cross Station had become an obstacle course, with entire families taking up permanent shelter in every corner, hampering commuters on their way to and from the trains. Women with small children sat on bundles of clothes, piles of blankets, along with suitcases, tin kettles, and even a primus stove or two.

Officious guards shooed them away, but when the guards left to attend to more arrivals, the people slowly drifted back again. Had they lost their homes because of the bombing? Or, like Archie's sister, were taking refuge for fear of more air raids? Newspaper vendors chanted the same headlines she had read at breakfast. The hoardings along the Strand announced a historic victory for the British and French.

'Have you seen the papers, Miss Merrill?' Archie greeted her at the shop door. 'Our lads are giving those Huns a seeing to and broke through the German lines.'

'I know, Archie, but the Allies have a long way to go before we can call this a victory.' The war was not going well at all. Hannah dumped her bag on the desk and shrugged out of her coat.

'We can't give up hope, Miss Merrill.' Archie's despondent expression made her immediately contrite.

'You're right, Archie. We can't. Look, I've got something to tell you.' She smoothed down her skirt with both hands, gestured him onto a stool and recounted what had happened the night before.

'He *was* a spy, then?' Archie sat with his knees together and feet splayed outwards.

'Does it matter now?'

'No. I s'pose not.' His initial shock turned to resignation. 'Is that why Constable Jones didn't turn up this morning? He's usually waiting on the pavement when I get here.'

'That is odd.' Hannah gave the street a searching look but there was no sign of him. Was the bookshop deemed of no further interest? 'If it's any consolation, I doubt Mr Carstairs suffered.'

'If he was a spy, he deserved to.' Archie sniffed and turned away, losing interest. 'And it's a shame about Jim- Constable Jones, I mean. He made a good cup of tea.'

Archie's lack of compassion showed Monty had made himself more disagreeable to the lad than she realised. As if sensing their bleak mood, Bartleby leapt onto the desk and nudged Archie's hand with his nose. Hannah stroked the animal's back, smiling indulgently. She found she looked forward to seeing the cat at the window when she arrived in the morning, his front paws planted in front of him, tail wrapped around his sturdy body and nose almost touching the glass. She had even stopped caring whether he caught any mice. The cat arched his back into her caressing hand, his muscles rippling beneath her touch, purring softly.

Had Inspector Farrell decided Monty had killed Lily-Anne and was now beyond his reach? A tidy conclusion she was not happy with, as Monty had been emphatic about not killing her. That someone else was there that night. But who?

She withdrew the postcard from her bag and studied the woman's face in the photograph for a moment. Seeing no resemblance to anyone she knew, she considered the words 'Hobart's Photographic Studio' printed on the reverse.

Shoving the card back into her bag, she hooked the handle over her arm and collected her coat.

'Archie? Would you mind the bookshop for me for a while? I'm going out.'

'Going out?' Archie appeared at a run, but she was out on the street before his plaintive voice reached her. 'You've only just got here.'

* * *

After a frustrating wait behind a line of ambulances queued up outside Charing Cross Hospital, the hackney drew up at an elegant four-storey Georgian building on the corner of Brewer Street, the words 'Hobart's Photography' etched in gold on the first-floor windows.

A narrow door beside a gentleman's outfitters at street level led into an entrance passage with a dog-leg staircase with turned balusters. The odours of linseed oil and disinfectant declared the building was well cared for.

On the first-floor landing, a half-glazed door opened on well-oiled hinges into a room, one corner of which had been laid out with a wingback chair, a potted plant atop a low table and a swagged blue velvet curtain slung behind. An oversized desk occupied half the remaining space, behind which sat a balding man with round wire-rimmed spectacles, the thick lenses of which distorted his eyes, making them frog-like.

'Excuse me, but are you Mr Hobart?'

'Old man 'obart sold up three years ago,' he replied, his flat vowels betraying his East End origins. 'Do yer want to make an appointment for a sitting?'

'Er, no. I don't wish to engage your services, Mr…?'

'Green. 'orace Green. I do glamour and promotion pictures on Tuesdays. If you come back then, I'll do you proud. Tall and slender girls like you are more pop'lar than the plump ones, though there's a market for everyone.'

'I'm not here to be photographed, Mr Green.' Hannah clutched the handle of her tapestry bag with both hands, resisting the urge to swing it at his head.

'Well, then. Saturdays are for families and children.' His amiable smile faded as he glanced furtively behind her, as if he expected to see a matron and a brood of youngsters.

'I'm searching for a friend of mine.' She held out the postcard. 'Have you seen her before?'

He balanced his spectacles halfway down his nose and stared at it. 'It's been taken here, all right. That chaise is the one out back. It's one of the specials, I'd guess.'

'Specials?'

'Another photographer chap hires the back room for what he calls "artistic studies". This is one of his.' He nodded to the postcard on the desktop. 'He distributes them through his own suppliers.'

'You don't sell them from the studio?' Hannah had assumed

the subject of the photographs commissioned them for their own use, but apparently not.

'Nah. He likes to keep 'em exclusive. He has a couple of models he works with.'

'Do you have his name?'

'Why do you need to know? His expression sharpened. 'You said you weren't here for photographic work?'

'That's right. I'm not,' Hannah said, disappointed but realising she might have pushed too far. 'I'm just looking for my friend. She's missing.'

'Are yer sure you won't change yer mind 'bout the pictures?' He drew his thumb and forefinger down his bulbous nose. 'Titled gentlemen pay good money for a picture of a lady like you. Nice eyes you've got. Aristocratic looking.'

'Quite certain,' Hannah snapped, unsure whether to feel flattered or insulted. 'Could you take another look?' Hannah held up the card again.

'Let me take a gander at the files.' He removed a folder from a cabinet behind him and opened it out on the desk. Inside, a larger copy of the same picture stared up at her, together with a handwritten list with dates and scrawled initials.

'You knew her straight away, didn't you?' She tamped down her annoyance in case he took umbrage and she lost what little goodwill he had.

'What if I did?' He shrugged, a smirk on his face she itched to slap away.

'Does she have a name, this model?'

'Depends. Is it worth ten shillings to you?'

Hannah hesitated. 'Five shillings.'

'Deal.' He spat in his pudgy palm and held it toward her.

Ignoring the hand, she pulled the file closer. The name 'Eliza

Brown' in block letters was written in the top right corner. 'Is this the name she gave you?'

'I thought she was a friend of yours?' His eyes narrowed, almost disappearing into the folds of flesh as he chuckled to himself. 'Who gives their proper name to a man who's seeing 'em with no clothes on, eh?'

'Exactly. Have you seen Miss Brown here recently?' Hannah produced two half-crowns from a pocket, placing them on the desk between them, but kept her finger firmly on the coins.

'Can't say I 'ave, no.' He scratched his ear with a stubby finger. 'Not since the photograph was taken, which was months ago.' He looked about to say something else, but bit it back.

'Mr Green.' Hannah grew impatient at the laboriousness of the task. She needed to get out of there before a potential spy turned up. 'I have no interest in whatever nefarious business occurs on these premises. I only want to find her.'

'Hey, I'll have none of that sort o' talk.' He snatched off his glasses and waved them at her. 'This is a respectable business. Nothing improper goes on 'ere.'

Hannah begged to differ, but this was not the time to debate the issue. If he was ignorant of how his photographs were used, it wasn't her place to enlighten him. Convinced he had told her all he knew, she removed her finger from the coins, which disappeared into his waistcoat pocket.

'Now you mention it, another lady asked 'bout Eliza a few weeks ago. She paid me more'n five shillings. And before you ask, she didn't give 'er name.'

'Could you describe her?'

'About your age, I would say. Pretty woman with blonde hair and eyes as bright as the sky. She kept chewing the finger of her glove, like she was nervous.'

Lily-Anne.

'I offered to take 'er picture too,' he said, getting into his stride. 'A proper portrait like, fully dressed and everything, but she weren't interested.'

Hannah glared at him, offended. He had offered Lily-Anne a formal portrait but assumed Hannah was there for a nude pose? 'And you're sure this lady asked about the same photograph?'

'Course, I'm sure.' He waved her away. 'Might it be worth another five shillings?'

'Depends.' Hannah leaned closer, ignoring the overwhelming sour smell of masculine body odour. 'What did you tell her?'

'Same as I told you. That this Eliza was one of those musical hall types. No, that's not right... she's an actress. Had to leave early once, 'cos she had rehearsals to go to.'

'Thank you for your help, Mr Green.' Hannah placed another two half-crowns in front of him. 'Good day to you.'

Out on the street, she paused at the kerb, and searched for an unoccupied hackney, when a shadow loomed at her shoulder. Her heart leapt and her every nerve prepared to bolt, when she heard a familiar male cough.

Groaning inwardly, she exhaled a slow breath and resisted the urge to run.

'Good morning, Inspector.' Hannah closed her eyes and turned around slowly. 'I didn't expect to see you here.'

'I'm sure you didn't, Miss Merrill. Might I ask what you're doing here?'

'If by 'here', you mean walking on a public street doing nothing untoward, I'm not sure what you're asking.' The way he glowered at her made her uncomfortable, but she refused to be intimidated.

His hand shot out and gripped her upper arm with such force, she was too shocked to protest. She garbled a weak complaint that he was hurting her, but ignoring it he steered her firmly into

Bridle Lane where an Arrol-Johnston motor car stood idling. Two uniformed officers closed in behind them, blocking her route back into the street.

Inspector Farrell guided her to the open rear door and gestured her inside. Hannah lifted her chin and regarded him down her nose to keep a semblance of dignity when she was being given no choice. Her right foot caught the running board and, losing her balance, she ended up sprawled across the back leather seat that smelled of saddle soap and tobacco.

'Should I be grateful this isn't a Black Maria?' She pulled herself into a sitting position and adjusted her dislodged hat.

'This isn't a joke, Miss Merrill.' He slid into the driver's seat, propped an elbow on the back of it, and glared at her over his shoulder. The lines beside his eyes deepened as he fought a smile. 'Or were you planning to engage in some part-time modelling to supplement your income?'

'That's not funny!' She glared at him. 'I haven't compromised your investigation, if that's what worries you. The chap at the studio has no idea why I asked about the postcard. Not the real reason, anyway.'

Several passers-by slowed at the entrance to the alley to watch the drama, prompting her to pull her hat brim lower on her face.

'His name is Helmut Greenbaum. He was born in Hamburg, and he works for us.'

'Really?' Her disbelief vied with admiration. 'Well, he certainly throws himself into the role. His accent is very convincing.'

'German nationals are useful informants in this business.' Inspector Farrell cleared his throat. 'It doesn't take much of an incentive to make them co-operate.'

'You mean the fact you haven't sent him to an internment camp?'

'Something like that.' He had the grace to blush. 'And you haven't answered my question.'

'Oh, all right.' She pulled the postcard from her bag and handed it to him. 'Lily-Anne Soames had this in her possession.'

'Then how did it get into yours?' He gave the card a cursory glance, but did not hand it back.

'I was more interested in why she kept it,' she replied, ignoring his question. 'I hoped Mr Green might tell me who the model is.'

'And did he?' She hesitated, and he added, 'You might as well tell me because I shall ask him.'

'Mr Green gave me a name, Eliza Brown, but nothing else.'

'And when did you intend to share this information?'

'You're already here, so it appears I didn't have to.' Then a thought occurred to her. 'Your being here cannot be a coincidence.' He cleared his throat, and she grinned. 'It's Weber, isn't it? He works out of Hobart's Studio.'

'Maybe you'll make a detective after all, Miss Merrill. But you hanging about here is not conducive to our catching him.'

'First, I'm not hanging about. Second, have you any idea how pompous you sound?' She held out her hand. 'Can I have the photograph back now?'

'No.' He slid the postcard into an inside pocket, climbed out onto the pavement and opened the rear passenger door. 'Leave the police work to us before you get into real trouble, Miss Merrill. And I don't want to see you here again.'

Several curt responses crowded her mind, none of which she voiced, and she exited the motor car more elegantly than she entered it.

'By the way,' he said, halting her as she turned to leave. 'Mr Carstairs's inquest will take place behind closed doors. There's no need for you to attend in person.'

Hannah nodded, relieved. Lily-Anne's inquest had been harrowing enough.

'Oh, and Miss Merrill,' he said when she had gone another ten feet. 'Do give my regards to your aunt.'

She sighed, but did not look back, furious with herself at having relinquished the postcard, though she resolved to find Eliza Brown before he did. But where would she begin? London had hundreds of theatres, dozens in the West End alone, but without the postcard, her chances of finding one unknown actress were slim.

Her angry footsteps brought her to the junction of Great Windmill Street and Shaftesbury Avenue to the frontage of the Apollo Theatre. An idea formed and, the hackney forgotten, she crossed the street, dodging between horse-drawn carts and surly pedestrians. At the box office, her enquiry was met with a disinterested shrug, followed by a suspicious glare from the doorman, which prompted her to make an abrupt departure.

The Lyric produced similar results, so, retracing her steps, she tried at the Palace Theatre, where an aggressive box office clerk implied if Hannah's husband took to loitering around their stage door at night, it was no concern of hers.

The manager at the Queen's only half listened to her request, then cut her off, saying he wasn't taking on any new actresses this season. Before she could explain, he instructed a spotty-faced lad wielding a carpet sweeper to show her the door. Wishing she had her Aunt Violet's skill at giving officious doormen and cheeky clerks the short shrift, she headed for the station.

Opposite Charing Cross Station, a poster advertised the evening's performance of *The Scarlet Pimpernel* at the Strand Theatre. Hoping not to encounter another superior doorman, she entered a lobby where a wooden board displayed photographs of the cast; most prominent were Fred Terry and Julia Neilson, dressed as Lord and Lady Blakeney. Below them was a list of supporting actors, too minor to warrant a photograph. Her smile widened in triumph when she reached the fourth name down, 'Miss Eliza Brown as Sally Jellyband'.

'Two front stall tickets for tomorrow night's performance, please,' she addressed the glass partition in the box office tucked into the corner of the foyer.

'You'll be lucky.' An overblown woman with frizzy salt and pepper hair clicked her tongue. 'Got a few in the gods for tonight, but the boxes are sold out and there's nothing in the stalls.'

Hannah's shoulders slumped in disappointment. Even if this Eliza Brown was the same person, she wouldn't be able to tell from there. 'When will any front stalls seats be available?'

'Let me see.' The woman scratched her head with a pencil. 'The first two seats free are for the evening performance on Wednesday the thirteenth.'

'I see.' It was over a week away, but would have to do. 'I'll take them.'

'That'll be nine shillings, miss. Curtain up at eight forty-five.'

26

Hannah half-heartedly listened as the minister intoned the committal service for Monty at the Margravine Cemetery in Hammersmith; a public cemetery opened to relieve overcrowding in the local church graveyards.

Hannah looked up in time to catch Darius watching her with a wave and a wistful smile. She was about to return it, but the sight of Cecily, a silent, statuesque figure in full-length black beside him changed her mind.

The last handful of earth landed with a thump on the plain pine coffin, a signal for the small group of mourners to drift away and gather outside the gates on St Dunstan's Road.

'That was awful,' Aunt Violet said, easing up beside her. 'Monty wasn't my favourite person, but he didn't deserve that pitiful send off.'

'He had no family, so Darius organised it,' Hannah said.

Her aunt's attention shifted to the road, and with a light touch to Hannah's shoulder, whispered, 'I'll be back in a moment.'

Inspector Farrell was about to climb into a motor car at the roadside. He smiled at Violet's approach, closed the car door and leaned his back against it, arms folded across his chest.

'Those two appear to be getting on very well.' Darius's soft voice in Hannah's ear sent a ripple of pleasure through her. 'Have you spoken to our Inspector Farrell yet today?'

'Er, no.' She fidgeted, following the direction of his gaze. 'He isn't very pleased with me at the moment.'

'What have you done to offend the constabulary?' Darius bent his head conspiratorially, making her pulse race.

'It's nothing, really.'

'Seems we are both in trouble, as I appear to have upset Cecily.' At Hannah's raised eyebrow, he added, 'I suggested we postpone the wedding because of this business with Lily-Anne and now Monty.'

'I gather she did not take it well?'

'Livid would be more apt. She complained I was unappreciative of the time and effort she had made with the arrangements.' His jaw clicked.

'I doubt being your fiancée is easy for her. I know little about her background, but she's about to marry into one of London's leading banking dynasties. Perhaps she's intimidated?' Hannah could not believe she was defending Cecily of all people, but hated seeing Darius so unnerved.

'Somehow, I doubt that's her problem, but you're right. I should be more perceptive.' He nudged her arm playfully, his smile widening. 'I wish I'd been so with you.' In response to her look of enquiry, he added, 'Do you recall the garden party at Marble Hill? Where Monty drank so much at luncheon he threw up in the ornamental pond?'

'Did he?' She recalled the occasion perfectly, though pretended not to. Gerald had spent the entire afternoon drinking champagne with a group of loud-voiced young men and completely ignored her.

'Gerald said he planned to propose to you before he went to France. I should have pre-empted him, but it was probably too late by then, wasn't it?' He touched her arm briefly. 'I had better get back to her or she'll sulk for the rest of the day.'

Hannah froze. Did he mean that? Or was it easy to say when he was safely committed elsewhere? Had he declared himself then, she would never have accepted Gerald, and he might not now be engaged to Cecily. How could he hold out a spark of hope, only to dismiss it in the same breath? Flustered, she brought a hand to her hat brim to hide her face, determined not to watch him go, her gaze alighting on her aunt just as she reached to pick a piece of fluff from the inspector's coat, her hand flattened against his lapel. He glanced down at her aunt's hand and up again, smiling into her eyes.

'How are you, sweetheart?' a familiar voice said at her elbow.

Hector Merrill, garbed in the finest black wool Saville Row could provide, smiled down at her. The immaculate suit made him look powerfully built when he was running to fat, and he had salt and pepper hair that even in his seventh decade leapt thickly from a low forehead. His eyes, the same hazel green as her own – although hers were wider and with thicker eyelashes – took in her face. He had eschewed the fashion of thick side whiskers and a full beard because of his belief they made him look like a badger or a retired army colonel.

'Papa! When did you get here?' Hannah moved to give him a hug, but at the last second remembered where she was. 'Why didn't you tell me you were coming?' She scanned the road, relieved to see there was no sign of her mother.

'Last-minute decision,' he replied in his customary clipped

tone. 'Came to pay my respects to Carstairs junior. His father was my clerk for thirty years, so it was the right thing to do.'

'I see.' Would he feel the same way when it came out his old friend's son was a traitor to his country? 'I'm glad you came, Papa. Have you spoken to Aunt Violet?'

'Briefly. She and that inspector chap told me Monty was hit by a grocer's van. Says you saw the whole thing?' At her silent nod, he added, 'Is it true he was suspected of killing Lily-Anne Soames?'

'It's complicated, Papa,' she replied vaguely, unwilling to get into explanations at a cemetery. 'The police are being circumspect, so I don't know all the details.'

'Huh. Monty was an incompetent waster, always was, but I still find it hard to believe him a murderer.' He cast a brief look toward Inspector Farrell. 'You're not in any danger, are you?'

'No, Papa.' *Not any longer.* 'You aren't here to drag me back to Surrey, I hope?' she said, only half-joking.

'Would it be so awful of me?' His mouth quirked at the corner. 'Your mother doesn't understand this working in Violet's bookshop notion of yours. She wants you home, where you'll be safe.'

'I *am* home, Papa.' She linked her arm through his, drawing comfort from his reassuring presence. 'And with airships capable of bombing anywhere in Europe, no one is completely safe. I'm in no more danger than you are.'

'You could always stay with Iris,' he said, grasping another option. 'She could do with some help with the children. She's finding it particularly hard this time.' His oblique reference to the fact Iris was pregnant again did not escape Hannah.

'That's... kind of her, but the last thing my dear sister needs is a house guest.' The idea of being nursemaid to three babies under three was more harrowing than any bomb. Not that Iris could be struggling, what with two nursemaids and a full complement of household staff.

'Well, I've said my piece. Can't do more than that.' He let the silence stretch between them, then said, 'Did you know the Benthams are back?'

'No. I didn't.' Her chin jerked up to meet his eyes. 'I assume they know about Lily-Anne?'

He nodded. 'It seems they weren't in the Far East at all, but Athens. The hotel in Singapore sent on Cavan's telegram, which reached them eventually. They caught the first boat back and arrived yesterday. They took the news badly, as you can imagine. Then what with all this mess…' He gestured vaguely at the newly dug grave behind them.

'Are they staying in London?'

'Cavan invited them to stay at the house in Chiswick, but they declined. Too many memories, so they are with us in Farnham. Terrible business about Lily-Anne. Wilfred told us she ran with a crowd who frequents a night club in Beak Street owned by some Canadian gangster? Young johnnies dance to jazz bands till dawn, lubricated by expensive champagne in the company of fast women.'

'You seem well informed, Papa.' She was about to reassure him Murray's wasn't nearly as bad as he imagined, but perhaps this was not the best time to mention she was also a patron, albeit an infrequent one.

'Have you seen how the chaps in those places dress?' he said, huffing a noisy breath. 'In bright yellow or turquoise waistcoats, and not a proper tie among them, only those ridiculous cravats. And monocles!' He snorted. 'And the tango, of all things. What's wrong with a good waltz, is what I say. And they all flout the "beauty sleep" law without regard for the consequences.'

This nomenclature for the new law that decreed public houses and dance halls were instructed to close by ten o'clock made Hannah smile.

'She was always a lonely girl at heart.' His distant look told her he recalled another time. 'But then Lily-Anne was lost after that scandal in oh-four. No wonder she went off the rails,' he muttered absently. 'Ah well, storm in a teacup. No point crying over spilled milk,'

'Lonely?' Hannah snorted. Her friend was always the centre of attention, while she was a wallflower in comparison. Then something he said alerted her. 'Scandal? What scandal, Papa?' she asked, wondering how many clichés he could trot out in one afternoon.

'Perhaps I shouldn't have mentioned it, sweetheart.' He consulted his pocket watch. 'Better get back or I'll miss dinner. Train leaves in forty minutes. Can I give you a lift? I've got a hackney waiting.'

'No, I'm fine. Aunt Violet drove us here. Have a good journey back and give Mother my best.' She bussed his cheek and gave him a brief, but firm hug.

'Your father looks well,' Darius said, as Hannah returned her father's wave as the hackney pulled out onto the main road. 'I had a quick chat with him when he arrived. He told me the Benthams are staying with them.'

'He mentioned it. Louisa is a close friend of Mother's so they will probably stay there for a while. They signed over the Chiswick Mall house to Lily-Anne when she married, so it's Cavan's now. Papa said they have no wish to go back there.'

'It must have been awful to be summoned home because their only child has been murdered.' He stared off over the graveyard. 'I remember being called to the headmaster's office when Mama died.'

Hannah's heart twisted at the memory. Darius's mother had been a sweet-natured woman who always reminded Hannah of roses and the colour pink. When he was fifteen and away at school, she had contracted tuberculosis. His father sent her to the coast to recover, but she died there, giving Darius no chance to say goodbye, making his loss particularly hard.

Snapping back to the present with a start, he squeezed her arm. 'Look after yourself, Hannah.' Knowing where his thoughts had gone, she watched him go with sadness. Would she ever be able to raise events in their mutual past once he was married? And should she?

* * *

Aunt Violet tossed her hat and coat onto a chair, slumped onto the sofa opposite and used the toe of one shoe to ease off the other. 'How stupid of me for wearing new shoes for a funeral. Too much standing about.' The offending shoe dropped onto the rug and she rubbed her toes with both hands.

'You and Inspector Farrell appeared to have a good deal to say to one another, Aunt Violet.' Hannah remarked.

'His name is Aidan. He has a Welsh mother and an Irish father. Quite a passionate combination.' She kicked off the other shoe. 'Incidentally, when were you going to mention your outing to Soho yesterday? Are you keeping secrets?'

'Who told you?' Hannah stiffened, then relaxed as it came to her. 'Oh, of course – Aidan.'

'He's worried you'll attract the attention of whoever killed Monty. He'd feel responsible if anything happened to you.'

'You didn't mention our visits to Hemmings and Mr Guppy in your little tête-à-tête, I hope?'

'Give me credit for some discretion.' Her aunt stared around the room as if searching for something. 'Darling, could I trouble you for a drink? Whoever heard of an internment without a wake?'

'Darius thought a discreet ceremony was preferable for a

suspected murderer and spy. Although I spotted a brace of reporters smoking behind a tree.'

'Speaking of Darius, I noticed he and Cecily are barely speaking. Is there trouble in paradise?'

'Something like that.' Hannah tried not to sound too gleeful. 'He suggested postponing the wedding because of the deaths of Lily-Anne and Monty.'

'Oh dear. I doubt those words filled Cecily with charitable sentiments?'

'Apparently not.' Hannah's cheeks heated as she replayed their conversation in her head while rooting around in the sideboard. 'Will sherry do?' Monty had thoroughly depleted the brandy supply.

'In the absence of gin, perfect.' Aunt Violet accepted the glass of dark amber liquid Hannah handed her. She relaxed against the upholstery, idly swinging one silk-clad leg, frowning at Hannah's empty hands. 'Are you not joining me?'

'No, I won't, thank you.' She resumed her seat. 'I've been thinking about things, and although I might be way off the mark, it works in my head.'

'Go on. Let's hear it.'

'My guess is, Monty sold or gave one of those postcards to Cavan as some sort of male comradeship thing. What if Cavan's interest was piqued, and he set out to discover who she was?'

'They began a liaison, you mean?' Aunt Violet pursed her lips in thought. 'Hmmm, I cannot see Cavan with a woman who poses for nude photographs.'

'Who knows what an attractive man might do when he sees an available lady?'

'Hardly a lady. She was practically naked in those pictures.'

'Stay with me, or I'll lose my train of thought. Perhaps this mistress killed Lily-Anne because she wanted Cavan to herself, so she lured Lily-Anne to the bookshop?'

'Lured her for what purpose? I doubt it was to ask her to divorce Cavan so he could marry her?' Aunt Violet's laugh was harsh and humourless.

'It answers the question of why Cavan was buying negligées at stage doors. He must have left the photograph lying around and Lily-Anne found it.'

'Some men have an inherent desire to be caught when misbehaving. It's a nanny thing. But why kill her?'

'I'm not at that point yet. Lily-Anne went to the studio to find out who she was, just like I did.'

'And what *did* you find out?' Aunt Violet pressed.

'I'm not saying. You'll only go running off to tell Aidan.' She dragged out his name teasingly.

'How mean!' Her aunt frowned. 'I thought we were in this together?'

'We were, until you started consorting with the enemy.'

'I swear I won't say a word.' She nudged Hannah in the ribs, almost spilling sherry over the sofa, only saving it at the last second.

'All right.' Hannah feigned reluctance, but she longed to show off how clever she had been. 'Her name is Eliza Brown, and she's an actress.' She scooted closer, her voice lowered, although there was no one to hear them. 'What if she killed Lily-Anne?'

Aunt Violet's glass halted halfway to her mouth.

'No, don't say anything. Listen. Say Lily-Anne met Eliza at my bookshop?' Hannah warmed to her theory. 'It's on neutral ground and a short walk from the theatre.'

Aunt Violet held up a finger. 'Point of order. How did Eliza Brown know about the bookshop?'

'I... I don't know. I haven't worked that out yet. Just surmise that's where they met. Lily-Anne demanded Eliza leave her husband alone, on pain of having her career ended.'

'How would Lily-Anne have done that?'

'Who knows? Have that postcard sent to her employer? Miss Brown had no intention of letting that happen because she wanted Cavan to herself. Maybe they got into an argument, and in a fit of temper, Eliza snatches the paper knife from the desk and stabs Lily-Anne with it? Who would suspect Eliza? She and Lily-Anne had never met. And Monty said there was someone else there that night. Maybe it was her?'

'So, do we know anything about this Eliza person?'

'Actually, I do.' Hannah paused for maximum effect. 'She's appearing in *The Scarlet Pimpernel* at the Strand Theatre.'

'Ooh, I love that play.' A dreamy smile appeared on her aunt's face. 'I saw the original performance in oh-six when the theatre first opened. Fred Terry made a wonderful Pimpernel. He's too old for a romantic lead now he's in his fifties, but if you manage a theatre, I imagine you can pick your own parts.'

'I've bought tickets for tomorrow night's performance,' Hannah interrupted, bringing a halt to her aunt's reminiscences.

'And you didn't invite me?' She pouted.

'I thought I just had.'

'Excellent. I haven't been to the theatre in ages.' Hannah was about to correct her, but she waved her away. 'Real theatre, I meant, not music hall.' Her empty glass clinked as she placed it on a side table. 'Now I really must go, or we'll lose our table.' Wincing, she forced her feet into her shoes.

'Table? What table?' Hannah blinked, thrown at the rapid change of subject.

'At Rules. Aidan is taking me for an early dinner. We arranged it at the funeral.'

'Rules? How could he afford that? He's a detective inspector, Aunt Violet, not a Lord.'

'No, but his mother owns a very lucrative London hotel.'

'So that's what he was referring to when he said his mother paid taxes?' Next time, she would pay more attention. 'I trust you not to tell Aidan what we're planning. We don't want him crashing through the door with a brace of uniforms in tow, ruining it.'

'As if I would. How about we meet at the Palm Court after you close the bookshop tomorrow afternoon? We'll have something to eat before the performance.' She gathered up her hat and coat and gave an airy wave from the door. 'Don't wait up.'

'Now who's keeping secrets?' Hannah muttered as the front door slammed shut.

27

The lights had gone down by the time they entered the auditorium, the play in full flow with every seat filled. They had to pick their way along the darkened aisle over pairs of feet, murmuring, 'excuse me' and 'so sorry' as they located their seats. The first act finished with a flurry of enthusiastic clapping as several boiler suited figures rushed onstage to arrange rustic tables, three-legged stools and the painted backdrop of a rustic French inn.

'Fred Terry isn't nearly as dashing as when I first saw this play.' Aunt Violet's parody of a stage whisper brought several dark looks their way. 'Oh, I think this is it. The *Fisherman's Rest* scene. What part is this Eliza person playing?' Aunt Violet focused a pair of opera glasses on the stage.

'She's the innkeeper's daughter, Sally Jellyband,' Hannah replied, shushing her.

'Hmm. The cast are wearing so much stage makeup, the girl's faces all look the same.'

'Excuse me, miss.' A middle-aged gentleman with a heavily waxed moustache leaned his head between their seats. 'I'm trying to listen to the performance.'

'I sympathise.' Aunt Violet batted her eyelashes. 'Might I suggest an ear trumpet? A friend of mine paid quite a reasonable price at—'

'Hush, Aunt Violet!' Hannah nudged her with an elbow. 'You'll get us both thrown out.' She took the opera glasses from her and trained them on the stage. 'I think I see her. But how will we get to talk to her? I'm not hanging around outside with the stage-door johnnies after the play.'

'I have an idea. Did I ever mention Fred Terry was a dear friend when I was younger?'

'Really?' Hannah replied, impressed. 'Julia Neilson is his wife, isn't she? Is she a friend too?'

'Friend might be a slight exaggeration, but I doubt she'll forget our last meeting.'

'Why, whatever happened?'

'Never mind.' Her aunt waved her away. 'We'll go backstage during the interval.'

A loud "harrumph" sounded behind them, prompting Hannah to hunker lower into her seat.

The curtains had barely closed for the interval when Aunt Violet dragged Hannah to her feet.

'Come on, or we'll get caught up with the crowds on their way to the bar.' She hustled her to the door at the side of the proscenium arch and between the scenery flats below; a dizzying profusion of ladders, access walkways, sandbags, pulleys and thick ropes. They passed a row of doors, each bearing an actor's name, most of them closed. The sounds of excited female chatter and good-natured arguing emanated from a room at the end. Just as they reached it, the door opened, and a girl dressed in eighteenth-century costume and a tall, curly white wig emerged; the panniers of her primrose gown filled the hallway.

'Excuse me. Where might I find Eliza Brown?' Aunt Violet asked.

'Well... er...' The actress gave the room behind her a fearful look. 'We're not supposed to have visitors in the dressing room during the performance.'

'What a shame!' Aunt Violet's face fell dramatically. 'I'm her cousin, and we've travelled down from Northumberland to see her. Our train leaves in an hour, so we won't even see the end of the play.'

'Well, as you've come so far.' The girl's indecision dissolved into daring. 'I'm sure a few moments won't hurt. I'll fetch her.' She darted back into the dressing room as fast as her cumbersome dress allowed.

'I hope we don't get Eliza into trouble,' Hannah said.

'More trouble than being arrested for murder?' Aunt Violet puffed a breath through pursed lips. 'Did you know I almost took up a theatrical career? My Ophelia was celebrated in my time.'

'Your time?' Hannah scoffed. 'Aunt Violet, you're not yet forty.'

'Hush, dear. Not so loud. Ah, here she is.'

A young woman garbed in the costume of a tavern wench, complete with frilled puffed sleeves and mop cap, approached; a less-likely killer Hannah couldn't imagine. Up close, she seemed much younger than in the photograph, despite her heavy stage make-up.

'Who are you?' She crossed her arms, frowning. 'Because I don't have a cousin, especially one from Northumberland.'

'Just a little harmless subterfuge.' Aunt Violet's disarming smile removed the suspicion from the girl's face. 'A friend recommended your performance, which we have so enjoyed. We wanted to meet you.'

'How kind.' Her surprised delight made her appear vulnerable, almost shy. 'Am I acquainted with this friend of yours?'

'You might be.' Hannah studied her face. 'Her name was Lily-Anne Soames.'

Eliza froze just as a raucous burst of laughter erupted from the communal dressing room. She darted a nervous look at the door.

'Perhaps there's somewhere a little less public where we could talk?' Aunt Violet said, instilling a hint of menace in her voice.

'All right.' Fear and defeat fought for dominance on the girl's face as she nodded at a door to her right. 'We can use Jane's room.'

The dressing room was exactly as Hannah had imagined; a tiny space dominated by a wide dresser with a massive mirror lit on either side by spirit lamps. The surface was invisible beneath piles of cosmetic tubes, powder puffs, sheer scarves draped across the mirror and costume jewellery. A clothes rail crammed with costumes in bright jewel tones ran along one side; a row of hooks on the wall held hats, scarves and feather boas in a riot of colour. The air was heavy with perfume, face powder, and mildew mixed with burned candles. An empty chair before a cracked mirror and a vast wicker trunk were the only seats in the room, so all three remained standing.

'How did you find me?' Eliza closed the door firmly behind her.

'Mrs Soames had a photograph of you from Hobart's Studio in her possession,' Hannah said.

'But—Cavan told no one about me.' Eliza brought a hand to her throat, her dark eyes moving between them in a near panic. 'You aren't going to cause problems for him, are you?'

'Aren't you more likely to do that?' Aunt Violet snorted. 'You were the one conducting a liaison with him,'

'Liaison?' Her fear dissolved into disbelieving laughter. 'What a ridiculous idea.'

'I don't see why,' Hannah said, determined not to let her aunt dominate the conversation. Eliza was her find, after all. 'Dr

Soames is handsome, wealthy and charming. Why wouldn't you consider him as a lover?'

'Because he's my brother!' Eliza snapped, then quieter, 'Half-brother, anyway.'

'Well.' Aunt Violet huffed a breath. 'I certainly wasn't expecting that.'

'Nor me.' Hannah frowned. 'I've known Cavan for years and he's never mentioned a sister.'

'No, well.' She hunched her shoulders. 'We were, what do they call it... estranged? My real name is Eliza Soames.' She glanced up sharply. 'But if you didn't know who I am, why are you here?'

'Lily-Anne Soames was my best friend. I'm trying to find out who killed her,' Hannah explained.

'And you thought *I* did it?' She split a horrified look between them. Several emotions crossed her face and her eyes narrowed. 'No, not me. You think it was Cavan who killed her?' She folded her arms again, jutting her chin. 'Some friends you are. Cavan's no murderer. He adored his wife. He would never harm her. Never!'

Hannah believed her. 'I'm sorry, I thought—' She faltered. 'We're hoping you might throw some light on the situation.'

'That's not what it sounded like,' Eliza snapped. 'Accused me, more like.'

'Well, someone killed her,' Aunt Violet interjected, just as the bell sounded to announce the end of the interval.

'I'm truly sorry we misjudged you,' Hannah said, liking this spirited, determined young woman, and that Lily-Anne would have liked her, too. It saddened her to realise Eliza would never have a relationship with her sister-in-law. 'My aunt and I would love to hear your story.'

'Well, I—' Eliza hesitated. 'I'm not in the ballroom scene, so I can stay a while longer.'

'How did you and Cavan become estranged?' Aunt Violet asked.

'Hah! And isn't that a story and a half?' She perched on the edge of the chair beside the mirror, leaving the wicker basket to Violet and Hannah. 'His father married my mother when Cavan was twelve. I came along a couple of years later, but Dad always favoured him, what with being a boy and the firstborn. After my mother died, I might as well have been invisible. Any money he had went straight to Cavan's medical school fees. Papa wanted to put me into service.' She snorted, adding, 'Get rid of me, more like. I ran away when I was fifteen.'

'Did you always want to act?' Hannah asked, admiring her obvious courage.

'It's as good a job as any.' Eliza shrugged. 'I came to London on the promise of a part which didn't work out. I got a musical hall gig at the Hackney Empire for a bit. Then I met Mr Terry, who offered me this part.'

'How did you reconnect with Cavan again?' Hannah asked.

'A couple of months ago, Cavan and a friend of his came to the stage door asking about me.'

'Did his friend give a name?' Hannah asked, convinced she already knew.

'Malcolm, or Milford. Or something like that. A handsome chap with a limp who sneered a lot. It seemed to amuse him Cavan had a sister on the stage. Like it gave him something to hold over him. It was the reason Cavan and me lost touch. He wasn't born to money, and when he qualified as a doctor, he became too proud to visit us in Clapham.'

'And marrying Lily-Anne meant he mixed with a different level of society,' Aunt Violet added.

'Something like that. But when he found me, he apologised. He said he would make it all up to me, and that our father had died, not that I cared much. Lily-Anne didn't know about me, but then who wants an actress in the family, eh?'

'Apparently he does, or he would never have gone to the trouble of finding you.' Hannah now imagined a scenario where Monty, in his blithe ignorance, offered one of his postcards to Cavan, who recognised the subject as his long-lost sister.

'He wanted to tell Lily-Anne, but I wouldn't let him. I didn't want to make things difficult for him.' Her mop cap had slipped forward over her forehead, and she shoved it back with one hand. 'I only attended the funeral because it meant so much to him. I borrowed a thick veil from the theatre wardrobe, so no one would notice me.'

'I did,' Hannah murmured, though Eliza did not appear to hear.

'Cavan found a respectable boarding house near Covent Garden market for me where the landlady won't allow gentleman friends over the doorstep.' At Hannah's enquiring glance, she shrugged. 'Actresses get harassed all the time by toffs. They assume because we dress up and go on stage, we're ready for anything. But now, with Lily-Anne gone, he wants me to come and live with him.'

'And will you?' Hannah recalled him saying how empty the house was. Having this bright, animated girl there would be good for him.

'I told him I'd think about it.' She shrugged.

'Well,' Hannah, feeling suddenly emotional. 'When you next see Cavan, you might mention Hannah Merrill and Violet Edwards would be delighted to call. My aunt is also acquainted with Mr Terry. Perhaps she could put in a word for you?'

'And as long as she doesn't mention my name to Miss Neilson,' Aunt Violet whispered in Hannah's ear.

'That's kind of you. And maybe it is time we behaved like

brother and sister again, I—' Eliza broke off as the door opened a crack, revealing a young woman in a similar "wench" costume.

'There you are, Eliza,' the newcomer said in a fierce, insistent whisper. 'They're calling for you. We're on in five minutes.'

Eliza raised a hand to show she understood before turning back to Hannah. 'I have to go, but if you find out who killed Lily-Anne, would you tell me? We never met, but Cavan told me so much about her. She sounded lovely.'

'We promise.' Hannah blinked away sudden tears. 'Oh, before you go.' Eliza halted on her way out and poked her head around the door. 'Did Cavan give you a silk negligée recently?'

'How did you know?' Her dark eyes beneath well-shaped brows showed a startling resemblance to Cavan. 'I had a tatty old cotton thing, and he thought I should look like a real actress like the other girls. It's beautiful and I've had so many comments about it.'

A distant voice called her name in a half impatient voice, at which Eliza gave a last grin and allowed the door to close behind her.

'Good recollection of the negligée,' Aunt Violet said. 'I had forgotten Mr Guppy's side-line.'

'But where does it leave my theory about who killed Lily-Anne?' Hannah said as she joined her aunt in the corridor.

'I have no idea, but how lovely to think Cavan has his sister back.'

'Lily-Anne is still dead, and I promised myself I would find out who is responsible.'

'Hannah, enough. We've been lucky this meeting with Eliza did not go horribly wrong, so stop this before you cause any damage.'

'Me? You were as keen to poke around as I was!'

'Possibly.' Aunt Violet straightened her shoulders. 'And it's been fascinating too, but I'm reluctant to test Aidan's patience... again. Also, don't ever tell Cavan that you have the postcard. He deserves peace of mind. Now, let's watch the rest of the play.'

'I object to putting this on me when you were the one who boasted about your connection to Mr Terry. And incidentally, what was that about not mentioning your name to Miss Neilson?'

'We'd better get back, Hannah, the interval bell rang minutes ago.' Aunt Violet tutted, ignoring her.

28

Returning to the darkened auditorium well after the re-commencement bell rang resulted in offering apologies, treading on the same toes as before, and eliciting similar grunts and hard stares from other patrons.

Hannah tried to concentrate on what was happening on stage but was soon aware of a repetitive *clunkety-clunk*, sound overhead; it was like a scrape of rusty train wheels, followed by a roar like a furnace charging up.

A low murmur of enquiring voices swept through the auditorium and grew louder; the players on stage broke off their speech, necks craned as they stared at the ceiling with varying expressions of confusion and fear.

'What's that noise?' Hannah whispered, leaning closer to her aunt, Violet's floral perfume filling her nostrils.

The words were barely out of her mouth when a thunderous crash rattled the rafters. A voice from the orchestra pit hollered he was going to die and had to be calmed by his fellow musicians, while feminine screams erupted from the stalls. Pieces of plaster flew from the ceiling and large slabs of plaster peeled from the walls onto the patrons still in their seats. The blacked-out windows shattered, followed by more cries as a cloud of plaster dust drifted from the ceiling, bringing half the audience to their feet to stand frozen in place, wide-eyed and silent. The auditorium lights flickered, then glowed again.

'Aunt Violet?' Hannah coughed as dust filled her throat.

'What happened?' Aunt Violet rose from where she had dropped to the floor between the seats.

'I'm not sure, but I have a horrible feeling.' Hannah helped her up and picked a sovereign-sized piece of plaster from the rose on her aunt's hat.

Mr Terry strode to the front of the stage, his arms spread wide and hands flapping in a call for calm.

'Attention, everyone, please.' His heavily applied makeup made him incongruous to the situation, as did his brightly striped pantaloons and grey, voluminous caped overcoat. The wave of worried mutters quieted to whispers, while those who had reached the aisles turned back to the stage.

'There's been an explosion at the rear of the theatre. The damage is minor, however, and everything is under control. If you'll resume your seats, the performance will continue.' Bowing, he left the stage, and the orchestra struck up the opening bars of 'God Save the King'.

'If they are carrying on with the play, it can't be too serious,' said a woman in a velvet evening coat further along the row.

'Sounded like an airship to me,' her companion raised his voice over the music. 'One of those German "L" range Zeppelins. We'd better get out, as there might be others not far behind.'

Another roar and a ground-shaking rumble sounded from further away, prompting a fresh wave of shocked gasps and whimpers as playgoers stumbled into the aisles, tripping over each other in a frantic scrum to get away.

Hannah grabbed her aunt's arm. 'Those are bombs falling, and the bookshop is right behind this theatre!'

'Well, I've no intention of waiting here for the roof to fall in.' Aunt Violet gathered her handbag and gloves, threw her fox-fur stole over her shoulder, and stood. 'Let's go.'

'I hoped you were going to say that.' Hannah scrambled over more stoic patrons and into the aisle with those who had also chosen to ignore Mr Terry's instructions.

A doorman barred the way to the rear doors, despite being jostled and shouted at by a group of people who demanded they be let through. 'Sorry, ladies and gentlemen, there's a massive hole in the other side of this door and it's jammed.'

'Aunt Violet?' Hannah clutched the back of her aunt's coat as a thought struck her. 'What about Eliza?'

On stage, Lord Blakeney addressed the ruthless character Chauvelin in melodious tones, as the audience who had remained in their seats brushed dust and bits of wood from their clothes as if nothing had happened.

'Eliza will be fine. The damage is to this side of the theatre.' Gesturing Hannah to follow, Aunt Violet shouldered her way back up the aisle and across the empty foyer, emerging into a strangely silent Strand. People in their best clothes lined the pavements on both sides, heads angled back, eyes wide and mouths agape as they stared upwards in fascinated horror.

Caught in the crossed beams of two powerful searchlights hung a glittering silver cigar shape of an impossible size, gliding slowly across the navy-blue sky. Splashes of flame erupted all around it; bullets fired from anti-aircraft batteries mounted on portable stands on the pavement, but none appeared to make an impression.

A motor taxi screeched to a halt on the road in front of them, the face of the driver horrified as he gaped at the sky through the side window. He fumbled frantically with the door and threw it open before he leapt out and ran off in the opposite direction, leaving his confused passenger, an army officer, in the rear seat.

Hannah stared at the distant airship gliding away to the south-west, majestic and yet deadly. 'Inspector Farrell was right. My finding the message made no difference.'

'It was too much to hope it would change anything,' her aunt reasoned.

Diners from side street restaurants continued to spill onto already crowded pavements, forcing them into the road where they impeded horse-drawn carts, motor taxis, hackneys and panicked pedestrians. Blinding flashes and ear-splitting booms sounded all around from the guns on pavements partly blocked by rubble from damaged buildings. Bodies dressed for a night out on the town lay among the rubble, and pieces of shattered glass lay everywhere, no window left unscathed. Firemen dragged hoses along already wet streets, but as soon as they doused one fire, another burst from a gaping shop window or hole in the road, small blobs of flame smouldering every few feet. Firemen moved from one to another, using axes to break up the debris and create gaps to stop the spread of the flames.

A sickly, sulphurous smell combined with the cordite and smoke from the various street fires. 'Aunt Violet, I can smell gas,' Hannah said.

'Keep moving. The first thing they'll do is turn it off at the mains.' Her aunt urged her around piles of rubble and broken paving stones. 'We must reach the bookshop before the wardens close the roads.'

A rumble and crash sent a cascade of roof tiles from a nearby building. Hannah leapt out of the way seconds before they smashed onto the pavement at her feet, sending shards in all directions. Sidestepping them, she clung onto her aunt's arm as they forced their way through the crowds flowing down the Strand like a wave towards Aldwych.

Policemen and stretcher bearers in khaki or wearing St John Ambulance uniforms attempted to clear the road for the ambulances, the high trill of bells filling the air as they crowded into the already crammed Strand.

Misshapen, dark red and black blobs lay on the roads or attached to buildings and lamp posts every few feet along the street. One had a bloody thatch of hair attached to it. Hannah slowed her steps to work out what was giving off the unmistakable smell of cooked meat, and froze as reality hit her. They were parts of human bodies. Her stomach roiled and her knees threatened to collapse.

'Don't look, just keep moving.' Aunt Violet wrapped her arm around her and urged her forward, only to be forced aside by a fireman dragging a hose along the street. Several more used axes to break up the debris to keep the fire from spreading. At intervals, bursts of flame rose through holes in the road ahead, consuming bare wood, fabric and stuffing from furniture hurled into the street by the explosions.

In Catherine Street, the blast had blown out the windows and doors of every shop and public house. Shards of glass lay in a thick layer on the road, like thousands of twinkling lights. A grating sound above sent them into the nearest doorway as a pile of loosened tiles slid noisily from a roof and smashed onto the ground a foot away. A piece of slate nicked Hannah's ankle, but she refused to stop, hoping the damage wasn't as bad as it felt.

A man in evening dress coming the other way staggered to one side to avoid her and slumped against an empty window frame of a shop, disinclined to move.

'Is he hurt?' Hannah paused beside him.

'I don't think so.' Aunt Violet leaned closer, then straightened.

'He keeps repeating something about a sixty-eight bus and that they're all dead.'

Hannah glanced along the street just as a policeman strode towards them with purpose, the beam of his torch bouncing off nearby buildings.

'Is anyone injured here?' he called from several paces away.

'We're fine,' Aunt Violet answered. 'But this man is in shock. He's mumbling something about a bus in Chancery Lane.'

'It's being dealt with, miss.' He gave a curt nod, indicating he knew what they referred to, then tucked his hand beneath the distressed man's elbow and hauled him gently upright. 'Come on, old chap. There's a Red Cross van near the station giving out tea. I imagine you could do with a cup.'

'The officer will take care of him.' Aunt Violet's voice seemed to come from a long way off. 'We have to get to the bookshop.'

Hannah nodded, her heart thumping as she concentrated on putting one foot in front of another. When they reached the bookshop, her stomach dropped. The glass of the twin bow windows had collapsed inwards, leaving the front door still attached to the frame, but hanging by one hinge. A large section of ceiling lay on the floor inside the front door. The first row of bookshelves had collapsed into firewood, scattering books with the spines broken that littered the floor; torn pages fluttered amongst the wood and glass. Theatre posters that were a feature and popular with their customers hung crazily on the walls, while the rack holding programmes representing fifty years of Covent Garden's theatrical history lay on its front. Archie's carefully arranged window display was an unrecognisable pile of plaster, dust and torn paper.

In contrast, the rear of the shop remained unscathed, shielded by rows of bookshelves around it. Some had lost most of their books, but even so, remained staunchly upright.

'Oh my, what a mess.' Aunt Violet sighed. 'But not to worry. Windows can be mended.'

'I suppose so,' Hannah murmured, then a sudden thought struck her. She hitched her skirt and with a horrified call of 'Bartleby!' leapt over the broken window frame and into the shop.

'Hannah, no!' her aunt's voice called from behind her. 'It's not safe!'

29

'The damage isn't at all bad back here, Aunt Violet!' Hannah picked her way over piles of books and broken glass, dimly lit by a shrouded, but still burning street light. 'The first row of shelves must have shielded the blast.' She silently thanked the original shopkeeper's forethought when he commissioned the carpentry all those years ago.

'Be careful, the roof might be unstable.' Her aunt cautiously followed her inside, her feet crunching on bits of wood and glass.

'It looks solid enough.' Hannah picked out a long crack in the plaster, but otherwise there was little to show for the blast that had taken out the storefront. The central desk, however, resembled a wounded animal brought to its knees, the heavily varnished oak scarred by flying glass, a section of panelling broken off by the fallen bookshelf.

Her foot slipped on a sheet of paper, threating to turn her ankle, but she righted herself without mishap. A low mewling sound came from beneath the collapsed desk and Hannah bent to where Bartleby's two blue eyes stared at her as if to ask if it was safe to come out. Scooping him into her arms, she gently stroked the fur beneath his chin with her finger. 'The Germans have gone, cat. You're safe now.' The animal butted her chin with his head as she tucked him into her coat. 'Aunt Violet, where are you?'

'In the storeroom,' her aunt replied, followed by a rattle and thud, then a cry of triumph. 'There are a couple of oil lamps in a cupboard. And some matches!'

Hannah's heartbeat racked up a notch as a shadow crossed the skeletal bookshelves and the figure of a man, his head bent to avoid a hanging beam, climbed over rubble and broken glass and into the shop. She swallowed, preparing to demand what he wanted when he straightened, stamped his polished shoes on the floorboards to dislodge the plaster dust, and looked up.

'Darius!' Hannah gaped as she tried to reconcile him with the scene before her. 'Goodness, what are you doing here?'

'I was on the Strand when the first bombs hit. Knowing your shop was in the next street we came to check if it was all right.' His feet slid on sheets of paper and loose pieces of rubble, making him stagger slightly as he approached.

'Well, as you can see, it isn't all right.' Hannah hugged the cat closer, grimacing as plaster dust tickled her nose from his thick pelt. 'Did you say "we"?'

A movement in the gloom drew her eye to where Cecily was also picking her way over the rubble to join them like a mare with laminitis, tutting at every step. She wore a long black evening cloak buttoned to the neck and a veiled hat that covered part of her face. Hannah was about to warn her she might damage her elegant clothes, but Cecily was listening to no one.

'I *told* you to take me home, Darius.' She grunted as she caught her foot briefly on a piece of wood. 'But no! You had to come and see this ridiculous little bookshop and risk us all being burned alive.'

'How nice, friends come to help us.' Aunt Violet emerged from the storeroom with a lit lamp, the dull yellow glow lighting up a smirk on her face that she did not even try to hide. 'No such luck about the burning, Cecily. But we didn't escape unscathed.'

Cecily glared at her and slapped the dust from her coat. 'None of us should be here at all. It's dangerous.'

'If you don't wish to stay, I'll find a taxi to take you home.' Darius's voice sounded tight with suppressed frustration. 'People have died tonight, and there are dozens of injured who need help.'

Hannah's grip on the cat tightened. It was so unlike him to be sharp with anyone, especially Cecily.

'And yet, here we are, at a bookshop!' Her smug expression challenged him. 'We aren't helping any injured at all, so might as well go.'

Hannah ignored her, groaning as the oil lamp revealed the full extent of the damaged shop spread before them. The destruction of the bay windows and door had brought down a section of ceiling, reducing the floor area by a third. She dared not look at Aunt Violet for fear of seeing the same dismay mirrored in her face.

'In good time.' Darius had apparently taken charge. 'We need to secure the shop against looters first, and – wait, did you hear that?'

'I didn't hear anything above all those sirens and bells. It's chaos out there.' Cecily's voice was irritated, but her eyes darted around nervously.

'Hush!' Darius held up a hand. 'It sounded like someone moaning.'

'I can hear it now, too.' Hannah followed the low moans to the left-hand bow window which had collapsed in on itself. 'Bring that lamp over here, Aunt Violet.'

Leaving Cecily seething in the centre of the shop, Hannah and Aunt Violet clambered over a pile of books to where a six-foot-wide slab of ceiling lay at an angle. Darius got there first and bent to peer underneath. 'There's someone under here! Give me a hand.'

Hannah set down the cat, which scurried beneath a corner of the overturned desk, then she helped Darius and her aunt pull books from the pile surrounding the broken window, revealing a figure in a light-coloured overcoat lying face down on the floor.

'It's a man!' Aunt Violet held the oil lamp closer, revealing a long gash on the man's head, surrounded by sticky blood. She placed the lamp on the floor while Darius levered the slab of ceiling enough for Hannah and her aunt to drag him out.

'One of your looters, perhaps?' Cecily snapped, though no one paid her any attention.

Darius slung the semi-conscious man's arm over his shoulder and lowered him onto his back on an empty section of the floor. Aunt Violet held the lamp high so his dust-covered features became recognisable.

'It's Constable Jones!' Hannah gasped.

Aunt Violet retrieved the second lamp, which she placed strategically on the edge of the undamaged bookshelves.

Constable Jones's eyes flickered open, and he raised his head and blinked. His eyes widened as they focused on the shattered front window. 'Good grief, who did that?'

'The Kaiser,' Aunt Violet said, rolling her eyes. 'Have we got anything to tie around this cut to stop the bleeding?' Hannah stared around, but everything was covered with a thick layer of plaster dust.

'I'll use this.' Aunt Violet unwound the cream scarf from around her neck and wrapped it around the policeman's head, tying it in a knot at the back like a turban.

'Darius, we really should go,' Cecily whined. 'This building could collapse any moment.'

'We aren't leaving until this man is taken care of,' Darius replied without looking at her.

'Don't worry, Cecily,' Aunt Violet spoke with barely restrained patience. 'You won't have to stay long. I think help is here.' She nodded to where two policemen, apparently scouting the surrounding streets were making their way over the damaged window.

'Is anyone injured in here?' one of them asked.

'This chap is,' Darius said from where he bent over Constable Jones. 'He's one of your lot, but I don't know why he was here so late at night.'

'He's here because I sent him,' Inspector Farrell called from the street, his face partly in shadow from his fedora and a single shrouded street light that was flickering wildly. 'I was on my way here when I was distracted by helping to clear the damage on Wellington Street. The main gas main has been badly damaged by the blast and the road is closed.'

'Why were you coming here?' Hannah took in his dirt-covered jacket and a rip in the hem of his trouser leg. He smelled of dirty water, smoke and a faint odour of gas.

'You were right, sir. Weber was hiding out in the flat upstairs.' Constable Jones eased upright onto an elbow, one hand to his bandaged head.

'He was what?' Hannah gaped. 'For how long?'

'The last couple of days, perhaps. I've been keeping an eye on the place, which is why I was still here when there was this massive bang and the front window collapsed on me.' Aunt Violet helped him to his feet, hauled a fallen chair upright, and eased him into it.

'Good work, Jones.' Inspector Farrell patted his shoulder as he passed. 'You'll be pleased to know your diligence paid off. He was spotted trying to board a train at Victoria about an hour ago. He's in custody.'

'Well, that's seems to have worked out well.' Cecily summoned a bright, if shaky, smile. 'The police have got their spy, and this man doesn't look badly injured, so could we leave now, Darius? Please!'

'How did you know Mr Weber was a spy, Cecily?' Hannah asked.

'I was about to ask the same thing, Miss Prentice. It is Miss Prentice?' Inspector Farrell made his way across the shattered window, kicking books aside as he went.

'It is, yes.' Cecily seemed to shrink inside her coat, staring at the shop like a trapped animal. 'I'm certain Darius must have mentioned it in passing.'

'I don't think I did,' Darius said, his tone measured.

'I would normally suggest we gather at Scotland Yard, but everything is chaotic just now.' Inspector Farrell nodded towards the reading corner. 'Why don't we adjourn to the chairs in the back there and talk? One of my chaps can take Jones to the hospital to get that nasty gash sewn up.'

'No, thank you.' Cecily eased back a few paces as he got closer. 'I don't have anything to talk about. Darius, perhaps you would summon that taxi?'

'I'm afraid I'll have to insist.' The inspector extended a hand towards the rear of the shop. Cecily looked toward Darius, who refused to meet her eye. 'Very well.' She approached the wingback chair Hannah had yet to dispose of, but chose not to sit.

Darius leaned against a remaining upright several feet away, but still close enough to be part of whatever the inspector had planned. Aunt Violet exchanged an enquiring look with Hannah, who retrieved Bartleby from beneath the desk and joined them, along with the two policemen and a slightly unsteady Constable Jones.

The noise from the street continued, punctuated by an occasional ambulance bell, the odd shouted instruction, and a rumble of wheels. Hannah wondered what they were all waiting for and why it had anything to do with Cecily. Even Darius displayed an air of anticipation until the inspector spoke.

'Miss Prentice, would you kindly remove your right glove?' Inspector Farrell asked, his request more like a command.

'My glove? Whatever for?' Cecily pulled her bag closer into her body, while resolutely refusing to sit. 'I'll do no such thing. What a ridiculous suggestion! Darius! Are you going to allow this?'

'For God's sake, Cecily,' Darius snapped. 'Do as the man says!'

Cecily's bravado dissolved, and she swayed as if she might faint. Then, with one last frantic look at the street, she gave the inspector a hard shove that sent him back a pace. Had he not been so close to a pile of books it might not have affected him too much, but taken sharply off balance, he issued a yell of surprise and landed on his back among the debris.

Heedless of the damage to her shoes and stockings, Cecily trampled books that covered the floor, along with shards of wood and broken shelves as she lunged for the street. Still holding the cat, Hannah froze, her mouth slack with shock as a uniformed officer helped Inspector Farrell to his feet.

Darius straightened and took a step towards Cecily, but Aunt Violet had grabbed Cecily's left arm in both of hers, tucked her shoulder into the hollow of Cecily's shoulder and pulled, forcing her onto her toes.

Grunting, Cecily clawed ineffectually at her captor's arm, her face contorted into a grimace as she struggled to disentangle herself. Then Aunt Violet hooked her free arm around Cecily's left leg and jerked upwards, unbalancing Cecily who toppled to the floor amid bits of plaster from the ceiling.

Aunt Violet loomed above her, Cecily's leg still held fast, rendering her unable to move.

Bartleby leapt from Hannah's arms and landed on an empty patch of floor, back arched, ears flat and teeth bared, hissing before scooting beneath an armchair.

'You can let go now, Violet,' Inspector Farrell regained his feet and grabbed Cecily's arm in a firm grip. 'She's not going anywhere.' He guided her to the wingback chair, placed his hands on her shoulders, and pushed her into it. 'Stay there. I haven't finished with you.'

'That was harder than in the practice sessions.' Aunt Violet huffed a breath upward through pursed lips and tossed a long curl of hair that had escaped its pins over one shoulder. 'Where's my hat?'

Retrieving it, Hannah brushed off a layer of plaster dust and absently handed it to her aunt while wondering what Cecily had to do with all this? And why the drama with her glove?

30

Panic flickered in Cecily's eyes as she stared at the shattered window, then the pile of debris blocking her way. She threw a hate-filled look at Aunt Violet on one side, and a plaintive one at Darius, who refused to look at her.

'Aunt Violet, how did you *do* that?' Hannah asked, awestruck, brushing plaster dust from her aunt's skirt.

'Ju-jitsu.' Aunt Violet grinned, blowing air through her lips dislodging a curl that hung over her left eye. 'Emmeline's bodyguards taught me.'

'Mrs Pankhurst has bodyguards?' Hannah crept closer, kicking aside a slab of plaster.

'She needed them.' Her aunt relaxed her shoulders, one hand pressed to the back of her neck. 'When the police broke up our marches, they liked to deliver punches to places which didn't show bruises. One chap broke one of my ribs once.'

'All right, Vi?' Inspector Farrell approached, and rubbed at a smudge on her cheek with his thumb.

Hannah's eyes widened. *He called her Vi!* No one ever called Aunt Violet that.

'Nothing I couldn't handle.' Her aunt's hair had loosened from its pins, hanging in dark, wavy strands over her shoulders almost to her waist, making her look younger than her forty years.

'Might we talk now, Miss Prentice?' Inspector Farrell brushed plaster dust from his trousers as he approached where Cecily huddled in the enormous chair, her knees together and hands in her lap as if trying to make herself as small as possible.

'I have nothing to say to you.' She lifted her chin, her eyes averted.

'Then I shall do the talking, shall I?' He spoke calmly, confident he was in control. 'Are you sure you don't want to be taken to the hospital, Jones? You might have a concussion.'

'I prefer to stay, sir,' the policeman said. 'I'd like to see the case through.'

Good for you, Jones.' Inspector Farrell clapped him hard on the back. 'Care to join us, Mr Clifford?'

'I'm fine here, Inspector.' Darius watched the proceedings from a distance, one shoulder against one of the three bookcases that remained standing, one ankle hooked over the other.

'We'll start again, shall we, Miss Prentice?' Inspector Farrell gestured to the policemen to take up their places on either side of Cecily's chair. 'Or perhaps I should call you, Miss Protheroe?'

'Protheroe?' Aunt Violet straightened 'Of course, the scandal. *That's* what all this is about.'

'What scandal?' Hannah snapped, frustrated. 'Would someone tell me what's going on?'

'Perhaps you might enlighten us, Miss Edwards?' Inspector Farrell surrendered the stage to her.

'I'll recount what I know.' Aunt Violet plumped up her chest. 'Some ten years ago, or thereabouts, Louisa Bentham embarked on a... liaison with a gentleman named Jonathan Protheroe.'

'Lily-Anne's mother?' Hannah gasped.

'Hush, or this will take all night,' Aunt Violet snapped. 'Wilfred Bentham discovered through a loyal servant that the pair planned to elope.'

Hannah was about to ask if that loyal servant was Mr Hemmings, but changed her mind.

'He took revenge by calling in a loan on Mr Protheroe's business that ruined him,' her aunt continued. 'He took his own life a year later.'

'They killed him!' Cecily blurted. 'Papa never recovered from the disgrace. All because of that whore, Louisa.'

'How come I never knew about this?' Hannah demanded.

'One doesn't discuss infidelity with schoolgirls, Hannah,' her aunt tutted.

'I see,' Hannah murmured. 'Or think I'm beginning to.' She recalled the year Lily-Anne was enrolled in her school. Her mother insisted they become close friends, hinting her daughter had suffered some unfortunate incident which was never explained.

'Wilfred took Louisa out of the country afterwards to keep her away from Protheroe,' Aunt Violet continued. 'And any other man she might take a fancy to. They've hardly lived in England since. No one knew what happened to Protheroe's daughter Clara.'

'Well, now you do!' Cecily growled. 'I was taken out of school, away from all my friends and forced to make a living teaching miners' brats at a Council Board School.'

Hannah might have felt some sympathy for her until that last comment, but now all she experienced was contempt.

'I never knew.' Hannah released her hold on Bartleby, leaving the cat to wander between the chairs.

'It was for you, Darius. For us,' Cecily sent him a pleading look, her gloved hands clasped together in her lap. 'I had to stop Lily-Anne, don't you see?'

'What did you do, Cecily?' Darius demanded, his voice like ice.

'Why don't you explain it to us, Miss Protheroe?' the inspector said gently.

'Don't call me that! My name is Prentice now.' Cecily's eyes sharpened in defiance. 'I hadn't seen Lily-Anne for years, then Darius took me to a dinner. The Soameses were there. I hoped Lily-Anne wouldn't recognise me, but I was wrong.' She glanced down to where Bartleby weaved between her feet. Tutting in disgust, her foot shot out, catching the cat's belly with the toe of her shoe.

The animal let out a high, indignant mewl and scampered beneath a chair.

Hannah started forward with a cry, but her aunt gripped her upper arm. 'Leave him, he's fine. I want to hear this.'

'Miss... Prentice. I'll ask you again. Kindly remove your right glove.'

At first, Hannah thought Cecily might refuse again, but this time her shoulders slumped and she tugged at each finger in turn. She slowly slid the gauntlet-style glove from her hand, revealing a puckered, semi-healed line between her thumb and forefinger.

'That cut looks infected. How did you come by it?' the inspector asked.

'It won't heal properly.' Cecily stared at it, her brow furrowed as if confused. 'I put honey on it, but that didn't work.'

Hannah leaned forward, frowning. 'What am I looking at?'

Inspector Farrell pointed. 'That cut was made by the hilt of a blade meeting something hard, say a rib. The blade stops short, but the hand holding it slips on the end of the blade, causing such a wound. It's quite common in stabbings.'

'Stabbings?' Hannah gasped. Her vision tunnelled, the room and its occupants blurring like a vignette photograph.

Cecily killed Lily-Anne?

'Did you and Mr Carstairs kill her together, Miss Protheroe?' Farrell asked. 'Or did you work alone?'

'Monty?' Cecily's harsh, humourless laugh made even Aunt Violet start. 'That spineless weakling? He made a decent enough burglar, but when Lily-Anne tried to blackmail us both, *I* killed her.'

'What exactly happened that night in the bookshop?' Inspector Farrell's calm tone was incongruous with Hannah's burning outrage and Darius's controlled silence.

'At Lily-Anne's dinner party, she heard Monty and me talking. She didn't know what it was about, but after the burglary, she guessed, as Monty was more affluent than usual.'

'The burglary of two hundred pounds from Dr Soames's study? The one which his wife denied?' the inspector asked.

'Yes. Cavan called the police, which spoiled her plan, so she claimed *she* had spent the money.'

'Because Mrs Soames intended to use it against them later?' Inspector Farrell said, seemingly for his own benefit, as he put the sequence of events together.

'Of course.' Cecily sniffed. 'Why else would she keep it to herself?'

'That night, Lily-Anne came here after the bookshop was closed to confront Monty.' Cecily sliced a hard look at Hannah. 'She didn't realise he had been sacked. Not that it mattered.'

'Is that when you stabbed her?' the inspector asked.

'You're getting ahead of yourself, Inspector.' Cecily's sneer of self-congratulation made Hannah squirm. 'I was at my home in Craven Street when Monty called me in a panic. He said Lily-Anne thought we were conducting a liaison and was going to tell Darius and Cavan about us and the robbery. I walked over here and told him to leave. That I would deal with her.' Her smile turned into a sneer. 'He couldn't get out of there fast enough. Lily-Anne agreed to keep quiet about the burglary if Monty stopped sponging off her husband and I ended my engagement to Darius.'

'Would she have been believed if she retracted her story?' Hannah directed the question at Inspector Farrell.

'Probably not,' he replied. 'Though I imagine Miss Prentice feared being exposed as Jonathan Protheroe's daughter more.'

'That happened years ago,' Hannah interjected. 'Why does any of it matter now?'

'Of course it matters!' Cecily jerked in her chair, the hands on her bag tightening into claws. 'If Darius discovered I'm the daughter of a bankrupt and a suicide who planned to elope with a married woman, he would never have married me... He is—was, my only chance to retrieve the life I had lost. A position in society, status, respect. I also wanted revenge for what the Bentham family did to my father.' She stared off as if looking deep into the past. 'Can you imagine how exquisite it was to be engaged to the son of the man who had helped ruin my father?'

'Joshua Clifford didn't ruin Protheroe,' Aunt Violet protested.

'But he didn't prevent it either,' Darius spoke for the first time since Cecily had begun her story. His closed expression betrayed nothing of what he was feeling. Shock? Outrage? Disbelief? Or a combination of all three?

'I tried to reason with Lily-Anne,' Cecily needed no prompting to continue, content to have all attention on her. 'She refused to listen. I gave her some cocaine to make her more... amenable, but that made her worse. She shouted that she finally had her chance to rid herself of both me and Monty.'

'Then what happened, Miss Prentice?' the inspector asked softly, their communal breaths held in anticipation of what would come next.

'I grabbed the paper knife on the desk and stabbed her. It was over so quickly... I barely remember doing it. Then I left.' She stared at her hand as if unable to believe that a small, but deep cut had betrayed her in the end. She peered up at Darius through her eyelashes. 'We had a lovely dinner at Elena's that evening, didn't we? An alibi you never questioned, Inspector.' A sly smile tugged at her mouth. 'I had you running around in circles for a while, didn't I?'

'You did indeed, Miss Prentice,' Inspector Farrell conceded calmly.

Hannah tensed, and Darius released a low, angry groan.

Chairs creaked, the only other sound the odd shout from the street or the bell of an ambulance.

'Why did you kill her here, in our bookshop?' Aunt Violet asked.

'I thought Hannah would get the blame. It seemed appropriate.'

'Appropriate? What did I do to deserve that?' Hannah demanded.

'What do you think?' Cecily's eyes flashed, and she issued a contemptuous laugh. 'Since your fiancé was killed you've hung around Darius like some harpy. Poor, faithful, unrequited Darius, who always runs when you call.'

'Why, you vicious bitc—' Aunt Violet leapt from her chair and lunged at Cecily, who cowered, an arm raised to fend her off.

Inspector Farrell grabbed Violet around her waist while she was in mid-stride and lifted her off the floor where she flailed uselessly.

'Now, Vi. Can't have you attacking my suspects.' A bemused but admiring smile lit his eyes before he lowered her gently to the ground. She pouted, tugged down her skirt with both hands, her eyes burning with unspent anger, their faces inches apart. His eyes roved her face, and his lips twitched. He looked as if he was resisting an urge to kiss her, while her aunt's glittering eyes and high colour suggested she would have let him.

'With the theatricals done with, might we continue?' Inspector Farrell brushed off each sleeve and adjusted his tie.

'Continue?' Hannah said, aghast. 'Isn't what we've just heard enough? This woman murdered my best friend!'

'I'm aware of that, and I apologise for the way you learned of it, but—'

A low rumble came from overhead and all eyes went to the ceiling. Cecily's eyes widened and with a terrified shriek, she leapt to her feet. 'The roof is coming in!'

Constable Jones leapt to his feet with remarkable agility for an injured man. Inspector Farrell pulled Violet away from the falling masonry, leaving Cecily to the two policemen; not that she needed any urging as she leapt over the debris on the floor like a steeplechaser.

Hannah swept Bartleby from a pile of books seconds before Darius gripped Hannah's upper arms and bundled her into the street, just as another low rumble started, growing louder, followed by a screech of wood separating as the entire roof collapsed inwards, sending up a cloud of dust into which pages from ruined books fluttered to the ground.

* * *

The shrouded street lights had been extinguished, the only light coming from the fires from nearby buildings and portable lamps on windowsills or hung from doorways, throwing long shadows onto the eerie street scene.

The pungent smell of cordite and charred wood mixed with the street odours of soot and manure stung Hannah's eyes as she surveyed what remained of the Covent Garden Bookshop. Crashes and shouts came from the teams of soldiers and firemen who still searched for survivors beneath collapsed buildings in nearby streets. Carts rumbled along the Strand, carrying the injured, makeshift bandages around their heads and limbs.

Hannah tried to summon a modicum of sympathy for Cecily, but failed. Among her other transgressions she had hurt Darius, who pretended not to see the look of longing Cecily gave him as the policemen led her to a police van parked on the corner. It was a look which showed she had truly loved him.

'Well, that was a revelation I didn't expect,' Aunt Violet chattered animatedly, energised by the evening's events. 'It was the most excitement I've had since Ruby Busby and I hid in St Andrew's crypt on Census night.' Hannah shuddered, and Aunt Violet laughed. 'Chin up, darling. You've been vindicated. You helped trap a German spymaster, and the murderer has been revealed.'

'With two people dead, it feels more like a pyrrhic victory, Aunt Violet. Wait a moment, vindicated? I was never a serious suspect. Was I?'

'Probably not.' Her aunt shrugged. 'You'll have to ask Aidan.'

'I don't think so. I can only imagine how seeing Cecily after so long would have roused Lily-Anne's feelings of abandonment. She missed her parents dreadfully, so the chance of getting revenge on the daughter of the man who had ruined her mother's reputation must have been impossible to resist.'

'Don't make excuses for her,' Aunt Violet scoffed. 'Lily-Anne was prepared to do anything to get what she wanted.'

'She didn't deserve to be murdered.' Hannah hitched Bartleby higher in her arms, his warm, soft body a soothing comfort.

Inspector Farrell materialised out of the darkness; tired, dishevelled, but quietly satisfied. 'It's been quite an eventful evening for all concerned.'

'How much did *he* know?' Hannah turned to where Darius stood in deep conversation with a pair of squaddies at the end of the street.

'Mr Clifford has been most helpful in this investigation; an uncommon trait in the upper classes when dealing with the police.'

'He's an honourable man, which doesn't answer my question.' Hannah appreciated how conflicted he must have felt to inform on his fiancée.

'I'll keep it to myself, if you don't mind. Incidentally, Miss Merrill, you said you might have something interesting to tell me this evening?'

'Beg pardon?' Hannah stared at him for a moment, then remembered her redundant theory about Cavan's sister. 'Er, no. It turned out to be a dead end.'

'A pity. I was looking forward to hearing your impressions of Miss Eliza Brown?' His eyes sparkled with mischief. 'Quite an impressive young woman, isn't she?'

'She's delightful.' Hannah refused to rise to his challenge. Had he known where she was going when they parted outside the studio in Soho? Probably. She glanced to where Aunt Violet was helping Constable Jones into an ambulance.

'It might be a naïve of me, Inspector, but I hoped the air raid would be called off when the German's message went astray.'

'Optimistic, rather than naïve. At least Weber is in custody, so some good came of it.'

'They'll only send more spies, won't they? The Germans.' He did not answer. He didn't have to.

'I didn't take you for a defeatist, Hannah Merrill.'

'Nor did I.' She surveyed the rubble-strewn street and holes in shop roofs with dismay.

'It might interest you to know,' he said, absently fondling

Bartleby's ears. 'When Weber was apprehended, he was found to have a list of prominent British subjects who have travelled to Germany within the last five years. The intent is to approach them and enlist them in the new regime when Britain loses the war.'

'Loses it? How presumptuous of them.'

'Those names are probably useless to the Germans now. And if not, it soon will be when we have contacted them all.'

They broke off as Darius approached, brushing dust from his sleeves. 'Those chaps are going to rustle up some boards to secure the bookshop until I can engage builders to complete the repairs.'

'That's so kind of you, Darius, and it's not even your shop.' A pang of conscience reminded Hannah he had lost two friends and a fiancée in this mess; the one person who least deserved it.

'It's no bother.' He stood to one side as Aunt Violet approached, glad of the distraction.

'There's no telling how many people have been killed or injured.' Aunt Violet sighed. 'If the War Office would set up sirens to warn people to take cover earlier, some deaths might have been avoided. Men on bicycles with whistles are less than useless.'

'They might change their minds after tonight,' Hannah said.

'Perhaps,' Darius said, apparently unconvinced.

'We must arrange to get you all home,' the inspector said, taking charge. 'I doubt there's a cab to be found tonight in all this chaos. That is, unless you drove here, Vi?' Farrell had abandoned any pretence at formality.

'I came by train.' Aunt Violet brushed plaster dust from her skirt, but it made little difference. 'We haven't even thought how to get home, have we, Hannah?'

'Might I lend you my motor car?' Darius offered, returning to his amiable self. 'I parked in Tavistock Place, so hope it's still in one piece.'

'Which of yours is it?' Aunt Violet asked mischievously. 'The Swift or the Rover?'

'The Rover.' Darius mirrored her smile. 'It has a starter motor, so you won't have to crank it. I'm going to stay here to help volunteers and soldiers from the nearby barracks. Even the local Boy Scout troop turned up and are doing a sterling job.' He moved to tuck Hannah's arm through his as he had done a thousand times, but drew back at the last second.

'How will you get home, Darius?' Hannah shifted the sleeping Bartleby into her coat, where he snuggled happily.

'I'll probably book into the Waldorf tonight and then fetch my motor car from your house in the morning.'

'Are you sure? You look tired.' Hannah longed to keep him with her a little longer.

'I'd rather keep busy. I doubt I could sleep, anyway. My mind won't stop working.' He stared off for a few seconds before shoving both hands into his pockets, his shoulders slumped as he walked away.

'He'll be all right, Hannah.' Her aunt encircled her shoulders with an arm, her voice soft. 'He needs to work through this on his own.'

'I know.' Hannah swallowed, burying her nose in Bartleby's soft fur, rewarded with a contented chirrup.

31

'I can't believe he's letting you drive it,' Hannah said, as Aunt Violet bunched her skirt in one hand and climbed into the driving seat of Darius's beloved Rover. 'He loves this vehicle.' Apart from a small tear in the canvas roof, and a long scratch on the bonnet, it was otherwise undamaged.

'How dare you! I'm an excellent driver, although I'm going to have to be very careful with all this rubble on the roads.' Aunt Violet pressed a button on the dashboard, grinning happily as the engine roared into life. 'Will you listen to that?'

'I'm more interested in taking a long, hot bath in our luxurious marble and chrome bathroom; exactly what I need right now. I feel all gritty and...' Her voice trailed off. 'What am I saying?'

'Something about a bath?' Aunt Violet craned forward and peered through the windshield as she carefully guided the motor car between piles of roof slates, potholes, and broken kerbstones.

'In the last few hours, we discovered Cavan is not a faithless murderer but has a secret sister. We came close to being killed by a German bomb, stumbled through streets of smashed buildings, holes in the road, and horribly injured people – not to mention actual bodies!' Her words tumbled out in a rush and she had to fight to catch her breath. 'The bookshop is a complete mess. Cecily will hang for murdering my best friend, and we're sitting in this luxurious motor car discussing baths.'

'Which do you prefer to talk about?' her aunt said calmly. 'German spies and murderers or how many people were blown up or crushed by falling buildings tonight?'

'None of the above.' Hannah's throat burned; her lips clamped tight as tears threatened.

'I thought not. Reliving every gory, heartbreaking detail won't change anything. This night will haunt us for a long time, but one day we'll be able to recount it to our grandchildren, who will either be overawed or scoff they don't believe a word of it. Either way, it's as it should be.' Her aunt stared ahead, her jaw rigid. 'We survived unscathed, as have those we care about. This war will leave no one untouched. Before it's over, there will be stories of loss and heartbreak to trump ours.'

'But how do we make sense of it all?'

'Perhaps we aren't meant to.' Her aunt sliced her a sideways look. 'Are you really taking that cat home with you? Ivy hates anything covered with fur that isn't dead.'

'She'll hardly notice. Now stop complaining about one inoffensive pussycat and slow down, will you?' Hannah wiped her wet cheeks with a grubby hand and dropped a kiss on the black furry ear sticking out above her lapel.

* * *

Hannah awoke as the door opened to admit Aunt Violet in a purple and white floral dressing gown she recognised as one of her mother's. 'It suits you better than it does, Mother.'

'I stole it the last time I visited Madeleine. She probably hasn't noticed.' Her aunt threw open the curtains on a rattle of brass rings, flooding the room with light. Her hair, so similar to Hannah's, hung in soft waves around her shoulders, her face scrubbed from her bath, making her look younger than her forty years.

Hannah yawned and burrowed under the bedclothes, reluctant to leave her warm cocoon. 'There's something I've been meaning to ask you, and I'm not judging you, but I cannot reconcile it.'

'That sounds ominous.' Aunt Violet left the window and perched on the bottom of Hannah's bed, making the springs creak.

'I'm talking about you openly flirting with Aidan Farrell.' Hannah placed her feet onto the floor and reached for her own dressing gown. 'You dining with Aidan is unfair to Eva.'

'And what does my seeing Aidan have to do with Eva? She knows I have my own friends.'

'Don't be obtuse, Aunt Violet.' Hannah shoved her arms roughly into her sleeves, tutting in annoyance when she realised her robe was inside out, so she had to remove it and start again. 'Mother can barely utter her name, let alone acknowledge she exists.'

'Ah, I can see I have some explaining to do.' Aunt Violet shuffled closer, her voice lowered though there was no one to hear. 'It's not what you think.'

'Then enlighten me.' Hannah wrapped the cord around her waist and tied it in front before sitting on her dressing stool and tugged a hairbrush through her hair with long strokes. Her aunt inhaled deeply, both hands clasped in her lap.

'Three years ago, I called at Eva's house for a suffrage meeting and found her in a heap on the bathroom floor after a severe beating from her husband.'

'Eva is married?' Hannah's hand stilled on the brush and she met her aunt's eyes in the mirror.

'She was.' Aunt Violet shrugged. 'Her husband was a Member of Parliament and refused to divorce her, claiming the scandal would ruin him.'

'Was?'

'Let me finish!' Aunt Violet rolled her eyes. 'I took Eva to hospital and once she was patched up, insisted she came home with me.'

'Poor Eva. Why didn't you ever tell me any of this?' Hannah twisted on the stool to face her.

'Because she begged me not to. Grandmama had recently died and left me the villa in Mortlake, so it was perfect timing.'

'I shall always be grateful to Grandmama for leaving us property. It might have raised a few eyebrows, but I doubt she cared.'

'She didn't. She was a staunch supporter of Millicent Fawcett in the eighties. She wanted us to have our independence. She left your mother a house too, but if there is a man in the world from whom no one needs protection, it's Hector. Now, can I carry on with my story?'

'Yes, of course. Sorry.' Hannah went back to brushing her hair.

'Between us, we devised a plan to convince everyone we were a couple in the hope it would prompt her husband to instigate divorce proceedings. Wife beating is not grounds for divorce compared to a woman leaving her husband for another woman.'

'I cannot believe this!' Hannah slammed the hairbrush down on the dresser. 'I've championed your lifestyle to my parents for years, and now you tell me it was all a sham?'

'I'm a little hurt your admiration for your maiden aunt stems from my unconventional lifestyle?' Aunt Violet clasped a hand to her chest in mock horror.

'No,' Hannah faltered. 'But I've defended you from sly remarks long before I knew what the word "lesbian" meant.'

'The masquerade was entirely necessary. Eva is now free to take up a teaching position at a ladies' academy in Eastbourne and will put the ignominy of being divorced for her alleged "unnatural practices" behind her.'

'And what about your ignominy? Surely your good name has suffered.'

'Hannah, I've been arrested four times, imprisoned in Holloway, and had my photograph in The Times throwing bricks at the House of Commons. I doubt I have a reputation left.'

'Does Aidan know about this arrangement with Eva?'

'Of course he does.' She rose and planted her hands on Hannah's shoulders. 'He understands why I did it. In his profession he sees far too much of the abuse some husbands heap on their wives, and it leaves him feeling helpless.'

'Hmmm, perhaps there's more to the man than I first thought. Even if he did toy with the idea that I was a murderess.'

'Now.' She squeezed Hannah's shoulders. 'Darius will be here soon, so let's find you something to wear?' She strode to the wardrobe and threw open both doors.

'What about this?' Her aunt clutched beneath her chin a dusky pink silk blouse with pearls running down the high collar, a navy-blue velvet skirt in her other hand. 'This will be perfect, and while you have your bath I'll go down and keep Ivy from bursting a blood vessel. She queued for hours to get six precious eggs and has ruined two of them while you're still dozing up here.'

* * *

Darius did not arrive in Chiswick until mid-morning, by which time Hannah had paced the floor for almost an hour before she finally spotted him at the gate, examining his Rover that Aunt Violet had parked behind her Sunbeam.

She wandered out to the front of the house, forcing herself to stroll with her hands behind her back. 'What are you doing loitering out here?'

'Wishing the last three years had never happened.' He looked up at the small, but neatly perfect Georgian façade of the house, his expression pensive, almost sad.

'If that was even possible, would we have done things differently?' Her pulse raced, anticipating what it might mean for her if he qualified his remark. 'Won't you come inside?'

'Could we stay out here? It's a lovely day and I've always loved the river.'

Her heart thumped uncomfortably as she followed him out to the grass verge that overlooked the water. Was he going away to get over losing Cecily? Had he come to say goodbye?

'I'm sorry about the bookshop. It's a total wreck.'

'Today, perhaps it is. But there's always next year, and the one after. I'll talk to Aunt Violet and see what she wants to do. Maybe she'll let me be a full partner and we can rebuild it.'

'I admire your resilience. You must love the place.'

I love you more.

The words hovered on her lips, but she could not say them. Not yet.

'Hannah, I need to talk to you.' His smile faded, his knuckles clenched at his sides before he relaxed them. 'About Cecily. I—'

Her stomach dropped, and she interrupted him. 'I'm so selfish. I haven't asked how you are. It must have been a dreadful shock finding out what she had done.'

'It's worse than that.'

'Worse how? She killed Lily-Anne. Stabbed her in cold blood. That's unforgiveable.'

'She killed Monty too.'

'But that was Weber. I saw the van he used to run him down. It almost hit me.'

'It was Cecily driving the tradesman's van. A grocer's van belonging to her cousin.'

'How do you know this?'

'Farrell put the pieces together, with my help. He warned me he was investigating her and questioned me about her background. I realised how little I knew about her, so I started digging.'

'Was it true Cecily had to teach at a council school?'

'Yes, but only for six months after her father killed himself. Her cousin stepped in and supported her. He told me everything, even proudly showed me his fleet of grocer's vans in his yard.' He planted his feet squarely on the ground, his hands clasped behind his back, eyes on the water. 'At the dinner party Cecily mentioned, I saw Cecily and Monty huddled in a corner together.'

Hannah gasped, and he laughed. A thrilling, almost joyous laugh. 'Not like that! Had it been, this mess might have ended differently. At the inquest, Cavan told me about the burglary and how Lily-Anne had insisted he withdraw his complaint to the police. There wasn't only money in Cavan's study.'

'Of course!' The truth hit her like a punch to the stomach. 'There was cocaine and opium in the house, too?'

'Good sleuthing, Miss Merrill.' He grinned. 'Inspector Farrell informed me Cecily and Monty were selling the stuff in nightclubs and private parties to finance her return to polite society.'

'So the woman posing as Cavan's assistant at the pharmacy was Cecily, not Lily-Anne?'

'Exactly. She deceived us all.' Darius inhaled a breath and stared off as if at a spectre of an unimaginable future. 'Cecily manipulated me from the start. I should have caught on sooner. Do you remember the night of Mary and Robson's party?'

She frowned. Why was he bringing that up? 'I do. It was a week after I became engaged to Gerald. Cecily arrived alone, but no one remembered having invited her.'

'I was, um... out of sorts that night, so Mary offered me their spare room for the night. When I awoke the next morning, I found Cecily lying beside me.'

'What? No!' Hannah's mouth hung open.

'My reaction exactly.' He winced, clearly embarrassed at the memory. 'Her performance was faultless; the way she pretended to wake slowly, then the gasp of shock when she saw me, the panicked clutch of the bedclothes. She was hysterical and insisted our only choice to preserve our reputations was to tell Mary and Robson we were secretly engaged.'

'You agreed to it?' His explanation answered all her questions about why they had got together.

'Reluctantly. I had a banging hangover. She even ordered a diamond ring from Garrard's on my account. As a prop, she said.'

'Why did you allow it?' Hannah paused, thinking. 'Wait a moment. You have an account at Garrard?'

'Doesn't everyone?' His mouth quirked into a lop-sided smile.

'Queen Mary might have, but ordinarily, no.' She slapped his wrist playfully, warmed by the fact he trusted her enough to reveal his humiliation. 'Oh, Darius. She must have had it all planned.'

'I know that now, but I could hardly abandon her after having defiled her.'

'Don't be ridiculous!' Hannah scoffed. 'You couldn't defile anyone. But why not place an announcement in The Times? Saying "The marriage of so-and-so will not now take place." I see them all the time.'

'I considered it, but when the woman I always wanted was marrying my best friend, I stopped caring.' He shrugged and turned back to his contemplation of the river. 'Then Gerald was killed, but it was too late.'

Hannah's cheeks burned at his words, words she had longed for him to say, and though she waited several heartbeats for him to expand on them, he did not. Instead, he seemed to shrug away his contemplative mood. His demeanour underwent a complete change from confessor to confident in an instant.

Did he regret having revealed his feelings? Were they both damaged beyond repair?

'Let's not talk about her any more.' He pulled back his shoulders and straightened to his full impressive height. 'I've joined the military arm of the Secret Intelligence Service. It's time I did my duty to my country.'

'You're enlisting?' Her heart jumped into her throat and a rush of blood in her veins made her dizzy. *This couldn't be happening. She couldn't lose Darius, not now.*

'My father got me in to see the bod in charge, who was impressed with not only my German, but they want me to complete a course solving codes and ciphers.'

'Will... will you have to go to the Front?'

'Not immediately. I—Are you all right, Hannah?' He frowned, his eyes darkening with concern.

'Yes, yes, of course.' She inhaled a deep breath. 'What were you saying?'

'I'll be in London for a while, but depending on how the war goes, I might have to go overseas at some stage. Even then, I'll be based at Command Headquarters, well away from any fighting.'

'You will come back?' After everything, how could he expect her to say goodbye to him as he went into a world with few good endings?

'The Cliffords came over in the Norman Conquest. We take a lot of killing.' He reached for her hand, his fingers warm and comforting while hers felt cold. 'And when I do, it will be because I know you'll be—'

A click of heels followed by the creak of the front gate announced Aunt Violet.

'Hannah, you cannot keep Darius all to yourself. Ivy has a pot of actual coffee brewing. You don't want to miss it.' She hauled him by one arm and steered him towards the house. 'Your father just telephoned to tell us you're planning a new career. You'll look so handsome in uniform. Won't he, Hannah?'

'Indeed, he will, Aunt Violet.'

Joining her at the door, her aunt raised her eyebrows at Hannah over Darius's shoulder.

Hannah shrugged helplessly.

Aunt Violet shook her head and preceded Darius into the house.

Hannah followed more slowly, resigned but not defeated. There was still time for her and Darius; when the world was less cruel and chaotic; they had put tragedy and their mistakes behind them.

Time would tell. They had plenty of that – God, and the war willing.

AUTHOR'S NOTE

The Holloway Brooch, designed by Sylvia Pankhurst, was awarded to members of the Women's Social and Political Union who had been imprisoned. Described as 'the Victoria Cross of the Union' the design is of the Portcullis symbol of the House of Commons, the gate and hanging chains in silver, and the superimposed broad arrow (the conflict symbol) in purple, white and green enamel.

ACKNOWLEDGMENTS

With grateful thanks to the brilliant team at Boldwood for bringing this series to life: Caroline Ridding for showing me the difference between a saga and a cosy mystery, Isobel Akenhead for her enthusiasm for my characters, editors Gary Jukes and Debra Newhouse for smoothing out of my clumsy phrasing. Special mentions go to Amanda Ridout, Sue Lamprell, Nia Benyon, Ben Wilson, Megan Townsend, Emily Ruston, Marcela Torres, Emily Yau, Marcela Torres and Sarah Ritherdon, [the last one just because,] Also my thanks to Boldwood's creative department for the stunningly beautiful covers.

My eternal appreciation also goes to my agent Kate Nash who has been with me all the way. And not forgetting the Historical Fiction Critique Group: AnneMarie Doust, Colleen Donnelly, Diane Scott Lewis, Jennie Pittam, Lisa Yarde-Bim, Maggi Andersen, Mirella Patzer, Rosemary Morris, Susan Cook and Ursula Thompson, who have read every word of this novel and shared their skills, encouragement and advice throughout.

ABOUT THE AUTHOR

Anita Davison is the author of the successful Flora Maguire historical mystery series.

Sign up to Anita Davison's mailing list for news, competitions and updates on future books.

Visit Anita's website: www.anitadavison.co.uk

Follow Anita on social media here:

twitter.com/anitasdavison
facebook.com/anita.davison
goodreads.com/anitadavison

ALSO BY ANITA DAVISON

Miss Merrill and Aunt Violet Mysteries

Murder in the Bookshop

The Flora Maguire Mysteries

Death On Board

Death at the Abbey

Poison & Pens

POISON & PENS IS THE HOME OF COZY MYSTERIES SO POUR YOURSELF A CUP OF TEA & GET SLEUTHING!

DISCOVER PAGE-TURNING NOVELS FROM YOUR FAVOURITE AUTHORS & MEET NEW FRIENDS

JOIN OUR FACEBOOK GROUP

BIT.LYPOISONANDPENSFB

SIGN UP TO OUR NEWSLETTER

BIT.LY/POISONANDPENSNEWS

Boldwood

Boldwood Books is an award-winning fiction publishing company seeking out the best stories from around the world.

Find out more at www.boldwoodbooks.com

Join our reader community for brilliant books, competitions and offers!

Follow us
@BoldwoodBooks
@TheBoldBookClub

Sign up to our weekly deals newsletter

https://bit.ly/BoldwoodBNewsletter

Milton Keynes UK
Ingram Content Group UK Ltd.
UKHW041721270923
429488UK00004B/85

9 781785 133138